KATLYN DUNCAN grew up in a small town in Massachusetts with her head always in the clouds. Working as a scientist for most of her adult life, she enjoyed breaking down the hows and whys of life. This translated into her love of stories and getting into the minds of her characters. Currently, she has published twelve books with HQ Digital and has ghostwritten over forty novels.

When she's not writing, she's obsessing over many (many) television series. She currently resides in Connecticut with her husband, kiddo, and adorable senior citizen dog (who will forever be a puppy at heart!).

Also by Katlyn Duncan

Barefoot on the Beach

KATLYN DUNCAN

ONE PLACE. MANY STORIES

HQ
An imprint of HarperCollins*Publishers* Ltd
1 London Bridge Street
London SE1 9GF

First published in Great Britain by
HQ, an imprint of HarperCollins*Publishers* Ltd 2020

ISBN: 9780008364922

Printed and bound in Great Britain by
CPI Group (UK) Ltd, Melksham, SN12 6TR

To J&J, "Finally!"

Chapter 1

All Renee Clarke wanted was to be alone to complete her work in peace. Waking up at the crack of dawn on a Sunday was her routine for claiming the private office at the co-working space in downtown West Cove.

But the tapping on the glass in front of her was hard to ignore. Renee focused hard on her screen, hoping Darby, the maintenance manager of the building, would move along. When she finally met his eye, he grinned with his large and brilliantly-white false teeth.

Renee removed her headphones and placed them on the wooden desk. The calming sound of waves from the ocean soundtrack faded away. The rush wasn't anything compared to at home where she could hear the ocean roaring in real time, but it was bearable twice a week when she removed herself from the comfort of her small office in the corner of her bedroom. The days she chose to work in the office building downtown were after her father Marcus's bocce nights at the local club, when he required more sleep. Renee didn't mind the distance either since their two-bedroom home wasn't exactly spacious, and at thirty-three years old, she needed her own space too.

"Good morning, Darby."

"Good morning, Miss Clarke," Darby said through the glass.

He continued to smile, and Renee had no idea how long they'd have to make pleasantries. There were times he talked to her for the entirety of the time she was there and a few instances where it was a quick hello. It was the way of small towns. Normally, Renee wouldn't have minded, but her working time outside the house was precious. Especially since she was paying by the day. "You know it's a holiday weekend, right?"

Renee stifled a sigh. "I'll be out by noon at the latest." Most were preparing barbecue meals for their Memorial Day celebrations, but Renee already had that covered. Her fingers tapped over the paper planner open next to her laptop. Shaded areas of various colors blocked out all her activities.

"No rush, Miss Clarke. You have a good day now."

"You too."

With a wave, Darby shuffled away, leaving her in peace.

As she replaced her headphones, a vibration radiated up her fingers. With barely a glance at her phone screen, she shoved it in her bag. It wouldn't bother her there. Everyone she cared about knew her morning work hours were from six to eleven, and she still had an hour to go.

Renee rolled her shoulders and inhaled a calming breath. The window across the hall was the only one facing the distant ocean, which was why she always chose that working space. It didn't quite match up to the golden dunes and the relaxing waves from the Long Island Sound in front of her house, but the sliver of water in the distance and the ambient beach sounds in her playlists were enough to get the job done.

Once she had centered herself, Renee glanced at Cait's grin staring back at her from the screen. Between projects, Renee had promised to help her sister set up a wedding website. It was a little over a month before she'd watch Cait walk down the aisle, and she couldn't help feeling the ten-year gap between them like a lead weight in her stomach.

Renee hoped Cait was making the right decision. Twenty-three was so young, and most of the tourists Renee observed in town over the summer months were older than that and usually traveled in groups of singles. If Cait waited a few more years, she could be sure she wasn't jumping into marriage too soon.

Jorden and Cait had been inseparable since high school, and Cait hadn't ever strayed. Renee couldn't help but worry that Cait had picked the only guy she had ever dated as her life partner.

Renee clicked the folder on the cloud drive, opening over two hundred pictures that Cait had shared. Some of the images were recent, but a lot of them were from years ago. Mostly Cait with Jorden and their friends, but a few sparked memories for Renee. Cait's childhood was much more carefree than hers. Tendrils of a black cloud hanging over her own childhood blurred her thoughts. She tried to push them away the moment they appeared.

When brides contacted Renee to work on their website, she tried to capture the essence of their relationship as much as possible. For most, weddings were a one-time event, and she wanted to add to that perfect experience that all brides desired.

Renee enlarged a photo of Cait and Jorden.

Jorden stood over a foot taller than Cait. Cait's fair hair was down, and the wind had paused its movement, splaying it over Jorden's bare, brown chest. If she hadn't known them since forever, she could have easily admired them on a billboard modeling swimwear. The photo captured the waves crashing over their feet. Jorden rested his cheek against the top of Cait's head as she displayed her engagement ring for the camera.

Renee couldn't count how many brides she'd worked with or seen on Instagram who had held photoshoots for their engagements, effectively making the "surprise" not so much. Cait was the exception and had one of the beachgoers take a picture the moment after Jorden had proposed. Her excitement beamed from her eyes and smile. Jorden's matched hers in the most beautiful display of love she'd ever seen. Renee's heart, hardened against marriage, softened slightly.

Another vibration radiated from the floor.

Renee peered at her bag, and her throat clenched. Twice in such a short amount of time? She broke her own rule and grabbed the phone. There were two missed calls from Cait. Cait was more the texting type so a phone call sounded alarm bells in her head. Her instincts pulsed through her as she dialed her sister.

Cait answered on the second ring. "Is everything okay?"

"Yes, of course." Cait's bubbly voice carried over the line.

Renee adjusted the phone against her damp palm. "You know I'm working." Work time was coveted and carved out for only one purpose. Renee had always had an entrepreneurial spirit and could compartmentalize her life enough that nothing short of an emergency would get in the way.

"Guess who's coming for a visit?"

"Who?"

"Guess!"

Renee glanced at the window, almost hearing time tick down until she had to leave.

"You know I'm no good at this."

"Fine." Cait dragged out the word. "Me! I'm coming to visit."

"I already knew that." Renee focused on her screen, uploading the engagement photo to the website. "The week before the wedding."

"Not then. Today."

Renee's fingers paused on the touchpad. "What?"

"Catch up here, Nay."

"Sorry, I wasn't expecting— You're coming here today?"

"I'm in an Uber on the way to you now."

Renee blinked a few times, wondering if an entire month had sped by in a matter of minutes.

"Don't worry. The GPS has crazy traffic on it. I don't know how you live here. But I'll see you soon."

"Cait—" The line went dead. It didn't make sense. After peeling the phone away from her face, she texted her father.

Cait is coming to West Cove?

Was this a joke? Why would Cait come for a visit, leave, and come back in the same month?

Without waiting for a response from her father, she quickly scrolled through the other webpages she had already made. Work distracted her, and she needed a minute to sift through her thoughts at the unexpected surprise. Besides, with Cait coming to West Cove, she'd want to see the website as soon as possible.

All the pertinent information was front and center on the main page: registry, address of the venue with an interactive map, and their hashtag #CaitGotJordened. She curled her lip, unsure if Cait would think it fit her plan. Plenty of weddings impressed her with their hashtags for guests to post on social media at all the events before and during the big day. Renee was still astonished by how people were so creative with them. Cait had insisted Renee pick theirs, and she hoped she didn't disappoint after an hour of searching online for what others had done.

The perfectionist in her didn't want to reveal the final product until it was complete, but Cait always got her way. These websites usually didn't take longer than an hour or so, but Renee wanted it to be everything Cait dreamed. It was a small gesture, but for someone who didn't believe in marriage, it was the only thing Renee could offer other than her services as a bridesmaid.

On the wedding party page, the only missing photo space was for her. Renee grabbed a picture of herself from Cait's Instagram. It was of her and Cait from the last time Renee visited Arizona. It was two years ago, so Renee's hair was in its highlighted phase but Cait looked stunning as usual. Renee doubted anyone would look too closely and notice she had gone back to her natural tawny. The night of the photo, Cait had forced Renee into a selfie at an outdoor restaurant. Even with poor lighting, the image captured their personalities. Cait with her over-the-top smile and Renee reserved as always. Granted, every time she went to Arizona, she was wary at every corner as she thought Cait might set up a surprise meeting with their mother.

Renee stopped herself there. Thinking of Isla wasn't going to help her already agitated mood. She packed her laptop and checked around the desk to make sure she hadn't left anything behind. Her stomach groaned.

Marcus hadn't responded yet, so she texted him again. **I'll pick up lunch from TCP. See you soon.**

Then she flipped over to the message chain she shared with Sadie. **I need a to-go order for three. Surprise me.**

Seconds later, Sadie responded. *Extra peppers, right?*

Renee shook her head. Sadie took every opportunity to mess with her, especially her tastes in bell-shaped vegetables. But what were best friends for? **Triple peppers.**

You got it.

* * *

The Coffee Pot sat at the corner between a craft store and one of the only massive parking lots downtown. As it was only a few doors down from the co-working space, Renee tended to stop by there often, especially when Sadie was working. As she wasn't much of a breakfast person—other than two cups of coffee before leaving the house—she always pushed her first meal closer to lunch.

The sun was almost at its peak, and the heat clung to Renee's skin. The distance from the beach meant the constant breeze off the water didn't offer the relief she needed to get through the warmer days. It was not even June yet, and the temperatures were already getting upwards in the eighties.

The glass front of the restaurant gave a clear view of the people inside. Renee didn't recognize any locals, so at least her visit would be short. At this time of year, most wanted to talk about the tourist season, but Renee had to get home to Cait.

Sadie rushed to the window and slapped her hands on it, before leaning back and laughing. She hadn't startled Renee, but the idea of the possibility gave Sadie the most satisfaction.

Renee laughed and shook her head. As kids, they had lived by the beach four doors down from each other until Isla had lifted Renee out of West Cove. During the pre-internet days, they had stayed in touch by writing each other letters. Renee had kept most of the letters from those dark eight years she had spent with her mother and Cait's family. Cait had been a byproduct of her mother's second marriage, which was the best part of the deal and had made it worth it for Renee.

When Renee moved back to West Cove after college, she and Sadie picked up where they had left off. Sadie's parents had moved south for half the year, while Sadie remained in West Cove with her husband. As Renee settled once more into life in West Cove, the two friends' lives had returned to a time where everything was perfect.

A couple walked out of The Coffee Pot, and Renee thanked them for holding the door before strutting inside. A rotating fan blew warm air into her face as she passed the counter filled with homemade desserts wrapped in plastic. Renee inhaled the scent of chocolate and cinnamon as she claimed her usual seat in the corner of the dining area. She had timed it perfectly as there were only two tables full. It was early enough that the breakfast crowd was gone, and the lunch patrons would arrive shortly.

Renee settled into her seat as Sadie plopped into the one across from her. Sadie blew a chunk of frizzy blonde hair that had escaped from her bun and wrinkled her freckled nose. Sunburned skin peeled from her cheeks. Sadie had moved away from the beach the moment it was possible. Her pale skin was never white for too long when the summers took over. Instead, a seasonal flush swooped in, and her avoidance of the beach intensified. "I thought taking care of three kids was hard. I forgot what tourist season felt like. This isn't getting any easier."

Renee grabbed the damp towel from her friend's hand and wiped the table in front of her. "It's not going to get easier, especially the weekends."

"Every year it starts sooner."

Renee nodded. The locals knew of the arrival of the season from the amount of traffic flooding I-95 each weekend. Unlike Sadie, Renee looked forward to the change. Only for three months out of the year, new faces appeared. There were new possibilities of people who could learn to love her hometown as much as she did.

"Your order will be right out," Sadie said. "I have to admit I outdid myself. But I need to ask why three orders? Have you found summer love already?"

Renee knew the mocking about her summer flings would come up soon enough, but at least she had a better excuse for the third order. "Cait's coming."

"Yeah, in a month."

"Today." Renee checked her phone. "Anytime now."

"Okay?" Sadie dragged the word out. "What's that about?"

"No idea," Renee said. "I don't see the point in her coming to visit, leaving, then coming again for her wedding."

"This wedding is going to be a disaster, isn't it?"

"I hope not." Renee couldn't help internally agreeing, but she wanted to believe that Cait had grown out of her carefree nature as she got older. As a kid, Renee was there to stop Cait from crossing a busy road toward the next shiny distraction. Renee's last visit at Cait's was stressful enough as Cait had insisted they stay out all night and then had a fit on her neighbor's porch wondering why she couldn't get the front door open with her key.

"Well, at least you can stay out of most of it until the bachelorette. Where are they doing it anyway?"

"No idea," Renee said. "I'm not involved with any of the planning for that party. Cait put that all on her friends."

"And the rest of it? On Isla the Terrible?"

Renee shrugged. "I'm not involved."

Sadie pressed her lips together.

Renee was desperate for a subject change. "Do you need anything for the barbecue tomorrow?"

Sadie grabbed her phone and opened her notes application. She was a compulsive list-maker. She had been since they were kids. "We could use some ice. Maybe an appetizer. Only if you have time."

"Not a problem. I'm looking forward to it. I know Dad is too."

"He loves any excuse for a party," Sadie said.

Any excuse to be the *life* of the party. Once Renee had moved back home, her father had changed from a depressed divorcee into a happy-go-lucky sort. Renee supposed after years of living without his daughter that he was glad to have her home. It did prevent any conversation of her moving out. Renee never wanted to leave West Cove. She was adamant that Marcus would not relive the feeling of being let down and neglected after her mother left him all those years ago, dragging Renee along with her. He didn't mind her living with him, and neither did she. For the time being, they were making up for the lost time.

A bell rang from the kitchen, and Sadie popped up from the seat to retrieve Renee's food. When she returned, Renee kissed her friend on the cheek and headed to her car. Before getting inside, she dialed Cait's number to update her location. If Renee timed it right, she should arrive home before Cait. The call went right to voicemail. Cait was probably on the other line—her sister rarely removed her gaze from the screen. She didn't leave a message, knowing she'd see Cait soon enough.

* * *

Renee drove through town on autopilot. West Cove was a relaxing place all year round, the only disturbance being wedding and beach season; the bed and breakfasts, inns, and rental properties filled with new faces and personalities, all adding a sense of change to the local haunts. Renee knew where to go in town at what times to avoid the crush of people visiting the strip of locally independent stores and the shopping outlet by the highway.

As she drove out of the quaint downtown area, space opened up on either side of the road. Like everywhere, West Cove had some chain food restaurants, but Renee's gaze drew toward the inn on top of the hill, which had gone through a renovation several years ago after a fire had almost burned it to the ground. The citizens of West Cove helped with money and time to restore it. Life poured from that building, and it was one reason she loved her hometown. It held history to her and the community.

The turn onto her street curved by the West Cove Country Club, where Marcus was a member and had been for most of his life. He was a legacy, yet Renee hadn't quite taken that step to join. She had all the family benefits of attending events with her father, but none of the commitments.

Out of all the places in the world to get married, Cait had chosen there. Renee had been both shocked and pleased when Cait had told her the location of the wedding. Cait claimed that she connected with West Cove as much as Renee had, even without the years spent there. Renee's life wouldn't be interrupted by having to plan a trip to another location, though she would travel across the world to see her sister get married. Marcus's contribution had been using his legacy within the club to secure the date for Cait's wedding.

The bend in the road curved toward the beach, and her shoulders relaxed. The left side opened up to the seemingly endless world above rippling water, while houses stuffed against each other filled the right side. They crowded each other in a battle to have unobstructed ocean views. Her home was the seventeenth one on the dead-end street. They were far enough away from the public beach that they weren't much affected by the bonfires and surge of tourists, but close enough to people-watch from the front patio during the lazy afternoons and evenings.

The pale blue cottage had been in their family before Renee was born. Renee spotted Marcus in his wooden rocking chair on the front porch and tossed him a wave. Her dad nodded his head as she pulled into the driveway, the familiar sound of rocks under the wheels signaling her arrival home.

The salt in the air clung to her nose as she inhaled deeply. Brandy, their thirteen-year-old chocolate Labrador, let out a lazy woof at her arrival. Renee lifted the bags from the passenger seat and climbed the steps with an infinite view of the water.

Brandy shuffled to stand up, fumbling with her unsteady paws. With a helpful bump from Marcus's foot, she rose and met Renee's hand in greeting. Her nose snuffled the bags of food.

Renee leaned the laptop bag against one of the columns and rubbed Brandy's ears. "There's a good girl."

Renee glanced at her father, sipping from a steaming mug of coffee. The sun reflected against his glasses so she couldn't get a read on him. "Don't think you're getting that greeting from me."

It might have been funny the first few times he had said it to her in the past. "Hey, Dad." She planted a kiss on his wrinkled cheek. His stubble scratched against her skin as he patted his hand against hers. His summer tan had already started from his days out playing bocce at the club, and soon enough, an unnatural bronze would settle in for the summer. "I wish you wouldn't work on the weekends. I miss our Sunday mornings here."

Renee made a show of checking her phone. "It's not morning anymore, and I did this with you last Sunday."

"My time here is limited."

Renee rolled her eyes at her father's dark humor. It had been more frequent lately. Only one of them found it funny. "I'm taking tomorrow off. You know I do it to keep up with all the work coming in."

Marcus shrugged before sipping from his coffee. Her dad's veins were tainted with caffeine from the amount he drank daily, yet he somehow slept more soundly than her. Retirement suited him better than most.

"Did you get my text?"

"I did," he said, glancing at his older-generation iPhone she had given him five years ago.

A high-pitched bark snapped from inside the house. It was a sound she'd only heard during Skype sessions with her sister.

Renee slowly turned as the sliding screen door opened.

Brandy backed away from the door, bumping her butt on the chair leg as Hunter, her sister's brown and white Shih Tzu mix, bounded onto the porch. Renee did a double take at Cait standing in the doorway, paying no attention to her menace of a dog.

"Surprise!" Cait rushed into her arms for a hug.

Renee inhaled her sister's hair, which hinted of raspberries and vanilla. Cait's thin arms packed more strength than she remembered. Hunter's sharp teeth gnawed on her toes. Even with the sincere regret in her choice in flip-flops, Renee couldn't help how her heart filled with the presence of her sister.

Chapter 2

The rush of the ocean filled her ears as Renee tried to piece together her morning. "I thought you were on the way?" Renee held her sister at arm's length. Cait's cheekbones were sharper than Renee recalled. Cait had mentioned some wedding diet she'd seen on Instagram a while back. Apparently, she had ignored Renee's insistence that she was already in great shape.

"I fibbed a little, Nay," Cait said.

"I haven't heard that name in some time," Marcus mumbled.

"It's going to be the last in a while." Renee reached down and shooed Hunter away. He looked at her, his underbite on display, and then barked. Cait only used that nickname when she was up to something. Now the phone calls and surprise visit made sense. Cait wanted something, and it took a trip across the country for her to ask for it.

Cait had only visited West Cove a few times after Renee had moved back home after college. It was so like their mother to want to get rid of a child for a whole two months at a time. Renee never complained. Cait's father, Jacob, had died when Cait was twelve—two years after his and Isla's divorce—which made Marcus an adopted father during the summers. Marcus adored Cait. Most people did.

"I wanted to take the month and experience West Cove in the way that we did as kids," Cait said.

Hunter started barking at a couple walking by. They were lugging two beach chairs, a massive canvas bag, and an umbrella to the beach.

"What about work?" Renee asked.

Cait lifted Hunter into her arms. She patted his head, and he angled his mouth to gnaw her vibrant pink, manicured nails. "Jorden and I found a temp to work in the office during the month before the wedding and for our honeymoon. It's a win for everyone."

Cait had gone to college for general studies where Jorden had gone for his business degree. He was on track toward taking over his family's business while hiring Cait to work in the office after their graduation. From the Instagram posting several times a day, Cait had found her perfect job. She wasn't ever tied down to any career in particular and liked going out at nights and on the weekends. Everything had fallen into place for her sister for her entire life. Renee wouldn't have wanted it any other way, and she was desperate to keep Cait from the messy childhood that she'd had herself.

"When did you put this together?"

Cait glanced at Marcus. "About a week ago now."

"I'm surprised either of you kept it to yourself." Even though they weren't related, Marcus and Cait had a shared trait that they were terrible at keeping secrets.

Hunter barked viciously at a jogger who ran too close to the house. Brandy started to whine. She peered up at Renee as if asking how long Hunter was going to stay.

"He'll get used to this place," Cait said.

Renee doubted it but said nothing. A whole month with that demon dog was well worth it if Cait was around. Though she wasn't sure if Brandy would be so patient.

"Do you need help with anything?" Renee asked.

"Nope," Cait said. "Papa Marcus already helped me."

Papa Marcus was another nickname from their past. Cait had been around eleven when she came to visit West Cove. She couldn't very well call him Dad. Papa Marcus came out one day, and it stuck.

"I need to go to the beach," Cait said, handing over Hunter to Renee. "I've been waiting for it for so long."

Hunter squirmed in her arms, and Renee kept him low against her hip in case he decided to bite her again. Her tight grip gave him enough of a warning to stop moving.

"Come, Nay."

"I'll be right there." Renee loved the feel of the sand under her feet, but a crawling sensation skittered up her arms and she needed a minute alone.

"Papa Marcus?" Cait asked.

"I'm headed into town. Do either of you need anything?"

"Nope!" Cait floated down the porch steps toward the road. By habit, Renee made sure her sister was across and over the cement barrier before she walked inside the house.

Brandy and Marcus followed her. Renee double-checked the door before letting Hunter down. He yipped and sprinted through the living room and into the kitchen. He charged upstairs before he started barking again. He was in the room directly above her. *Her* bedroom.

Renee glanced at Brandy, and she stared back. "It's only for a month." She scratched Brandy's head before the dog padded toward her bed next to the dining room table.

"I guess no one is eating," Renee said more to herself. She placed the bags on the table and lifted the steamy containers from inside.

"I never said that." Marcus walked over to the table and accepted the container from her. "She wanted to surprise you. And you seem surprised. Annoyed, too."

"It's fine." Renee crossed the room and opened the refrigerator. The momentary burst of cool air relieved her flushed cheeks. The work schedule she had meticulously planned crept into her mind. There wasn't a lot of room for entertaining Cait.

Marcus cleared his throat. "I know anytime someone says that, they aren't. I lived with your mother for two straight years of 'I'm fine' before she filed for divorce."

Renee grabbed three water bottles before closing her momentary oasis. "Well, I'm not going anywhere. And 'fine' is fine right now. I'm happy to see Cait. I'm surprised, is all."

"I think having her here is a great thing. She brings a smile to your face."

Renee handed over a bottle. "I smile all the time."

"Not like you do when she's around."

Renee leaned against the counter and glanced out the front windows. The top of Cait's head was visible from the beach. Being there for Cait from the moment she was born had certainly given Renee a purpose and helped distract her enough from her own life with Isla.

"It's going to be tight in here." There were only two bedrooms upstairs, and with Hunter around, it would be best for Cait to keep him in a locked room when she wasn't there. Hunter could have her room for now.

"We'll figure it out."

"I'll set up down here for the time being." Renee returned to the living room and opened her laptop bag.

Renee pondered her life for the next month. She'd stay on the fold-out couch. While she preferred to work in her room during the week, Cait could make herself busy with the beach so Renee could work during the day. Maybe not in the morning, but she could shift her schedule if needed.

Her calendar stared back at her. The week of the wedding was light, but she had filled up her schedule for the summer since a lot of people were taking vacations or working from home while their kids were out of school. Renee looked for areas where she could plan for quality time with Cait during the week. There were intermittent chunks throughout her block scheduling, but not much. Cait required a lot of attention. Renee wiped a hand over her face, moving her hair away from her damp neck. It was possible to shift some of her client work to the evenings, leaving more time during the day.

"Take a break from work and go see your sister," Marcus said from the kitchen.

Renee snapped the laptop closed. "I thought you were leaving."

"You brought me home some delicious food," he said. "I blame you."

Renee cradled the two containers in her hand and balanced the waters in the other. "See you later."

Her day off tomorrow gave Renee enough of a buffer to figure out what she needed to do. Having a plan prevented Renee from overthinking. With Cait in town, nothing was more important at that moment.

* * *

The sun was high in the cloudless sky, creating a sparkling effect on the water. Renee dropped her sunglasses over her eyes and crossed the road. The concrete barrier was short enough to straddle. Once her feet hit the sand, she kicked off her flip-flops and buried her toes in the coarse warmth.

To her right the private areas of the beach continued. Colorful towels and umbrellas peppered the sand while sunbathers sacrificed their bodies to the warm rays. A group of kids tossed a Frisbee around between shrieks of laughter.

The public beach had even more people. The warmer temperatures and holiday weekend gave way to more tourists flooding the shore.

Cait stood in the water with her jeans rolled up a few inches above her ankles. The edges were already soaked. Her hair was piled on her head. Like the water, the sun's rays made her hair glisten.

"How was your flight?"

Cait sighed. "Long. I sat next to this guy who wouldn't stop talking to me about his boring finance job."

"You didn't say anything?"

"Numerous times! And I was sure to mention Jorden like five times. He spoke more to my chest than my eyes, though. I have yet to figure out how to make them tell guys off."

"Well, this is your vacation, and you can get all the rest you want. I'll set up on the couch bed, and you can have my room."

Cait wrinkled her nose.

Renee plopped down in the sand. "Your stuff is already in my room, isn't it?"

"I knew you'd give up your room for a guest." Cait sat too, reaching for a water bottle.

Renee couldn't ignore the widening pit in her chest that told her Cait had more planned for her than she'd already let on.

Renee peeled the top from her container, revealing a chicken wrap.

Cait curled her lip at the thick grilled cheese and fries in hers. "Swap with me?"

Renee handed over her sandwich. "How are the wedding plans going? Everything all set?"

Cait bit into the wrap. Her words unintelligible around her bites.

Renee waited for her sister to finish, but Cait immediately took another bite. Renee's stomach clenched, and the lunch no longer seemed appealing, even though it smelled heavenly.

It took two more bites before Cait spoke. "I can't be expected to see a picture of a cake and decide. It's the most important day of my life."

"Do you need help? We can do a cake tasting while you're here."

Cait's eyes widened, and a sigh floated from her lips. "Really? You would help me out?"

"Sure."

Cait chewed on her lip. "Nay . . ."

It was the same almost-whine that Cait always attached to a problem. Renee ground her teeth. "It's more than just the cake, right?"

Cait slapped her hands against her legs. "Planning an entire wedding by myself is hard."

"All right, well, what's left?"

Cait blew a raspberry, and her gaze slid away from Renee. "I only have the dresses picked out and the vendor deposits."

"So, the flowers, food, music . . ." Renee trailed off, expecting Cait to stop her. She didn't.

"You work from home, so I figured you'd be able to help me. I'm not good at organizing stuff. Besides, you know all the people here. I'm sure they would rather deal with you than some stranger."

The excitement for Cait's visit, which she had convinced herself was a welcome blessing, quickly weighed on her. "Freelancing doesn't mean I don't work, Cait. You can't expect me to do all of this."

Cait shook her head hard enough that wisps of hair fell from her bun. "I'm not asking you to. It's my wedding after all. We could go to appointments together. I want to make this day perfect for Jorden. His parents had left money for his wedding in their will. They were so generous that I don't want to ruin it."

Renee bowed her head. Of course her sister wanted to make sure Jorden's parents' legacy was intact. "Nothing you could do would ruin it."

"It's a lot of pressure, Renee. You'll never know that unless you give up your hatred of marriage."

"I don't hate marriage." The lie fell out before she could stop it. Watching two marriages fall apart under different roofs had soured the sacrament. Over the years, she had to defend her view by denying it altogether. Not with Cait, though. "I support you."

"I know you do. Which is why you could take this as an opportunity to help plan a wedding since you'll never have one."

There was nothing Renee could do other than help. But if it

meant immersing Cait in her world in West Cove and making her sister happy it was worth it. "Okay, I'll help you."

Cait squealed and embraced Renee. "I knew you would help. This is going to be so fun!"

Renee wasn't sure *fun* was the word she'd use. "I need to stay on schedule with work. We have to make a plan and stick to it."

"You're in charge. Like my personal wedding planner. Tell me where I need to be and when." Cait ate more of her sandwich with a grin on her face.

As they ate, Renee counted the days to the wedding. It seemed much closer than it had a half-hour ago. Instead of only producing the website, Renee was now in charge of much more than that. Why hadn't Cait been honest from the start? If she had told Renee about her problems a month ago, Renee could have easily adjusted her schedule. She instantly regretted filling her days before the wedding, but how could she have known this was going to fall on her?

The conversation drifted to Jorden. The smile across Cait's face was the most genuine and excited she'd ever seen from her sister.

Renee would do anything to keep Cait happy. It was only a month. In the grand scheme of life, it was nothing but a blip. Besides, after Cait was married, Renee didn't know when she'd see her sister next before marital obligations took over. With the idea of helping with the wedding settling in her chest, Renee shoved her doubts away for the moment. They could do this together.

Chapter 3

The next morning, Renee woke as a low vibration shuddered the bed. Her eyes peeled open to find a grumbling Hunter sitting inches from her face. Cait had warned Renee that Hunter was an early riser, yet she thought the dog was locked in her bedroom upstairs.

"Go back to bed." Sharp pain radiated down her neck, and she remembered that she wasn't in her own bed but on the lumpy mattress from the sleeper sofa.

Hunter answered with a bark.

"Shh, all right." The night before, Cait had given Renee and Marcus instructions on how to care for Hunter if she wasn't around. The twelve-pound ball of fluff ate three times a day with unlimited treats. Both the food and treats were some foul-smelling organic brand. Marcus and Renee had silently agreed to store the food in a cabinet closest to the door at the back of the kitchen. At least the fresh air from the screen door might lift the stench from the house.

Renee pulled at the sheets, and Hunter let out a yip. He was small, but his barks were forceful. Enough to startle a sleeping Brandy curled on her bed in the corner of the room.

The ache in Renee's neck traveled down her spine as she sat up.

Hunter leaped from the bed and skittered into the kitchen. She piled the blankets in the narrow pantry and folded the mattress back into the sofa and adjusted the cushions on top.

Marcus and Cait were notoriously late sleepers, but Renee did a double take at the clock over the stove. It was a rare day for her to sleep past seven, never mind eight. Last night after dinner, Cait had gone to bed early to cure her jet lag. Renee took advantage of the time and worked until around midnight on projects she had originally scheduled for later that week.

Brandy glanced up at Renee from her bed, and she rubbed a hand under her chin. "Good morning, sweet girl." Brandy licked her hand and stood. She stretched out before padding behind Renee toward the kitchen.

Hunter sniffed at the cabinet with his food before running over to Renee with his sights set on her feet.

Since she wanted to keep all of her toes, she fed him first before filling Brandy's bowl. Once the coffee was brewing, she headed upstairs to shower. There was only one full bathroom in the house, and Cait always took longer than necessary in the morning.

There was no rush as Sadie and her family were the party-all-day types, but Renee looked forward to relaxing by the pool, surrounded by her friends and family. The warm water flowing from the shower should have soothed the ache in her back, but tension rose within her as all she could think of was the to-do list swirling in her mind for Cait's wedding. At the top of her list was recruiting Sadie for help with how to stay organized. Renee knew enough about her sister to realize that she would have to do most of the planning. If Cait hadn't already done what was needed, she wouldn't start now.

After gently rousing a blurry-eyed Cait, Renee left her sister to get ready on her own. Marcus was already in the kitchen, pouring himself a mug of black coffee.

In the corner of the room, Brandy and Hunter were at a

standoff. Where Brandy usually ate a leisurely meal, Hunter had devoured his and he licked his chops for more. More specifically, the remainder of the food in Brandy's bowl.

"Come on, outside," Renee said to Hunter. Yesterday, she had looped a long cord around the railing outside.

Brandy perked up at the word *outside*, and ambled out first. She hobbled down the steps, and Renee closed the gate before hooking Hunter to the chain. He snorted and paced the edge of the railing, investigating the small patch of grass below.

It was Brandy's only break from Hunter, and Renee wished there was a place she could hide from the devil dog too.

* * *

Later that evening, they arrived home, sun-soaked, and surprised to find two of Brandy's toys ripped to shreds on the floor. Brandy coveted her stuffed animals. But Ricky the Raccoon, and Barry the Bear were no longer whole. Their parts and tufts of fluffy white stuffing were spread across the room.

Cait clicked her tongue. "Bad Hunty."

Renee gathered the pieces of stuffing and fabric from the floor. Brandy watched her intently.

"Goodnight, girls," Marcus said. "I'm off to bed."

"Night," Renee and Cait chorused.

Marcus was lighter on his feet after visiting Sadie's hot tub more than once that day. The aches in his bones were usually less intense in the summer.

Hunter yipped and spun in a circle.

"You need to go out, boy?" Cait hefted Hunter into her arms and kissed his cheek. They vanished outside while Renee continued to clean the mess that Hunter had made. Brandy trotted over to Ricky's head and sniffed. "We'll get you some more toys when he leaves, okay?"

Cait reappeared and sunk into the recliner with a long sigh.

23

One hand cradled her phone while the other flipped the leg rest open. "Hunter doesn't like stuffed toys. He destroys them."

"No kidding."

"Do you have a pet store around here? I can pick up some rope or rubber toys." Cait never took her eyes from her phone screen.

Once Renee cleared the room of the massacre, she piled up the cushions from the sofa and pulled out the bed. The edge bumped the open recliner.

"Oops," Cait said as she swiveled the chair in the other direction.

"Did you have a good time today?"

Cait's yawn formed around the word, "Yeah."

"Why don't you go to bed? You can catch up on sleep since you don't have to be up early tomorrow."

"Or any day if I don't want to. This is the life, Renee. I wish I had a freelance job."

Renee stiffened. "I get up at five every morning."

Cait pulled a face. "Why? You can make your own schedule."

"You know I'm not a night person."

"Yeah, well, if I had your job, I'd never get up early."

Then you wouldn't make any money. Renee bit the words off as Cait's phone rang. Her sister sprung from the chair, and it smacked the edge of the bed.

"It's Jorden. I'm going outside to take this. He has to see how close we are to the beach. He didn't believe me!" Cait bounded out the front sliding screen door and left it open behind her. She held her phone at arm's length while Jorden's tinny voice filtered into the house. Cait turned the camera around to face the direction of the water. The sun was almost entirely set. Even though it was pretty on the screen, it was nothing compared to real life.

"This is going to be great for all the pictures. I told you, Denny."

Renee sneaked over and closed the slider, spotting several insects gathering nearby. Hunter was enough of a pest.

Cait walked across the street and sat on the barrier, showing Jorden the beach. A swell of pride filled Renee's chest that her sister was as happy with this place as she was. While it had so many terrible memories from Renee's childhood with Isla, she had lived there longer as an adult. Enough that the good replaced the bad.

Renee barely had the fitted sheet on the bed before Hunter started barking uncontrollably from the back of the house. Renee glanced outside, and saw that Cait was still across the street. She hustled over to the door and let him inside before he annoyed the rest of the neighborhood.

He darted to the cabinet and lifted his sharp claws and pawed at the wood.

Renee shooed him away. "Stop that." He hadn't marked the cabinet yet, but she didn't want a physical reminder of him in her kitchen when he and Cait inevitably left. He sat once he spotted the bag of treats. Renee chose one shaped like a tiny bone. He gobbled it up and swooshed his tail for more.

Renee asserted her dominance and refused, closing the treats away. Hunter shimmied past her into the living room, and onto Brandy's bed.

Brandy tried to scoot away, but she wasn't quick enough before Hunter settled into a tight ball between her legs.

Renee sighed and glanced outside. At least when Cait came back in, she'd take Hunter upstairs.

"Only a few more minutes," Renee said to Brandy.

Brandy harrumphed and made herself as small as possible against the intruder.

* * *

Those few minutes turned into forty before Cait came back. It was enough time for Renee to get ready for bed and read the first three chapters of her book club novel for the month. She was hosting the Wednesday after the wedding.

Once again, Cait left the door open a crack. She yawned again and then winced. "Oh, no."

"What is it?"

"We didn't have time to take Hunter for a walk today since we were gone."

"I'm sure it's fine."

At the word "walk", Hunter pounced and skidded to the slider door. With her dog's life in danger of the road, Cait slammed the slider shut.

Hunter barked and jumped against her legs.

Cait chewed on her lip. "Nay?"

Renee dropped the paperback book on her face, willing herself to disappear for the next ten minutes.

The bed shifted, and Cait tickled her toes. Renee pulled her foot away. "Please? I won't ask you any other time. I'm so tired. Jet lag and all that."

Renee pushed aside the book. "You could have taken him out while you were on the phone."

"You know I don't think ahead like you." Cait yawned again.

Renee shoved her bookmark between the pages. "I'm not going to accept any more jet lag excuses after tonight."

"Yes, Mom," she said with a smirk.

Renee removed the sheet and padded to the door where she had parked her flip-flops. She wiggled her toes around the strap and grabbed the leash by the door. It was Brandy's, but Renee didn't want to search for Hunter's. He liked to play with it, and she didn't have the patience at the moment.

Brandy rarely took walks anymore, but they tried to get her to the beach a few days a week. She loved the water, but there was no way Renee could handle Hunter in the waves. Besides, she wanted to be in and out with this dog.

"Night!" Cait trilled from the stairs, and Renee waved her sister away.

* * *

Outside, a cool breeze rolled off the waves. The moon shone bright, high in the sky, and between that and the streetlights, there was enough illumination for her to see there was no one else on the beach. She crossed the street and walked along the sidewalk next to the barrier.

It wasn't until she passed three of her neighbors' houses that she regretted her clothing choice. In shorts and a tank top with no bra, everything was out there.

Hunter dragged his nose against the ground as they practically sprinted down the street. A short, fast walk was just as effective as a long, slow one. At least that was what she told herself. Hunter veered to the left, tugging the leash toward a grassy area. While he sniffed around, Renee peered at the moon. With the crash of the waves in front of her, she inhaled deeply, releasing the tension in her shoulders.

A splash of liquid smacked her in the cheek before two more hit her forehead.

"Come on." Renee tugged the leash, and Hunter strained as he sniffed the spot. Two more tugs broke him loose from whatever he found, and he eventually followed. They kept the same quick pace as before. A bright pair of headlights appeared at the other end of the road. Renee launched onto the steps of her porch, and Hunter huffed his displeasure with the pace she had set. She ducked inside as the car pulled into the driveway next door.

Safely inside, she peered through the window at the idling truck. Renters frequently stayed at the Hardy house during the summer, but Marcus hadn't told her of anyone coming there that week. Usually, Marcus had an idea when people were coming in and out of the houses on their street. As a rule, all the home-owners looked out for each other.

Hunter bit at her toes, and she slid her foot backward before grabbing his collar. She unhooked the leash and patted his butt. "Go upstairs now."

For the first time since knowing him, he listened. His little footfalls scampered up the stairs.

Brandy sighed, and Renee gave her a good scratch behind the ears before turning out the light.

The truck door slammed from outside. Her heart raced from the run, but her eyelids were heavy. Renee slid into bed. The familiar squeak in the Hardys' screened back door creaked before it slammed closed with finality. Renee briefly wondered about her temporary neighbor before she drifted to sleep.

Chapter 4

Renee woke to the sound of tinkling claws against the hardwood floor. They were heavy enough to pick out which dog was up without opening her eyes. Brandy settled her jowls against the bed. A snuffling, wet nose filled her hand. An exasperated sigh came next.

"Outside?" Renee croaked.

Brandy lifted her head, and her ears perked up.

Renee peeled herself off the bed. The sunlight barely peeked over the horizon. Hunter wasn't frantically scratching at the cabinet. Cait must have kept the door closed all night.

"Come on."

Brandy trotted behind her through the kitchen. The clock on the stove read six-fifty. There had been no reason for Renee to wake that early. She wanted to start with Cait's wedding planning, so she'd put off her client calls to the end of the week, and none of the vendors opened until at least nine.

Renee opened the door for Brandy, and she ambled onto the landing and down the steps. Renee closed the screen door in case Hunter decided to break out of the bedroom and follow Brandy outside. It was time for coffee. Renee added more water than usual to the machine since Cait was there. She prepared Brandy's bowl of food, and that brought Hunter down in a flurry of fluff. His tiny black nose sniffed the air before he sneezed and trotted over to the pantry.

Already learning from past mistakes, Renee left Brandy's bowl on the counter and scooped out the gag-inducing wet food for Hunter. After setting it down, he charged after it as if he hadn't eaten for days. Brandy still hadn't come up, so Renee opened the back door and whistled for her. Brandy usually heard her kibble from outside and hobbled up the stairs without her having to call. Not this morning.

Renee whistled twice more. "Brandy!"

The familiar clinking of Brandy's tags didn't ring out in the air as they usually did. Renee walked onto the landing and peered over the railing. No Brandy.

Renee's heart skittered in her chest. The screen door slapped closed, and Renee swooped down the steps. "Brandy!"

Brandy never ran off. But she was getting older. Renee couldn't help but wonder if the dog got confused and wandered away. She rounded the corner of the house and sprinted to the road. Her heart slammed in her chest at the thought of a car striking Brandy. There must have been a rabbit or squirrel nearby to entice her away from her normal routine.

Both sides of the road were clear, but Renee couldn't spot Brandy on the beach either.

Harsh breaths fluttered out of her. *Where would she go?*

Renee walked to the back of the house again to retrace Brandy's steps. There was only one way out of the back area and that was the path she had taken. The only other logical way to go was—

A Brandy-sized paw print caught her eye. Now that she saw it, she couldn't unsee the trail of them. They were under an overhang, which had kept that spot of the neighbor's driveway dry. The truck from last night had a Massachusetts license plate.

The renter wouldn't be happy if he found a strange dog going to the bathroom on the property. She jogged over to the truck, fully expecting to find Brandy doing just that but she was nowhere to be seen. As Renee neared the house, she found something much worse.

The back door hadn't closed all the way, and there was a space just enough for a chocolate-Lab-sized body to squeeze through. If she had any doubt, the paw prints leading to the door and then disappearing inside were the finishing touch.

Renee ground her teeth together and debated her choices. It wasn't her place to tell others to keep their doors shut, mainly because most residents in West Cove didn't even lock their doors. It wouldn't be a warm welcome for the renter to find a strange dog in his house. Rocking on her heels, she contemplated her next choice. If she were inside the house and got caught, it would be even worse than finding a dog inside. But if she could get Brandy out of there before the renter saw, then she could avoid an awkward conversation. With the excuse on her tongue, she grabbed the door handle and opened it. The renter would have to believe that it was a mistake. Heat gathered under her arms and she wiped her damp hands against her shirt. This was a terrible idea. Yet her body propelled her forward.

"Brandy!" she hissed. Renee prayed that Brandy would listen to her for once that morning, but she had no such luck. The scent of bacon floated in the air. It had to be what drew Brandy inside.

The sunroom was much cooler than it was outside, forcing a cascade of goose bumps to erupt on her arms. Renee peered around the piles of garbage bags, beach chairs, and fishing equipment for her dog.

A fishing rod lay across the floor, threatening to trip her. Renee sighed. The door to the kitchen was open wide. The old girl had barged in with no apologies. If she ran into the renter,

Renee would have a lot of apologizing to do. The next week or so would be incredibly awkward when they passed each other. Her throat tightened.

Even though she hadn't been in the house for years, it looked the same as the last time she was there. The summer between her junior and senior years of high school brought her into that house more than a few times. Her stomach quivered at the memories of the boy she'd spent most of her vacation with.

The kitchen had the same vinyl flooring with various shades of brown in diamond shapes, just as she remembered. Renee clicked her tongue, another warning that Brandy needed to get out of there. The tempting bacon popped and sizzled inside a pan on the stove. The burner was off, and Renee's stomach swooped. The renter was up, but somewhere else in the house. Had Brandy interrupted him making breakfast, and he ran off to call animal control?

Renee rounded the oval table and chairs opposite the countertop in the galley kitchen. A female voice locked her in place at the threshold to the living room.

"Record-breaking highs are expected for the end of the week," the familiar voice said. Jeannine Lynch, the local weather girl.

Renee's chest deflated. It was just the news. Inside the wood-paneled room, an older television sat on a stand with a surface just large enough to hold the device, which had to be a relic from the early Nineties. A couch stood opposite from it, hosting a familiar elderly dog who sniffed the air in her direction.

Brandy turned her head, and her tail thumped the surface of the brown couch. Like every space Renee had seen so far, the house was exactly as she remembered.

"Come on," Renee said, looping her finger under Brandy's collar. It took considerable force to pull her down. Brandy snorted and settled onto the floor and shook. Her tags slammed against each other, sounding like an alarm bell. Her glossy eyes fell everywhere except in Renee's direction.

Hard footfalls careened down the stairs. Renee's heart hammered in her chest as a man appeared at the bottom across the room from her.

They both were at a standoff.

The words burst from Renee before she could stop them. "I'm sorry. She never does this. I-I live next door . . ." Renee's words trailed off as a spark of recognition flooded her.

The man was in the middle of tugging on his shirt, revealing the grown-up face of the boy she had lost her virginity to all those years ago.

"Luc?"

Luc blinked and shoved away his mop of sandy blond hair. Even though the only light in the room emanated from the television, the depths of his hazel eyes weren't the type she could forget. In the sunlight, they shifted toward green, while at that moment they were a darker shade of brown. He hadn't shaved, so sprigs of hair hid the chiseled cheekbones that she'd traced with kisses over that eventful summer with him. Her insides warmed and twisted at the same time.

"Renee?" He broke out into a wide smile. His teeth were perfectly straight now, given the last time she saw him, he had a mouth full of braces. "Wow."

As she had been last night, she became fully aware of the state of her dress. Still in a tank top and shorts, the cool morning air, and most definitely Luc's presence, affected her body in ways she didn't want.

Renee crossed her arms over her chest. "I didn't know you were here."

"I didn't expect you either." He stepped closer to her, and the tingles spreading from limb to limb intensified. They moved lower this time. A fresh, clean smell radiated from him. His damp locks hung over his eyes.

"I live with my dad." Renee loved West Cove, but Luc didn't have enough context to know she'd gone to college and then come back. She'd never been embarrassed about her lack of growth before. He probably thought she had never left.

"Marcus. That's great," he said, rubbing the back of his neck. Brandy shook again.

Luc chuckled, a deep, hearty sound.

"This is Brandy."

He scrubbed a hand over Brandy's head and her tail ticked in time with the touches. "She sneaked in here while I was making breakfast. I was just headed out to find the owner, but it looks like you've found me."

"Guess so." Renee let out a high-pitched laugh. She stopped herself and shook her head, wondering where that had come from.

"I, um, never thought I'd see you again."

Now that she was hyper-aware of her body, she noticed the dampened accent around his words. As teens, he had a thick Boston accent, giving her enough fodder about his "R's" to tease him. Luc had changed in so many ways, yet from his standpoint, she hadn't changed at all other than her age.

"I should get going." Renee reached for Brandy's collar again before backing away from Luc. "Sorry to interrupt your morning."

"I was up anyway." Luc shrugged. "I'm an early riser. I'm helping out at the high school for the girls' volleyball clinic starting next week."

"You're a coach?" Renee bumped against the doorframe as Luc slipped by her. He was at least a head taller than her. She didn't recall such a difference when they'd first met.

"I'm a teacher and a coach." Luc opened the cabinet above the stove. "Do you want some coffee?" He reached up to grab the machine, revealing a sliver of his sinewy frame between the waist of his shorts and the hem of his shirt.

Her eyes watered as she focused on his face instead. "I'm already making some next door. Thanks, though."

"No problem. I'm guessing we'll see a lot of each other now considering."

"Considering what?"

His full lips quirked into a smile. "Considering we're neighbors."

"Oh, right. How long are you here for?"

"At least until the Fourth. The clinic ends that week."

Brandy trotted toward the sunroom, understanding that she wasn't getting the bacon she had wanted.

Luc started to fill the reservoir of the coffee maker. "I guess I'll see you around, then?"

"Yeah." Luc shot her another grin and she smiled back. "I mean, yeah, of course."

"It's really good to see you, Renee."

Words were hard to form, as if her brain had dumped them to fill up with her last memories of Luc instead. The entire night they had spent together before he had left for good without another word. Their last kiss . . .

Renee tossed out a wave and stumbled out the back door. Outside, the air cooled her burning skin, and she was finally able to breathe.

* * *

Brandy was already halfway across the driveway toward the house, leaving Renee behind. "Now you're in a rush to get home?"

The dog peered over her shoulder as if to say, "keep up!"

As Renee trudged up the steps, she replayed the conversation with Luc in excruciating detail. She could have done without the breaking and entering, and the chance meeting with Luc. She wished it would have unraveled a different way. Even more memories flooded her mind.

"Morning!" Cait trilled from the half-bathroom.

"Morning." The comfort of her home enveloped her, and Renee collapsed on a chair, hiding her face in her hands.

"Pour me a coffee?" Cait asked before the toilet flushed.

Renee stood and headed for the cabinet with the overflow of mugs. The two she had in her hands clanked against each other. The sound snapped her thoughts together, and she took a deep breath to calm her trembling hands.

Cait bounced into the room, the bun on her head flopping to one side.

"Thank you!" Cait grabbed the mug from Renee's hand and then stopped. Her nose wrinkled and she stared at Renee. "What's up with you?"

"Nothing. That was mine, by the way."

"You have another mug right there. And don't change the subject." Cait paused, and Renee could almost hear the questions in her sister's mind. Questions she wasn't prepared to answer just yet. "Where were you? I heard you calling for Brandy outside. You woke me up."

Renee turned away from her sister, overly focusing on pouring her coffee. "Brandy got loose. I found her in the house next door."

"She was inside?" Cait slid into her chair and held out her mug to Renee. "Sneaky little girl." She rubbed Brandy's back, and the old girl sat down, wanting more.

"Yeah." Renee filled her mug, wanting to delay the conversation as long as possible. It wasn't as if Luc was going anywhere and Cait was the only one in the house who knew about her brief relationship with him.

"Someone is renting there?"

"Luc Hardy," Marcus's voice carried from the stairwell. He shuffled down, and Hunter yapped at the new person in the room. Marcus didn't bother to pet Hunter until he stopped jumping and nipping. "The owner's nephew."

As if Cait didn't already know.

"Luc Hardy!" Cait shrieked. "No wonder you look like that."

Renee shot her sister a glare. Of course, Marcus had no idea about Luc and her all those years ago, and she didn't need to inform him anytime soon. Or ever.

"Brandy sneaked into the house this morning." Renee glanced at Brandy, slowly munching away at her food as if she had done nothing wrong. "He's here until July to help with the high school volleyball team." She tried to keep her tone light and conversational, hiding the prickling embarrassment pinching at her skin.

"Until July, huh?" Cait's face split into a wicked grin. "That's a while to reconnect."

Renee ignored her. "You didn't tell me he was coming, Dad."

"I didn't think it was a big deal. It's better than an unknown renter." With four beds in that house plus the sofa, there had been plenty of summers where groups of college kids took over the house and Marcus wasn't shy about calling the police for noise ordinances and bad behavior.

"That place still looks the same," Renee noted.

"It needs a lot of updating." Marcus gestured for Renee to scoot over. He poured himself a coffee and settled in his chair. "I've told Audrey there are plenty in town who could help for cheap. She never took us up on the offer."

"Maybe Luc is helping," Cait said.

Marcus blinked. "Maybe. What else did you talk to him about, Renee?"

Renee spotted her reflection in the microwave door and balked. Had her hair been like that all morning? She smoothed the tattered brown nest down as if somehow erasing the memory from both her and Luc's minds. "Not much. I was just there to get Brandy. He arrived late last night, so I didn't want to bother him."

"You seem to know his whereabouts pretty well."

Renee took a long pull from her coffee, ignoring Cait's thin eyebrows jumping up and down. She was enjoying this too much.

Marcus leaned back and watched his daughter for a few seconds before shaking his head. "I have no idea what you two are on about, and I'm not sure I want to."

Cait burst out laughing, and Renee tossed a dish towel at her. Her sister moved quickly to the side to avoid it.

"I know you're allergic to hard work, but you can put the dishes away while I start on breakfast." Renee opened the refrigerator and reached for the carton of eggs she'd picked up from the farmers' market the other day. For some reason, the scent of bacon filled her nose. Then the onslaught of a shirtless Luc popped into her mind. Squeezing her eyes closed only solidified the details of his body. How was she going to get through a month of this?

"Don't be upset." Cait lifted a dish from the rack.

Marcus stood and clicked his tongue for Brandy to follow him outside to the front patio. It was their spot in the morning and Hunter didn't waste the opportunity to chase after Brandy.

Renee doubted Brandy would leave Marcus's side, unlike earlier when she invaded Luc's home. It was so unfair. Renee waited for a beat before turning to her sister. "I'm not mad, but he can't know about Luc. It's incredibly awkward. Please just tone it down a bit."

Cait rolled her eyes. "It was like a million years ago, Renee. Besides, I'm sure he would never think the guy next door and his daughter were together *together*."

Renee balked.

"So, is he hotter than he used to be? He has to be. I can practically see the drool on your lips. Give me the details!"

Renee swiped at her mouth and gathered her supplies before moving to the other counter, away from her sister's curiosity. She cracked four eggs on the side of the bowl a little harder than necessary. "There's nothing to say."

"So, he *is* hotter?" Cait said, bumping her hip against Renee's. "Hand me the whisk?"

Cait handed her a spatula.

"That's not a whisk."

"It works the same."

Renee reached across to the wire rack for the whisk. "He isn't unattractive."

"So, I'm right?"

"He was cute that summer, in a teenager-y way, but he's, like, gorgeous now. And he's nice. Which makes it so much worse."

"Why? There is obviously some attraction there."

"It's been years, Cait. Are you still in love with your first fling?"

"You know I am," Cait said.

Renee shook her head. Cait was the exception.

"Are you embarrassed because you broke into his house looking like that?" Cait half-smiled and cringed.

If Renee could ever make a physical manifestation of how she felt about that morning, Cait's expression would be it. "It wasn't my finest moment."

"Well he slept with you once. I'm sure after showering you'll increase your chances exponentially."

Renee focused on whisking the eggs into a yolky soup. "I'm not going to sleep with him."

"Don't close that door so quickly. You said he's hot. Is he married or does he have a girlfriend?"

"I have no idea."

"And when was the last time you had sex?"

Renee whipped around, making sure Marcus was still outside. He might have been out of earshot, but the slider had a screen. Their conversation wasn't exactly private.

"The last I heard you went on a date was a year ago."

"That was with a tourist, and there was no sex involved." Renee didn't even recall his name. That hazy night buried itself somewhere deep in her mind, where it belonged.

"So, it's been longer?"

Renee whisked the eggs, making enough sound to drown out Cait.

"I need your help, so I'm not going to push you. But don't discount him. He's only here for a little while. This might be the chance to have fun for a change."

"I have plenty of fun."

Cait indicated her shorts and waggled her eyebrows. "Not fun enough."

Renee swatted at her sister. "All right, that's a bit gross coming from you."

"I'm not a prude, Renee. I live with my fiancé, and you were the one to give me the sex talk."

Another way that Isla failed Cait. Renee wasn't sure she had done the best job, but for a twenty-six-year-old, she'd had enough experience to give her little sister advice on safe sex.

"Don't become an old lady before your time. I'm going to shower. Let me know when breakfast is ready."

Cait skipped up the stairs while Renee concentrated a bit too hard on whisking. Her hand cramped and she shoved away the bowl. She needed a bit more caffeine. Sipping from the mug, she drifted into the living room.

Hunter sat by the screen door, his tiny tail at attention. Small whines came from his throat. Marcus turned in his seat to look through the window at her.

"Scrambled okay?" she asked as if coming over to him had been her plan all along. The draw from the house next door was unbearable. The window gave her full view of it. Luc's truck was still there, and she wondered if she had had any effect on him too.

Probably not. There wasn't a ring on his finger or any hint of a woman at that house, but she couldn't get involved with him. Not when their families were so intertwined. Not when his time in West Cove was so short.

Didn't stop you the first time.

Renee's cheeks burned.

"Whatever you want to make. You know I don't care." Marcus's voice snapped her out of her thoughts. He glanced next door as if he knew what she was thinking.

Renee broke away from the door and went back into the kitchen, determined to scramble the eggs, along with Luc, out of her mind.

Chapter 5

After breakfast, Cait insisted on spending the day at the beach.

Renee placed the final clean dish from the rack into the cabinet. "We need to get started on the planning."

Cait glanced at her floral sundress. The ties from her bikini peeked out around her neck. "It's my first full day here. I haven't had a beach day yet. Can we push it to tomorrow?"

Renee understood why none of Cait's plans were confirmed. "No, we can't."

Cait stuck out her bottom lip, the way she used to do when she was a toddler. As a teen, Renee used to flick her fingers at that lip, which would cause Cait to tumble to the floor in a fit of giggles.

"Nay, don't be like that."

Renee sighed. "How about we take the time and make appointments for this week?" She doubted the vendors would have space to fit them in that day anyway.

"Yay! You're the best."

"I said 'we.'"

"I know, I know," Cait said, reaching for her phone. She tapped away as Renee brought the coffee machine parts to the sink to soak.

Renee's phone pinged from the table several times in a row.

Cait placed her phone on the counter and swooped her hair back into a bun at the very top of her head. "Those are from me."

"What are?" Renee asked.

"The list of vendors. That's my part."

"Cait, that's not what we agreed to."

"I don't know anyone here, remember? You said you would call them. After that, I'm all in, okay?"

Renee tapped the screen of her phone and sifted through the emails. They were forwarded from each of the vendors asking for confirmation of times, and some even had attachments of surveys, which Cait hadn't filled out.

Renee counted seven of them in total: the bakery, the venue, the DJ, hair and makeup artist, the dress shop, florist, and photographer. It seemed comprehensive and a little overwhelming. Cait wasn't the organized type, and Renee wondered how long she had expected to put off these details.

Some of the emails were a string of follow-ups that Cait had chosen to ignore. Renee recognized all the names from the emails. They were established businesses in the area, and she knew a few of them would need smoothing over before she could ask them to make an exception for Cait. Some might not have held the date open without the proper responses.

The sliding door closed, and Renee glanced up from her phone. Cait was already outside, crossing the street with a towel under her arm.

A grumble vibrated in Renee's throat, and Marcus chuckled from his spot on the couch.

Hunter rushed to the door and barked in Cait's direction.

Renee crossed her arms. "What's so funny?"

"You can say 'no', you know."

"What else am I supposed to do? She's done nothing. She chose West Cove for her wedding. I can't let her have a bad time."

"I understand." To Renee, it sounded like he didn't. She climbed the stairs to her bedroom.

Renee hadn't been in her room since last night. The amount of clothes covering every surface made it look as if Cait's suitcase had exploded. She wondered how much of it was from Cait being careless versus Hunter's need to make every room a mess. His quick feet hurried up the stairs, and Renee closed the door before he could invade her space. A soft *thump* sounded from the other side. A whine and a bark came next. But Renee needed to get her work done before she could join Cait at the beach.

A bra hung from the side of her computer monitor, and Renee delicately tossed it on the bed before logging into the desktop.

First, she checked her schedule and answered emails. She left Cait's emails as UNREAD and moved on to the rest. A few clients wanted updates. She fielded those she could answer with a few sentences before opening Cait's emails. The only way to work through them was to jump in.

Her phone buzzed. It was a text from Cait. *Are you coming?*

After I plan your wedding, sure. But Renee didn't type what she wanted to and instead sent a thumbs-up emoji.

The bakery was the first email on the list, and cake tasting seemed like the perfect place to start. West Cove Country Club wedding packages included local vendors. But it was up to the bride to select the details. Cait had done half the work, and it seemed like Renee was in charge of the other half.

Sprinkles and Crumbs was the go-to place for any baked goods in the local area. The owner, Eileen, answered.

"Eileen, it's Renee Clarke."

"Hey! I'm a little swamped this morning—how can I help?"

"My sister, Cait Ingram, has a wedding on the Fourth—"

"That's your sister?" Eileen's cheery voice faltered. "I've been trying to get in touch with her for about a month now."

"Sorry about that, I'm working with her to finalize the details. Can we come in this week?"

"I was about to write her off, so good thing you called. Let me get my calendar." Shuffling sounds filled her ear as she flipped open her own calendar on her monitor. They found a date and time that worked for them, and Renee plugged it in.

"I appreciate this."

Eileen grunted. As she hung up, Renee briefly wondered if Cait's intention of having the locals want to help would do the opposite and hurt Renee's contacts within the town. It seemed unlikely but scheduling the meetings sooner rather than later would help preserve those relationships. As she confirmed more appointments, the weeks ahead of her needed a lot of rearranging. The feeling of accomplishment somewhat overpowered the worry knotting her stomach.

When she finished, she looked at her work calendar. Most places weren't open on Sundays, so she made a mental note to head over to the co-working space then.

Renee sorted her work—shifting more of it to the weekend.

This is only temporary. She wasn't a stranger to working under tight deadlines, but there didn't seem to be enough hours in the day. As long as she kept to her schedule on top of the wedding plans, everything would work out. She could host her sister and give her the best vacation and wedding while completing her work tasks.

By the time Renee was settled enough in her accomplishments for the morning, the clock read nine-thirty. How had it been forty-five minutes since she had sat down? Two more messages came in from Cait, insisting she come to the beach, and Renee finally conceded.

* * *

Renee's bathing suit was a bit more modest than Cait's as her body wasn't quite the shape it used to be in her twenties. She stared at her sister's almost concave stomach as she approached her lying on her towel facing the sun.

Cait rolled onto her belly and pulled her sunglasses low over her nose. "It's about time."

"I spoke with all the vendors."

Cait's jaw dropped. "All of them?"

"Yes."

"That didn't take long."

Renee spread her blue and white striped towel next to her sister and smoothed the edges. "It wouldn't have taken you long either."

Cait took her sunglasses off and folded her arms in front of her. She cradled her cheek in her hands, turning away from Renee.

"Cait, I want to know why you didn't ask for my help earlier."

Cait shrugged, still not looking at her.

"At the very least, I deserve an explanation. I filled my schedule with a lot of work, including your website. Is everything okay?"

Cait sniffed and turned her head to rest on her other cheek. "Everything is fine. Jorden is so busy with work, I didn't want to bother him with all this."

"What about your other bridesmaids?"

Cait rolled her eyes. "I love them, I do. But none of them are married or even engaged. They don't understand. I wanted to do this with you but wasn't sure how to ask."

Renee reached over and smoothed a chunk of Cait's hair out of her face. "You can ask me anything. Anytime."

Cait smirked against her arm. "I thought wedding stuff wouldn't be on that list."

Renee settled against the towel, peering up at the sky. "I want you to be happy no matter what. Even if you choose to spend your life with a ball and chain."

A sprinkling of sand peppered her side, and Renee grinned. Cait wiped her hand on her towel.

There was a moment of silence, growing heavier by the second before Cait said, "You blame Mom for all of it?"

Renee ground her teeth together, holding back the venom she wanted to spew about Isla. Cait had never seen their mother at her worst. She had divorced Marcus when Renee was eight, then divorced Jacob before Cait was a teenager. Cait and her father's relationship never suffered, and whenever she was around, Isla doted on Cait. Babysitting, feeding, and carting Cait around to activities had been Renee's job.

"I've made my own decisions." Years of therapy at college had formed a well-rounded, independent individual. But that dark thread weaving through every prospective relationship was tinged with her mother's influence. Renee rarely spoke badly about her mother to anyone other than Sadie. Since Cait hadn't been there for the dark times, it wasn't fair for Renee to taint that relationship as well.

"I think you'd make a beautiful bride, and someone very happy."

The sound of an engine roaring to life floated over the barrier from Luc's truck. It took effort for Renee not to turn around to catch another glimpse of him. One instance of seeing her in partial clothes was enough for a lifetime.

"I know you want to get a peek," Cait said.

Even with her eyes closed, Renee heard the smile in her sister's voice.

"You still have a plus-one for the wedding."

Renee couldn't help the snort bubbling out of her. "Luc? Yeah, right."

"Why is that so hard to believe? Did you see a ring? If not, he's fair game."

As far back as she recalled, her mother never wore a wedding ring through any of her marriages. "That doesn't mean much. He could have a girlfriend."

"Why don't you ask him? What's the worst that could happen?"

I could embarrass myself more than I did earlier this morning.

"Who else are you going to ask?"

"I've been to weddings alone before." More than she wanted to count.

"There's a wedding party dance after the first couple dance. Who are you going to dance with?"

"Dad?" Renee cringed saying it. As much as she loved her father, she couldn't help the swirling glee within her stomach at the thought of dancing with Luc instead. It was completely ridiculous but enough to make her consider it.

* * *

The rest of the day at the beach was the most relaxed Renee had been in a long time. Work usually filled her mind but sitting in the sun with Cait allowed her to sink into the moment.

Cait did most of the talking—as she always did. But Renee missed being the listener. Even with the waves as their soundtrack, she fell into the memories of putting Cait to sleep when she was a kid or listening to what happened during her sister's day.

Their mother had left Renee to care for her child while she did whatever she wanted, but Renee wouldn't want her life any other way. Cait was the perfect result of all that heartache, and she couldn't wait to show their mother how good of a job she had done for Cait when she was the one to help put the wedding together with her sister.

Chapter 6

The first appointments to get Cait's wedding in the right direction were with the florist and photographer. Renee gave herself time in the morning to work at the co-office space before picking up Cait for their ten o'clock appointment.

Renee wasn't much of a dreary-rainy-day type person, but she appreciated the thick gray clouds in the sky hovering over them. At least Cait couldn't force Renee to attend to the appointments alone with an excuse of another "beach day".

"Did you eat?" Cait asked, getting into the car. She wore a pair of micro jean shorts and a tank top. Cait shivered, and Renee grabbed a spare hoodie from the back seat and handed it over.

"Thanks." Cait shoved her arms in the sleeves. As she turned away, Renee noticed the dark circles under her eyes. She blinked, wondering if she had imagined them.

Cait lifted her makeup bag from her purse and started doing her foundation using the miniature mirror attached to the visor.

"You sleep okay last night?"

"Of course," Cait said quickly. "Your mattress is super comfortable."

"I know," Renee said with a smirk. "But make sure you eat

enough. Sometimes Dad isn't good at making food outside the essentials, so feel free to raid the cabinets."

"Okay," Cait said, dabbing her concealer brush under her eyes.

Renee opened her mouth but didn't press the issue. Cait did what she wanted. She had since she was a kid. Pushing her to get over this diet would only get the opposite result she wanted.

"What's first?" Cait asked cheerily as Renee backed out of the driveway.

"Greene Stems Florist."

"Oh, I've been looking forward to picking out the flowers. It's my favorite part of weddings."

"What are you thinking?"

"Well, the scheme of the wedding is pinks and grays. The guys' suits are gray, but I'd like to have pink boutonnières. For the bouquets, I was thinking pinks and whites. I have a whole Pinterest board full of ideas."

At least that would help the initial process. As much as Cait seemed to want Renee to take care of the details, letting Cait take over where she shined—talking to people—would make the time go by so much quicker.

* * *

Downtown West Cove was bustling with people for a weekday. Summers seemed to carry their own schedule with the vacationers coming and going as they pleased. During most times of the year, Renee didn't have to worry about parking. Now, the only free spots were at the bigger plazas, quite a walk from the florist. Renee wasn't in a rush to get in and out of the area as they had plans, but it wasn't convenient.

When they reached Greene Stems, Cait practically skipped through the door. Inside she twirled around and made a show of inhaling the scent around them. Pops of color peeked from various vases and displays across the space. A glass-front refrigerator took up half the size of the room, showing intricately arranged bouquets held by elaborate vases.

Cait peered around the room with a loud gasp. "This place is so adorable."

"I'll be right with you!" a husky female voice called from the back.

"Renee! Look at these."

Renee wandered across the room to Cait, who stood at a handcrafted wooden table. Cait flipped through a binder filled with photographs from other weddings. The binder was arranged by color, filled with hundreds of pictures.

"What do you think of this?" Cait landed a finger on one of the pictures. It was the scheme she was looking for.

"Pretty," Renee said about the bouquet.

Cait groaned and flipped to the next page. "I don't want pretty. I need perfect."

"They're just flowers. You know everyone is going to be looking at you, right?"

"When I look back, I don't want to have any regrets."

Renee couldn't imagine Cait regretting anything about her wedding. These jitters seemed to be consistent with a lot of brides, and Renee understood her sister wasn't immune.

"Good morning," Francis Greene said, squeezing her body through the narrow space between the edge of the counter and the front window. "Sorry about that."

Francis's grandfather had opened the shop ninety years ago, and she had taken over for the last forty. She was well past retirement, but she didn't look a day over fifty. Sprigs of flowers stuck to the tight curls on her head, looking more like a messy, floral headband.

"Francis," Renee said, kissing her soft cheek. "This is my sister, Cait."

"Oh, I remember you," Francis said. "You were a little menace when you were a child."

Cait glanced at Renee.

"She has a great memory," Renee said with a smirk.

Francis snapped her fingers as if plucking the memory from thin air. "You came in here with Marcus, sticky with ice cream on your hands, wanting to touch all my babies." It gave Renee a little thrill to see her sister squirm a bit.

"You remember cutting your finger on that rose thorn after I told you not to touch it?"

Cait smiled and laughed. To anyone else, it would have seemed as if she had brushed it off, but the tinge of red in her cheeks said otherwise.

"While these are beautiful examples, I thought I'd show you what I was thinking. Take a seat at the table, and I'll be right back."

Cait and Renee sat at the handcrafted table. Renee smoothed her hands across it at the beautiful craftsmanship. Marcus used to refurbish furniture, so she appreciated the attention to detail. The placard on the side read, Bower Designs.

Francis returned, holding a tall vase. She hefted it onto the table as if it weighed nothing. "Alternating tall and short centerpieces works well for a room that size."

Renee and Cait stood. Renee couldn't take her eyes off the assorted types of blush pink flowers. Matching sprigs from Francis's hair were in the bouquet. She must have put it together for them right before they arrived. Several ivy-looking plants cascaded out of the vase nearly touching the table.

"With the regulation candles, these arrangements do sparkle."

"Francis, this is amazing," Cait said.

"It's my job." Francis stared at that centerpiece with a critical eye before moving one of the flowers over about a centimeter. She let out a satisfied grunt when she was done. "Besides, the Clarkes have been good customers of mine. I wanted to make it special."

Francis winked at Renee, and Cait reached back to squeeze her hand. "It's perfect. Thank you."

"My pleasure. Now, let's look at bouquets."

* * *

The meeting with Francis took well over an hour and a half. Now that she was involved with the decisions, Cait had a lot to say. By the end, she and Francis were in perfect agreement on the arrangements.

Walking out of the florist, Renee mentally checked flowers off her list. If all the appointments were that easy, they could figure out the wedding in no time.

They weren't due to meet with the photographer until one, so they had time to head over to The Coffee Pot for an early lunch.

Renee's shoulders relaxed as they entered the restaurant. Cait seemed lighter in her steps too. Renee had put too much pressure on the appointments. It was easy enough.

Since it was a weekday, Sadie wasn't there to chat with about the wedding. She was home with the kids during the week, but Renee was happy enough to unwind with Cait and get her opinion on how the meeting with Francis went.

The moment they sat at the window seat, Cait flipped open the menu. "This place hasn't changed a bit, has it?"

Renee grinned. "Not at all." The only update to the menus over the years was laminating over the same list of dishes. The specials were updated on the blackboard over the hostess station every day, yet the three-page spread had been the same for as long as Renee could remember.

"I'm starving," Cait said, glancing toward the kitchen, which made Renee suspect that Cait hadn't eaten breakfast that morning. It wasn't like Cait to lie to Renee, but she had a way of stretching the truth.

Greer Huntley shoved through the double doors, holding a tray filled with food. The gray-haired co-owner of The Coffee Pot donned her signature impassive scowl. She called it her "concentrating look", and those who knew her well enough didn't hold it against her.

Greer spotted Renee and lifted her chin as if to say, "I'll be right there."

"Do you know what you want?" Cait asked.

"Sure do," Renee said.

"I bet you order the same thing every time."

"I have a rotating menu of about three items."

Cait smirked. "Of course you do."

Greer peered at the other patrons as she walked over to the table. She lifted a pen from behind her ear before posing it against a paper pad. "What can I get for you?"

Renee nodded for Cait to go first. "I always like to try the local flavor. Can you suggest something?"

Greer blinked, and for a moment, Renee thought she was going to give Cait a line about not having time for her. Instead, Greer tapped the end of her pen on her cheek. "That depends on how hungry you are."

"We're doing wedding planning today, so I'm plenty hungry," Cait said with a smile.

"Greer, this is my sister, Cait."

Then the impossible happened, Greer flashed her teeth in a wide grin. "I always feel like people are just lazy with that question, but any family member of Renee's has to be sincere or else you wouldn't bother with them, isn't that right?" Greer sat back on her heels and tapped the end of the pen against her lips. "We have the Greer special: triple meat breakfast platter with eggs and French toast. The quadruple stack of buttermilk pancakes with or without chocolate chips. If you're looking for lunch, I have the bacon supreme turkey club sandwich with a heaping supply of fries."

Cait's eyes widened. Since she had arrived, Renee hadn't seen her sister eat more than a few bites of anything. When Cait ordered the Greer special, Renee rolled her shoulders and shed the weight she'd held there. Cait's thinning out might have been due to a combination of stress from the wedding planning and traveling.

Greer left the table with their orders. Cait propped her arm on the table, resting her chin in her hand.

"You got through to Greer. Most people can't get past the grumpy side of her."

"I remember," Cait said with a sigh. "After the meeting with Francis, I realized that I want to be a part of this place too. Just like you are."

"You don't need to try that hard to fit in. Everyone loves you."

Cait rolled her eyes. "Everyone here loves *you*. They're tolerating me because of that."

Renee wasn't sure where the dip in confidence came from. "You and Francis got along well this morning. You didn't even need me there."

Cait shrugged.

For a moment, Renee contemplated digging into the issue further, but the sudden appearance of Luc outside the restaurant stopped her. No, it wasn't just his appearance. It was also the woman next to him. Even at their distance, Renee sunk into her chair, her shoulders curving inward.

Cait didn't notice since her eyes were on her phone. Renee's attention was equally glued to Luc as he and the woman with scorching red hair walked over to a white convertible parked across the street from the restaurant. Renee wasn't a lip-reader, but from their body language—the closeness of their bodies and the way her hand brushed against his as he held the car door open for her—they knew each other very well. Cait's earlier question about Luc's singlehood had an answer. Especially when the woman tweaked Luc's chin before sitting in the car. He grinned at the woman as he closed the door and lingered on the sidewalk watching her drive away.

Well, that's that.

It's not like Renee was going to start anything with Luc over the summer, but the sense of relief she should have felt never came. The urge to know more about the woman surged through her out of nowhere.

Cait's phone erupted with music, breaking Renee's attention from Luc.

"Sorry," Cait said before picking it up. Her gaze locked with Renee. "Hey, Mom."

By habit, Renee stiffened. She didn't recall the last time she and Isla had a conversation. Isla's efforts to "connect" involved Christmas and birthday cards, which had eventually stopped a few years ago. She had never been a mother to Renee. Marcus and Jacob had been the only responsible adults in her life. With Jacob gone, the list became even shorter.

Greer returned with their sodas and dropped two paper straws on the table.

Renee found it hard not to strain herself to listen to the conversation, pretending not to care. Cait's posture straightened as if their mother was sitting next to them.

"I sent you a text," Cait said, glancing at Renee, then at the table. "Yes, sorry. I can text you the details later. I'm having lunch with Renee right now." A pause. "Uh-huh. Okay, bye."

Cait cradled the phone in her hands. "Mom said hi."

Renee mustered a smile.

Cait swirled her straw in her soda and sipped from it. "She wanted to know what's going on with the wedding. I had texted her to check the website."

"It's not up yet."

"Yeah, she wanted me to tell you that."

"Why doesn't she know any of the details?" Renee already knew the answer, but she wanted to hear it from Cait.

Cait sighed. "She hasn't been a part of much of the planning. Work is busy, I guess."

Renee didn't want to get into whatever her mother was up to but had the feeling that Cait was trying to bridge the gap between them. It wasn't the first time. Cait hadn't noticed the strained relationship between Renee and their mother until about five years ago. At the time, Isla was seeing some guy almost half her age and going out every night to bars and clubs. Her distance from Cait forced her to catch on to their mother's ways.

Cait had experienced a part of Isla's selfishness when their mother had abandoned Cait at the airport, leaving her youngest daughter stranded. Renee had to send her sister enough money to cover the two-hour ride home. It was the first time in a long while that Renee had voluntarily called Isla. In that same fashion, it went right to voicemail where Renee unloaded on her mother to the recorded line.

Miraculously, Cait had received a new car several weeks later as a graduation present from Isla.

Renee hadn't mentioned it since.

"What's she doing now?" Renee asked, to keep the peace. She didn't need Cait to worry about how she'd react at the wedding when Isla arrived. Renee wasn't even sure what that would look like. Though, she had time.

"A temporary job. But I've been helping her look for something more permanent."

Renee pushed away from the thought that Cait had that same carefree spirit as their mother. No matter what environment Renee hoped to give her, there was always that genetic link between her and Isla. While Renee had stressed safety and independence, Cait sat in front of her with no career aspirations and getting married before twenty-five.

A dark cloud started to form over her head as it always did with the thoughts of her mother.

"I hope she's not upset that I came here early to ask you for help."

"Why would she be upset?"

"I think she wouldn't mind helping me, but West Cove isn't exactly her first choice."

Greer appeared at their table and plopped two plates of food in front of Cait and Renee.

Cait opened her mouth wide. "Wow. This is a lot."

"Eat up," Renee said, sensing the conversation about Isla was over. Good riddance.

* * *

The photography studio, Sullivan Meeks Productions, was at the edge of the downtown area, sharing space inside of a large Victorian house. Sullivan had been a transplant of the town about two years ago. He was in his forties yet could have been mistaken for older with his thinning hair and shortness of breath from walking down the stairs. "You have a great face for the camera. Have you ever modeled before?"

Cait's nostrils flared. Renee sensed she had given the guy on the plane a similar look. But at least Sullivan kept his gaze at eye level.

"I'd like to see some of your samples," Cait said, lifting her chin defiantly.

Sullivan smiled at her. Even annoyed, she disarmed him. "I have a stack over here. But first, tell me what you're looking for. Sometimes my brides want candid. Some want more formal. Well, the mothers and mothers-in-law do." He chuckled and lifted a red handkerchief from his pocket before swiping it across his sweaty forehead. "I can also do a mix of both."

"I think more candid," Cait said, glancing at Renee.

"Have a seat."

Cait and Renee sat on the leather love seat opposite the desk. It yawned under them as they sunk into the thick cushions. Renee adjusted herself until her butt was on the edge to keep it from swallowing her whole.

Sullivan stacked two albums side by side in front of them, before grabbing three more. "You can have them matted or flush-mounted. I'll give you some time, and you can let me know your thoughts."

"Thank you." Renee opened the one in front of her. The albums weren't like the wedding photos from her parents' wedding. Theirs was a three-ring binder with clear plastic slots for the photos. These were certainly the more formal type of portraits. The one in front of her was exquisite. The pictures were embedded in the thick page. She smoothed her hand across the smiling faces of the bride and groom and their wedding party.

Cait had the matted one, and she seemed equally enamored.

As she had done at the florist, Cait fell into her vision for the wedding. Sullivan took notes while regaling them with stories of some of the weddings he'd photographed.

Renee wasn't sure about his boastful nature, but he did good work.

When they left, Cait seemed as energized as she had before she had spoken to Isla. On the way home, Renee noticed a change in her attitude as well. At least her influence was helping Cait. She hoped to keep that up for the remainder of her visit and during the wedding. No matter what antics Isla came up with.

Chapter 7

The next day, the dress shop rescheduled Cait's appointment since there was an issue with the tracking number, and it hadn't arrived yet. The saleswoman assured her they would call the moment it arrived. As the alterations had already taken place in Arizona, the final fitting was all they had left on their to-do list.

It was the one wedding event that Isla had been there for, mostly because Cait hadn't tried on numerous dresses. Only one. The exact dress from Isla's wedding to Jacob.

Renee kept her shock to herself that Isla had kept such an heirloom, as well as the fact that it had been white. She wasn't a new bride, but her mother never paid much mind to tradition. In the divorce from Marcus, Isla had demanded more than half her share. She hadn't kept anything from their life together, instead selling their possessions to fund an entirely new wardrobe for herself while Renee arrived at a new school across the country in clothes she'd already outgrown. A wedding dress might have made some money, but Isla never ceased to surprise her when she least expected it.

Renee and Cait only had the bakery appointment left, and by the time they had returned home for dinner, they were strung out on sugar and could barely eat the hamburgers Marcus had grilled for them.

In their sugar high, they had agreed to share a bottle of white wine at the beach. They sat on low chairs, the waves crashing over their feet, as they talked about their past and growing up together.

Renee fell into the memory of her sister visiting over the summers when she was younger. Cait remembered so many of the details that Renee hadn't even noticed. Through their conversation, Renee saw West Cove through her sister's eyes. She finally understood why Cait wanted to have the wedding there. West Cove had been the most consistent part of her life, and Renee was happy to have been a good influence on her sister in that way.

* * *

Renee woke with a start as a grinding sound filled her ears. Hunter yapped his displeasure, while Brandy trotted out of her bed and toward the back door. Between her whining and Hunter hopping onto the recliner to get a better look outside, Renee didn't need her alarm clock anymore. She reached for her phone, where she had left it on the side table to charge. The cord was on the floor but not her phone. It wasn't on the floor either.

The grinding sound started again, and Renee peered out the window across from her.

Luc was outside in the driveway in a white T-shirt and baggy shorts leaning over a table saw. A block of wood fell to the ground, and then he started measuring the larger piece once more.

He must not know about the noise ordinance over the summer. It didn't start until eight on weekdays.

"Can anyone get sleep around here?" Cait groaned from the stairs. She shuffled into the room and flopped onto a chair.

"Can't let the dogs out?" Renee asked, only half-joking.

"Maybe I would be more alert if someone's alarm didn't wake me up."

"What are you talking about?"

"Your phone was blaring some ridiculous sound."

Renee glanced at the clock above the stove. It read eight-thirty-five. "Where is my phone, Cait?"

Cait waved her hand at the countertop. "What's wrong?"

Heat surged behind Renee's eyes as she spotted two missed calls and a voicemail from her client. "I had the alarm set for a reason, Cait." She rushed past her sister and nearly tripped over Hunter before stumbling up the stairs. She threw on the first dress she saw, sprinted to the bathroom, and brushed her teeth while combing her hair.

"What's the hurry?" Cait asked as Renee flew past her.

"I have work." Renee slung her laptop bag strap over her shoulder. At least she had the foresight to prepare her stuff the night before. "Which is why I set the alarm. Don't do that again!"

"What about my dress?"

"Let me know if they call."

"They already did." Cait showed her phone as if that made any difference.

"Make an appointment for after one."

"You want me to call them?"

Renee whirled around on her sister. She failed to keep her voice steady. "Cait, I have to go."

Cait muttered her dissent, but Renee didn't have time to unload on her sister. Hunter nipped at her heels, and somehow Renee managed to get out of the door without injury. She hoped she still had a client to rush to.

* * *

By some miracle, Renee managed to retain her client after her inexcusable tardiness. The fiery ball in her chest hadn't cooled much since that morning, and she couldn't go home just yet. Renee headed to the co-working space instead.

Having Cait in town was proving to be a little tricky. While they had fun together, Renee had to do better with her own schedule.

When she arrived in the space, most of the desks and offices were already taken by others. She took a chance and wandered to her normal spot with the view of the distant ocean, but of course, someone else had claimed it.

A desk in the corner of the room had tall dividers on either side with enough privacy and no view that she could work at in peace.

Renee was one click away from turning on airplane mode when a text came in from Cait.

Dress shop appointment at 1:30

I'll be there.

* * *

On the way to Unveiled Bridal, the sun blazed across the concrete, and the humidity clung to the air in thick waves. Renee smoothed her hair down before giving up on the frizzy mess. She'd dropped her laptop bag at her car and grabbed an elastic for her hair.

Unveiled Bridal was a five-minute walk from her car. Renee weaved through the influx of people walking down the main strip downtown. Charming families and couples strolled leisurely by the stores, some stopping to window-shop. Renee skirted them most of the time but found herself caught between two groups holding town brochures and figuring out the best place to get ice cream.

There was no shortage of great ice cream in town, and the thought of it made her mouth water. She hadn't eaten anything since the morning but could easily swap lunch for a sweet treat. Cait would love it, and Renee could ease into an apology about her behavior that morning. She hadn't intended to snap at Cait but turning off her alarm had crossed a line.

Renee arrived at the corner shop near the main intersection of the strip. The windows wrapped around one side of the block to the other, displaying elegant mannequins sporting glittering white gowns. Satin fabric bloomed around their feet as if they were standing on the softest clouds. Pearls and sparkling jewelry dripped from their necks and ears.

Renee had never had the urge to walk into a bridal shop. A traitorous pinch in her chest made her wonder what it would be like to walk into the store for herself. The other stores in town took on a whole new meaning to her as Cait introduced her to the wedding world.

Renee's phone pinged with a message from Cait.

I'm in the dressing room. Where are you?

Be right there.

Renee dropped her phone in her bag and walked inside.

Nadia Portnov floated over to Renee, her face blank. Her red-stained lips twitched but didn't quite form a smile. She was as elegant as the mannequins in the windows, and as stoic. Renee had never seen her without her slicked-back chignon at the base of her thin, long neck. Her flawless pale skin made her appear frozen in time. Nadia didn't need heels, as she towered over most women in town—and some men—but the nude stilettos added those extra few inches to her height.

"Your sister is in the back. Please look around while my associate dresses her."

"Thank you," Renee said.

Nadia dropped her chin, elongating her prominent nose, and briskly walked toward the back of the room. A thick red curtain concealed the dressing rooms. Outside of it was a white leather love seat, a circular stand for brides to appear larger than life coupled with a golden-trimmed trifold mirror.

Renee weaved around the white bridal dresses at the front of the store through toward the love seat. A hallway opened up to her right, and pops of color filled the racks spanning the length of the store. At least Cait had already chosen the blush-colored dresses for the bridesmaids. Renee had ordered hers online and already had it fitted to her frame a month ago. At least she wasn't in charge of the other bridesmaids. Dealing with the details of the wedding was enough for her.

Renee plopped onto the love seat, staring at herself in the mirrors. Her slouched posture did nothing for her appearance, so she sat up straighter.

Cait's voice floated through the thin opening in the curtain before Nadia flung them open to reveal the bride.

Renee's first reaction was a tightening in her throat as she held back the vision of her grown-up little sister. As the dress came into full view, Renee could almost feel the intricate lace pinched between her fingers. As a child, she had sneaked into her mother's room so many times to imagine her own wedding. The dress hugging Cait's body wasn't Isla and Jacob's wedding day dress, instead it was Isla and Marcus's.

Had Cait known and lied to her? No. It had to be Isla. Everything wrong with her life was Isla's fault. Renee couldn't believe that she had lied to her daughter about which wedding dress she wore.

Cait's smile beamed, but Renee's faltered. Her skin tingled with discomfort, and a sinking sensation pooled in her stomach as Cait stepped onto the circular stand displaying the A-line wedding dress. It was simple, yet elegant. It was perfect for Cait.

Once again, Isla had ruined what could have been a perfect moment.

Cait wiped a tear from her eyes and glanced at Renee through the mirror. "I didn't think I would cry."

Searing heat moved behind Renee's eyes. Revealing Isla's lie to her sister bubbled up and died on her tongue.

Nadia spread the train of the dress behind Cait, and Renee stepped aside.

"We didn't do many alterations," Cait said. "It was as if it were meant for me."

Renee swallowed the truth from her sister. Instead of painting

Isla as the liar, Cait would always remember how her sister ruined her dress fitting with the real story. Even though she didn't speak the words in her heart, it was Isla who had tainted this moment. What else was new?

Her smile faltered, but Renee pushed more effort into it. "You look beautiful."

Cait squeezed her sister's hand and peered at the dress through the mirror.

Nadia reappeared with a shimmering tiara, which caught the beams of the lights above them, throwing glowing beads around the immediate area.

Cait barely had to dip her head for Nadia to adjust it in her hair.

"Magnificent," Nadia said with a brief smile.

Renee's anger dissipated as Cait slipped into the role of the bride. She continued to smile and complimented the dress, while keeping quiet about all the curses she had wanted to throw at her mother.

* * *

After the fitting, Cait practically skipped out of the dressing room. With Isla's dress only a few feet away, Renee felt as if the world were closing in on her. She was desperate for distance and tempted Cait with ice cream to get as far away as possible.

"Are you sure you don't have to work some more?" Cait asked as they crossed the street toward One More Scoop—the oldest ice cream parlor in three counties.

"You have me for the rest of the day." Renee held the door open for her sister as a wave of cool air enveloped them.

The checkered black and white tiled floor led up to the ice cream bar where a glass case housed the homemade selections. There were never more than four flavors at a time, which put them in demand through the summer. Three teen girls and one boy worked the line which was already ten people deep in front of them. The room was a mix of families and groups of college-aged tourists.

"What's your favorite?" Cait asked, lifting on her toes to glance at the selections.

"The cookies and cream is my usual go-to, but I haven't been here in a while. They might not have it in stock."

The chalkboard menu attached to the wall confirmed her suspicion. They had a gluten-free and dairy-free sorbet, moose tracks, candy crush, and birthday cake flavors.

Cait used Renee's shoulder to balance as she stood on her toes to get a closer look.

The man at the front of the line turned with his bowl of ice cream, and Renee jolted at seeing Luc again. She moved away from Cait, and her sister's arm fell from her shoulder.

Cait scoffed. "Renee, what are you doing?"

Renee glared at the floor, willing herself to disappear. The memory of Luc with that woman appeared in her mind as that was the last time she'd seen him.

"Renee?" Luc's voice struck her.

There was no use in hiding anymore.

"Oh hey," she said. "I didn't see you there."

"Are you Luc?" Cait wore the most mischievous grin Renee had ever seen.

Renee glanced at the door, wondering how quickly she could run out of it. No excuses came to mind about why they needed to leave at that moment. Especially since they were still in line.

"I am," Luc said, offering his hand to Cait.

She shook it, while looking at Renee. "I've heard a lot about you."

Luc dipped his spoon into the bowl and tasted the ice cream. It looked like he had gone with the birthday cake flavor. The ice cream was good at One More Scoop, but the way Luc's mouth curved around the spoon made it appear divine. "I hope all good things?"

Renee had an idea this conversation wasn't going to go where she wanted. "Luc, this is my sister Cait. She's getting married at the country club on the Fourth."

"That's great," Luc said. "Congrats."

Cait beamed. "Thank you! Renee is helping me out with the last-minute details."

Last minute was the right phrase for it.

"Did you come to town with your family? Or girlfriend?" Cait asked.

Renee let out a strangled sound, which turned into a forced laugh. There wasn't any room for her to warn Cait to stop prying without Luc noticing.

"No, I came here on my own."

The lie came so easily. Though, maybe the woman outside The Coffee Pot was a fling. They seemed to be familiar with each other. At least more than friends. The woman wasn't a local. A question blurted from her lips even though it was none of her business. "I saw you with someone yesterday."

Cait's eyes widened. Renee hadn't told her about the woman. The line moved up, yet Renee didn't budge from her spot.

Luc glanced at the ceiling with slightly narrowed eyes. "Oh, that was Claire." He took another bite.

"Who's Claire?" Cait purred.

"My ex," Luc said.

There was no sign of worry that he had been caught, or any emotion behind his statement.

"She lives here?" Cait asked.

"No, she was dropping off something for me on the way down to New York for a trip with her family."

Renee nodded a few times too many as she absorbed the information. She had no reason to pry into Luc's life other than her curiosity.

Renee stepped in the open spot in front of her to separate herself from him.

"Well, I should get going," Luc said. "I'll see you later."

"Definitely, neighbor." Cait winked at him and giggled.

He laughed with her before scooping more ice cream into his mouth.

"Bye," Renee croaked.

"Next!" the guy at the counter called for Renee, and she tore herself from her spot and sprinted over to order.

Cait sauntered up to Renee. She fully expected Cait to order, instead she said, "He is way hotter than you said."

The teen boy at the counter stared at Renee with wide eyes, as if they were talking about him.

"Just order," Renee said under her breath.

"Candy *crush*," Cait said.

"Cute," Renee deadpanned. "I'll have birthday cake."

They slid over to the cashier, and Renee pulled out her wallet to pay.

"You really downplayed Luc, Renee. And catching him with another woman was ingenious to find out if he was single."

"That wasn't the plan." Renee handed the money to the teen girl. The boy who had scooped their ice cream brought over their bowls. He grinned at Renee.

Renee peeled herself away from the awkward encounter with the boy and Cait.

"Let's go outside," Cait said.

Renee peered out there to make sure Luc had already gone.

The small patio gave front-row seats to the sidewalks and streets, separated only by an intricately designed wrought-iron fence. They took a bench seat outside, facing the road. Cait was already three spoonfuls into the ice cream when they sat.

"Oh, this is good," she moaned. "Why haven't we come here sooner?"

"To be honest, I haven't been in a while."

"You live here."

"When it's open, tourists live here too. Most locals stick to the outskirts of town or buy ice cream from the store."

"That's blasphemy," Cait said, licking her spoon.

Renee grinned. "Not when the local stores purchase pints from these places."

"I want ten pints," Cait said.

"I think we can arrange that." Getting Cait onto the topic of ice cream was easy, but she wasn't sure she avoided the conversation of Luc entirely.

Chapter 8

On the one day Renee intended to sleep late, it wasn't Cait or Luc who woke her. Hunter's wet nose snuffled against her jaw before yapping directly in her face. Her eyes sprung open to his panting open mouth, which reeked of those organic treats.

Renee rolled over and peeked at the kitchen. The cabinet door was slightly ajar with the bag of treats toppled over on the floor. "If you throw up on my bed, you're sleeping outside."

Hunter barked, and Brandy jostled awake. She licked her lips and shoved off the floor, shaking off her sleep.

Renee flipped over onto her back and tried to bury herself under the covers, but Hunter's hopping around and Brandy's low whine forced her to give up.

At least it was past nine in the morning. Renee wished she could have slept in all day like her sister and Marcus. It was Marcus's late night tonight, so she knew he had his earplugs in and was sleeping as late as he possibly could. With Hunter already downstairs, Renee wasn't sure when Cait would roll out of bed.

Letting the dogs out and making the coffee took less than five minutes. Instead of sitting at the table by herself, she went out to the front porch. Between the breeze and the shade from the roof, she knew it would take some time for the coffee to warm her. She lifted a blanket from the back of the couch and wrapped it around her body.

Brandy trotted after, and Renee tossed Hunter a rubber animal from the bag of toys she'd bought the day before when she and Cait were in town. Hunter immediately took to the toy squirrel as if it held treats inside.

Renee hoped that would last as long as it would take to finish her first coffee. She left her phone inside, appreciating the soothing sound of the crashing waves across the street.

Brandy slid to the ground beside her, propping her head on her paws. She let out a sigh, and so did Renee. The rocking chair gave her a sense that she was on the ocean herself, slowly moving with the waves.

Down at the public beach, several groups of people were already securing their spots on the sand for what was to be another perfect beach day. The houses on her end gave off sleepy vibes as no one had risen yet, and the private beach was empty.

It wasn't until after cup number two that she noticed any signs of life in her immediate area other than the seagulls.

"Morning," Luc said from his driveway.

Renee stiffened at the sudden intrusion and relaxed when she realized it was him. Well, slightly. His presence seemed to put her on edge, and not in the worst way. "Morning."

Luc smiled. He was dressed in navy swim trunks and a black short-sleeved T-shirt with an intricate design of a guitar and drum set on the front. The logo was faded with age, and she had no idea if it was from a band or a brand. "You must do this every morning. What a view."

"I'm usually working around this time."

Luc opened the door to the bed of the truck and slid out two bags about the length of Brandy with her tail fully extended. They were both marked with the word HARDY on the sides. "Where are you setting up?"

"A beach volleyball net?" He gestured toward the water.

Renee pressed her lips together. "You're bringing the girls here?" *To the private part of the beach?*

Luc dropped his sunglasses over his eyes, concealing those pools that still hadn't ceased to draw her in. "Is that a problem?"

"No," she said quickly, even though the idea didn't sit right with her.

"You were such a rule-follower as a teen too." Luc grinned.

"I was not." A lie.

"I already have the permits from the city to conduct the camp here. The public beach is unpredictable with the number of people, and I don't need the girls more concerned with whatever their friends are doing around them. The competitions will take place across town at the park beach. It's much quieter here and there's more space to stretch out. Since I am on this property, I do have a right to keep up with whatever equipment I want directly in front of the house, but I can take this down every day if you think it will bother anyone. Well, other than . . ."

Her jaw dropped, and with another smile from him, she could tell he was teasing her.

Or flirting.

Renee was out of practice with flirting. Especially when it came to people she knew. She preferred the casual flings with tourists during the summer months. Technically Luc was a tourist too. She immediately shook the thought from her mind. "It doesn't bother me."

Luc closed the door of the bed and balanced the poles against the truck as he gathered the gear in his hands. He juggled everything around until Renee couldn't bear to watch him anymore.

"Do you need help?"

"Sure."

Renee's chest clenched. Her intention was to be polite; she thought he would have said no.

"I can do it myself, but it might be easier with two people."

Renee shot out of her seat, bumping Brandy's foot in the

process. The dog jerked back. Renee shot her an apologetic look before placing the mug on the small table next to the chair. "Come on, girl. Inside now." Brandy stood and shuffled into the house. After she'd made herself at home in the Hardy house the other day, she couldn't trust Brandy again quite yet.

Hunter raced to the door and reached his little body in a stretch with his paws against the screen. Renee flicked her finger at the spot above him, and he jumped down and snorted at her.

It was close enough to ten that if Hunter woke Cait or Marcus with his yelping, they wouldn't have too much of an excuse to be upset with her for allowing Hunter to run amok in the house.

Renee didn't bother with shoes since she'd have to take them off anyway. But she couldn't help checking herself out to make sure her clothes were appropriate for this kind of work. Her night-shirt—an old black T-shirt from a Billy Joel concert at Madison Square Garden from years before—covered up any main exposure parts while her shorts were long enough to keep her modest. She approached Luc. "Can I take one of those?"

Luc handed over the poles while he balanced the bags on his shoulders. "Have you ever set one of these up before?"

Renee checked both sides of the road before they crossed. "Can't say that I have."

Luc cleared his throat. "It's not that hard when you get used to it."

The sun hadn't quite made the top layer of the sand warm enough to be comfortable, but Renee loved the beach no matter what the weather. She sunk into the sand while Luc faltered slightly. She reached out to steady him but brushed her hand against his arm instead. "Sorry."

"No need," he said. "I need to get my sea-legs is all."

"How long have you coached beach volleyball?" For as much as Luc Hardy took up her thoughts each time she had spotted him, she hadn't learned much about him or his stay in West

Cove since the morning they had reunited. Other than his ex dropping into town too.

"This is my first summer."

"Really?"

"I coach indoor volleyball. But I've played beach volleyball since college. I pitched it to the high school."

"How come?"

"Aunt Audrey isn't doing so well, and she wanted me to check in with the beach house this summer. She's trying to sell it off and wanted some help fixing it up to get the most out of the sale."

Renee couldn't imagine a different owner of the house. Audrey was the landlord before Renee was born.

"I figured while I was here, I could keep cash flow coming in to help with the repairs."

"That's smart."

Luc placed the bags on the ground by their feet. They were in front of his house but far enough from the surf that the water wouldn't touch the net unless there was a storm swell. Renee imagined he would take it down if bad weather was coming. In their community, weather was always on the minds of the beach locals. Floods and hurricanes had caused serious damage over the years, and safety was of utmost importance.

"I usually take up a job over the summer anyway. I can't sit still too long." Luc unzipped the bags and placed the pieces of the net on the ground, along with two white balls and a hammer.

Renee watched the way his hands moved over all the pieces, aligning them on the sand.

He lifted one black pole and adjusted it to a marked length before starting on the other one. Once those were at the same length, he went for the metal stakes.

"Three on each side." Luc handed a set to her.

They were half the size of her arms with a sharp point on one end.

He pointed at the spot next to him. "Place them here."

Renee put one down. It fell over. "Here?"

"You can use some force. It's an approximation. It doesn't have to be perfect."

Renee tried again, tossing the stake side down a little harder until it stood up in the sand.

"Good, the other two can go about two feet on either side."

Pride pinched at her chest at the accomplishment. It wasn't much, but spending time with Luc was as relaxing to her as sitting on the porch with her coffee.

"Hold it steady," Luc directed as he looped the straps from the poles into the top of the stakes. He hammered them down until the sand halfway hid them before he lifted the other pole and headed down closer to the water.

"Aren't you going to finish that?"

Luc shot her a smile, which created a swooping sensation in her gut.

"I have to make sure everything is lined up properly before doing that."

The net stretched out between the poles. This time the pole was a lot harder to keep in place while Luc strapped it to the stakes. He left her there while he moved further down the beach. He turned around and locked eyes with her. Or maybe it was the net. She moved away from the pole to make sure. Luc's stance didn't waver. "Go back to the first one and put some pressure on the right side."

Renee did as he asked, and he nodded. "Perfect. Now, don't move."

Luc hammered the stakes on her side to the ground and when back to his observation. They repeated the steps until he was satisfied with the state of the net, and it was firmly in place.

Renee understood what a pain it would be to take this down every day, especially without help. She rescinded on her rule-following.

"Play with me," Luc said.

"I don't know how."

"You were more of a soccer person if I recall?"

Luc had a good memory. Renee barely recalled his parents' names or what high school he went to, but their time spent alone was fresh in her mind. It was enough to create a wave of shivers down her spine, despite the warm weather.

"It's similar, just hit the ball with your hands, not your feet."

"I haven't played since high school." For two semesters, before it became apparent that Isla wasn't giving Cait the attention the kid needed.

"I know, I'm just trying to make you feel more comfortable. But I can teach you. We worked on this net together, you and your sister can use it as much as you'd like."

At the mention of Cait, she glanced at the house.

Both Cait and Marcus were on the porch now, staring at her and Luc. Cait offered an exaggerated wave. From what she could tell, Cait stayed put across the street, but Renee had no idea for how long. They didn't have any weekend appointments for the wedding, so Cait's day was free to torture Renee in front of Luc.

While she was lost in her thoughts, Luc had retrieved the ball. "The game is straightforward, and it comes down to three moves: bump, set, and spike."

Renee knew enough about seeing the game casually on the beach and television to understand what a spike was. The net towered over her, and she couldn't imagine how she'd ever get high enough to make that move.

"We're going to focus on a bump for now. Lock your hands together like this." His arms formed a long triangle, and one set of fingers covered the other curled in a fist.

She twined her fingers together, focusing more on her arms than hands.

Luc touched her hands, forming the shape he wanted. They were much larger than hers, and she submitted to him moving them. His weight against her sent a rippling through her middle. "There." His statement was soft and low.

As he moved away from her, she slowly and unconsciously leaned toward him like a flower to the sun. When she caught herself, she pulled back a little too forcefully.

Luc lifted the ball from the sand and moved about five feet away from her. "Let's start easy." He tossed the ball, and she bumped it back to him.

It landed in his hands. He smiled. "Perfect."

"That was an easy toss."

"Okay, I'll make it a little more challenging for you." Luc moved back, doubling the distance between them. She bumped it back to him several times before he positioned her facing the net. He jogged to the other side of it and tossed the ball over. Renee bumped it back, grazing the top of the net.

They went back and forth a dozen times before she understood how to position her feet and get some air on the ball. She found herself grinning until Luc lifted his shirt off his body and tossed it to the bags on the side.

The sun reached for its highest peak, and Renee became aware of how her dark shirt absorbed the heat and the sight of Luc's chest created a sheen of sweat across her body.

The longer he stood there, the more she wanted him to take off more than that. Irrational thoughts swirled in her mind, making her miss the next two throws from Luc. She was aware of every part of her body, which crackled with sparks the longer they were together.

Then, the urge to flee took over her body, but it was Luc who broke the spell.

Luc ducked under the net, stopping a foot away from her. The hairs on his chest glistened with sweat. As she didn't want to stare, she instead locked eyes with the miniature version of herself in his sunglasses. "Do you want to take a break? I made lemonade last night. I could use a taste tester."

"Sure." Renee could have refused based on preferring water, but she wasn't ready to let Luc go just yet.

After collecting the empty bags and two balls, they walked toward his house. Renee was shocked that her family wasn't on the porch still. She hoped that Marcus knew Cait and her antics well enough to bring her inside to give her and Luc privacy. Or possibly they realized that Renee wasn't going to feed them breakfast and decided to do it themselves.

Renee was even more grateful that Luc went to the front door, as there was less time for her family's interaction with her and the possibility of forcing her to rescind the invite into his home. Like the back of the house, the front had a sunroom with screened windows facing the beach. In the winter, Marcus put the glass in to protect the house from the weather. It was his contribution to Audrey's home and keeping the neighborhood under his watchful eye when the locals were gone.

They entered a narrow hallway through to the galley kitchen. The air was much more relaxed in the house, but Renee's temperature still spiked. It was one thing to be alone with Luc in a wide-open space like the beach, but in the house, she couldn't help the prickling heat of embarrassment pinching her and beckoning her to leave as soon as possible.

"I tried a recipe I found online. Audrey used to have lemonade here all the time, but she had the powdered kind."

"There's nothing wrong with that."

"Well, I was trying to be different. I bought these lemons at the farmers' market."

"At the church?"

He raised a questioning brow. "Yes."

Every week on Thursdays, the parking lot of St. Bridget's Church was filled with tents from local farmers with their produce and crafts. Renee had meant to take Cait there earlier in the week but had forgotten about it entirely with the wedding plans. She preferred to shop local when she could.

Luc opened the refrigerator, and Renee leaned against the counter. "What are you doing to fix up the house?"

He revealed a glass pitcher with lemons floating inside. The liquid was almost clear with a slight yellow tinge to it. "Want to see the list?"

"Is it that bad?"

"There's a lot of little things. Mostly cosmetic. I'm handy, but I'm not messing with the electrics or plumbing."

"I have a few people in town I could recommend."

"Thanks." Luc grabbed two glasses from the cabinet. He poured lemonade in both and handed one to Renee.

He clinked the glass against hers before drinking.

Renee sipped from the edge, and the sour liquid flooded her mouth. The urge to spit it out came hard and fast, but she managed to swallow. The aftertaste was unbearable.

Luc choked it down, then stared at the glass as if it had personally offended him. "Wow, that's bad."

"It's certainly lemonade," she choked out.

"Don't drink that." He reached out for the glass, and their hands brushed. "Now I know why Audrey stuck with the powdered stuff."

"At least it's reliable."

Luc pulled a face and dumped the contents of the glasses and pitcher in the sink. "How about some water?"

"I should get going." The room started to close in on her the longer they were together. He was so nice and charming but Renee felt the familiar stirrings that she wanted to ignore entirely. If he were a tourist she'd just met, it would be easier to get to know him without any feelings attached. But with Luc, they had a history. Even a short one spoiled the idea of getting closer.

"Was it the lemonade?"

"Not at all."

"I'll be sure to have something better next time."

Next time.

"Oh, I wanted to let you know Marcus offered to help around here with the renovations too."

"He did?" Marcus tended to work harder than his body could handle. Luc had said the list was long, so he probably would let Marcus do as much as he wanted.

"Just make sure he takes care of himself."

"Will do. I'll see you later."

"Bye." She went out the front door. The salty air filled her lungs as she inhaled deeply.

Renee left the property, crossing the driveway to the porch. She fully expected Cait to ask her every detail about Luc, and she hesitated on the steps.

Marcus appeared on the sidewalk, coming toward her.

"Where were you?" Renee asked, glancing at Olivia's house. She was a widow who had lived next door, almost as long as Marcus had been here. Renee had hung out with her kids over the summers until they had moved on with their lives. They weren't the type to visit often outside of holidays, and Marcus helped out when he could.

"Where were *you*?" he asked with a pointed look at the Hardy house.

It appeared as if neither of them wanted to talk about their mornings.

Touché, Dad.

Chapter 9

For the first time since Cait had arrived, Renee sank into the new routine with a better handle on the balance between work and her sister. Strict boundaries of her time seemed to work with Cait, even though Cait always had some opinion about Renee leaving her alone for long periods. The only way to cure that was by showing Cait her finalized wedding website design.

Within seconds, Cait had forgiven her and spent the rest of the night sending the link to all her friends and wedding guests. Even after a rather nasty request from one of her bridesmaids about the ability to change her picture on the website, Cait responded well to the work Renee had done. Renee wished she could have finished sooner, but Cait's excitement tossed any guilt aside from putting work before her sister.

Cait's trial for hair and makeup went well enough on Tuesday that she had insisted on heading into New Haven for the day. They walked the New Haven Green and visited the area's shops and restaurants, Cait putting her best face forward. She snapped selfies and posted them to Instagram and some new platform that Renee couldn't remember even after Cait told her numerous times. Cait claimed #nofilter on all of them with no apologies.

The DJ gave Cait homework to figure out the dances she and Jorden agreed on for various activities during the reception. While Cait insisted on several selections, the radio personality asked that she think it over before finalizing anything. He had given her a list of songs categorized by most popular. Cait called Jorden and they talked for over two hours about the list.

The meeting with the venue coordinator was scheduled late afternoon on Thursday. It was enough time to afford Renee to work in the morning while gathering all the necessary materials for the coordinator at West Cove Country Club. Renee had organized the details and confirmations with all the vendors in a small binder she had found in her desk drawer. She was almost an official wedding planner and wanted to look the part.

The drive to the country club took all of five minutes as it was just a little further down the road, a part of the same beach where they lived. It was secluded by the natural jetties, which made it perfect for those who weren't excited to have tourists wandering onto the property during events.

Renee had been there a handful of times for fundraisers and events, but the sight always took her breath away. It was an elegant haven, nestled in her hometown. Through the intricate metal gates, bright green grass with rounded bushes on either side of the gravel road led to the main building. The building was over a hundred years old and had been through a major renovation several years ago. It was three stories and held a massive banquet hall along with the ocean view she knew and loved.

"It's so much better than the pictures," Cait said, practically leaning out the window.

"You picked a great place. Wait until you see the views."

They parked in a small visitors' lot off the side before walking up the main steps to the front double doors. Renee pushed the door open, allowing Cait to go through first.

The foyer was a vision of white marble floors with gold accents curving through the trim molding. Down a hallway at the back of the room stood floor-to-ceiling windows with a view of the private beach that was exclusive to members.

Prudence Rose's clacking heels loped across the stone floors toward them. Her electric blue dress fused to the curves of her body. It was modest enough for the country club but dressing it up with heels instead of flats could turn it into a dress to go out in the city. She was pushing forty, but a stranger would have no idea. Prudence was one of the lucky ones who always had a fresh face with barely any makeup.

Renee had her fair share of conversations with Prudence. Whenever Renee attended an event with her father, Prudence always insisted Renee find a fiancé so she could help with her wedding at the country club. Little did she know, Renee never planned to get married, never mind having Prudence involved. Her pushy attitude never helped the conversation, and Renee tended to steer clear of the Jessica Rabbit lookalike as much as possible.

Prudence's glossy pink lips parted as she took in Renee and Cait. "It's so good to meet my bride finally." She air-kissed Cait.

"Nice to put a face to the name," Cait said.

Renee handed Cait the binder.

"We met with all of the vendors this week." Cait handed over the binder, and Prudence plucked it from her hands. Her nostrils flared as she flipped through it. "Cait, I told you that I would have handled all the details for you. You didn't need to bother Renee." Her smile was fixed to her face as if waiting for Cait to come up with the perfect excuse as to why she hadn't.

Renee shot a look at her sister. Prudence's name hadn't come up at any point in the wedding planning. Renee would have remembered and insisted that Prudence took over.

Cait brushed them both off with a wave. "I wanted to do it myself."

A balk would have been rude enough, but Renee couldn't

help the strained sound lodged in her throat. Cait wasn't getting away with hiding her reason for what she had put Renee through since she arrived. Cait had rushed her into all these meetings and decisions so she could force Renee into handling everything. Prudence could be opinionated and a little over-the-top, but that was her job. Not Renee's. Cait needed to offer a better explanation.

Prudence licked her finger before turning each page. "Looks like we have everything taken care of?"

"Yes," Cait said.

Prudence snapped the binder closed. "Well then, let's get on with the tasting." She lifted her wrist, revealing an Apple watch. "We have a few minutes until Chef's ready. Do you want to see where you will be getting married?"

* * *

Prudence and Cait walked ahead of Renee, matching each other step for step. Off the hallway, floor-to-ceiling windows opened to the ocean view. It was a beautiful sight that the country club highlighted wherever possible. Prudence waved her hand toward where the cocktail hour and reception would take place. The doors were closed, but Prudence winked at Cait before opening the doors with a flourish.

Cait let out a little squeal, grating on Renee. She wanted to be as excited as her sister, but the conversation from before stifled any positive emotion she could muster.

The cocktail hour would take place in a room with a massive balcony. About a dozen high-top tables were already set outside with water views.

"The food stations will be over here with the selections that you choose today. Passed hors d'oeuvres will filter through the guests as well. The bar is over here."

The stone bar sat at one corner of the room. They barely had a moment to take in the space before Prudence was on her way again toward the ballroom.

"You're under the three-hundred-guest mark, so everyone will be on this level," Prudence said, glancing at the second level.

There was only one event Renee had attended where the second floor was used. She and her father sat up there, distant from the dance floor and DJ for the charity event. While Renee didn't mind detaching herself in that way, none of Cait's guests would feel left out.

Renee glanced inside. The round tables were already covered with white tablecloths, spreading out from the square wooden dance floor in the center of the room. It seemed lifeless without people and music, but the atmosphere held the same elegance as the rest of the club.

"Now, for the ceremony," Prudence said with a wide grin. Her teeth were blindingly white.

Cait caught Renee's eye and let out another little squeal. As long as the weather held up, she and Jorden would get married on a cement pavilion with the ocean as their backdrop. Their guests would see Cait standing under the flowered archway as the rush of the breeze from the water cut over the land. The image of her sister walking down the aisle with Jorden was a vision that swelled within Renee, causing an ache in her chest. Strong emotions usually didn't overcome her much, but this wedding was going to challenge that.

Renee stayed a few steps behind while Cait walked down the narrow aisle surrounded by chairs for another event, probably taking place later that day. Once Cait reached the edge where the pavilion started its descent onto the lower beach, she turned around and grinned.

Prudence bumped Renee's arm conspiratorially. "I think she's happy."

"Me too."

"Can we go to the beach?" Cait asked.

Prudence checked her watch again. "Go ahead."

Renee and Cait walked the soft sandy path toward the shore of the private beach. "We should make a list of photographs we want for Sullivan. I'd love a bunch down here."

"We can make that happen." Renee wondered if she should have taken Cait to the club as their first appointment. It seemed to light a wedding planning fire within her.

They walked the beach for a few minutes, lining up shots. Cait asked Renee to put them in the notes app on her phone for future reference.

"Well, what do you think?" Prudence asked after they circled back to the pavilion.

"It's everything I dreamed of," Cait said.

"That's what I like to hear," Prudence said. "Now, let's head inside for the tasting. You won't be disappointed with Chef's selections for your menu. We only use locally sourced ingredients, which make our dishes the freshest possible."

They entered one of the smaller meeting rooms on the first floor with tall floor-to-ceiling windows with breathtaking beach views. The heat from outside clung to Renee's skin, drinking in the air-conditioned space. A fully set table sat by the windows. There were six chairs around the table with the settings of all different colors. Only two settings were missing.

"Feel free to choose the setting you would prefer for your guests," Prudence said.

Cait walked around the table twice before settling on the white plates with a rose gold accent around the one smaller and larger plates nestled together, with matching rose gold utensils.

"Very elegant," Prudence said conspiratorially.

"Renee?" Cait asked.

"It goes well with the theme."

Cait nodded, seeming satisfied.

Prudence's attention snapped to the other side of the room before she waved her hand over. Two people entered the room.

The first, a girl who couldn't be past twenty dressed in a white shirt with black slacks. She held a large tray in front of her filled with several plates topped with delicious-smelling food. The other was a slender man with the sharpest cheekbones Renee had ever seen outside of the Hollywood tabloids. He wore a pristine white double-breasted jacket with his graying hair slicked back away from his face.

The girl placed the tray on the empty table next to them and stood with her hands clutched behind her back, awaiting instruction.

"It's so nice to meet you," Chef said with a thick New York accent. "Which of you is the bride?"

He locked eyes with Renee first, but she shook her head—almost too violently. It was as if the wedding had germs that could infect her. Her involvement with Cait's was the closest she wanted.

Chef's narrowed-eyed expression disappeared as he turned to Cait. "We have the selections for your cocktail hour for you to try. Please sit and allow us to fill your bellies." He let out a small chuckle before lifting two plates from the tray. He placed them onto their table at both of the empty spots before gesturing for them to sit.

They tasted miniature meatballs, tiny cheeseburgers, crudité cups, bite-sized flatbread pizzas, and various cheeses.

With each bite, Prudence barely gave them a chance to taste before asking their thoughts.

"Everything is delicious," Cait said as they moved on to the main meals.

"Since you weren't able to send in your selections, I put the order in for what I thought you would like."

Cait didn't miss a beat. "It's all great. Anything we choose will work."

"Wonderful," Prudence said with a smile.

Renee wasn't exactly hungry anymore after the hors d'oeuvres, but they tasted two types of salads, and the three choices for dinner: chicken, beef, and a vegetarian option.

"Anyone with a food allergy will be treated with an individualized meal to their exact specifications," Chef noted after placing the entrees on the table.

They ended the tasting with a selection of chocolate-covered fruit and several miniature pastries. By the end, neither Renee nor Cait could take another bite.

* * *

"Good thing we already did my fitting," Cait said as they walked toward the car.

"I'm not sure I'll be able to eat anything until your wedding."

The temperature had risen since they had been inside, and their full stomachs slowed their pace.

On the way out of the property, Cait gushed about the venue. The food selections had been a distraction while they were inside the club, but the same uncomfortable tingling within Renee at Cait's lie surged through her. Pushing the point might ruin the good day they'd had together, but she deserved an explanation. If there had been a miscommunication, they could clear the air and move on. If not, well, Renee would handle that when it came.

"Why didn't you let Prudence help you with the wedding plans?"

Cait shrugged, still staring out the window at the grounds of the country club. "She doesn't know me like you do."

"Cait, it's her job to do these things."

"I wanted to do them."

"*You* didn't do them. You asked me to organize all of this. Answer the question: why?"

Cait shrugged, a sign she wasn't going to say any more.

Renee immediately thought of her client and how Cait almost

ambushed that working relationship over an alarm clock waking her too early. "What? Now that I've already done everything for you, you're going to give me the silent treatment? Real mature."

It was a good thing Renee was driving, so she didn't have to watch her sister react to the dig.

That didn't stop Cait from speaking, though. "I'm so sorry I wanted to do this with you, Renee. I'm such an inconvenience to your perfect life here."

"All right, well, if you're going to be like that . . . If you wanted my help, you should have asked me months ago. Not weeks before your wedding at the risk of losing all of your vendors."

"I thought I could do it. But there's so much pressure around weddings. You have no idea."

"I do now!"

"I didn't want a stranger to plan my wedding when I couldn't handle it myself. I didn't think you would mind. I was wrong."

"Don't be like that."

"Like what?" The snap on the end of Cait's question flared up walls within Renee. They'd had arguments in the past, especially when Cait found her voice around thirteen. Renee knew when to stop and when to push. If she pushed now, her home wouldn't be a comfortable place to stay for either of them. The best thing to do was let it go for now, and it would smooth over eventually. Renee wasn't upset with Cait for wanting help from her, but she wished that her sister had been honest instead of making it seem like she didn't have the opportunity for help from a professional wedding planner.

* * *

It wasn't until they finally arrived home that Cait detached from her phone for the amount of time it took her to open the door and sprint inside. After their fight, Cait hadn't looked away from the screen or uttered a word. Renee hated to think of Cait writing awful things about her to her friends and Jorden. As the more mature one, she had to act like the clueless one who wasn't bothered. Hammering the point into Cait wasn't going to get either of them anywhere. Cait would get over it—she always did. All Renee had to do was bide her time.

Instead of going in the house and dealing with Hunter, Renee walked around to the other side, pretending as if she wasn't looking for Luc. There was no harm checking in and saying hello. At least it would give Cait some time to herself to cool off.

Someone grunted from inside. Someone who sounded suspiciously like her father. Renee surged forward and almost smacked into her father as he stumbled through the door with Luc on his heels.

"Dad?"

"I'm fine, I promise." Marcus massaged his side.

"What happened?"

Marcus stood straighter, adding a slight wince to his expression, while Luc's eyes widened with guilt.

"It's nothing." Marcus waved her off. "It's just a twinge in my back, is all."

"From what?" Renee glanced at Luc.

"We were bringing down boxes from the attic." Luc scratched the back of his neck. His eyes didn't quite meet hers.

Renee checked out her father. He had stopped walking, but his teeth indented in his lip hard enough to leave a mark. "Let's get you inside and see if we can ice it."

Marcus waved a dismissive hand at her. "I'm fine."

Renee couldn't even look at Luc. He said if Marcus helped, he would take care of him. The weight of the fight with Cait pressed against her. Marcus didn't need to help Luc, and now he was hurt because of it. Prickling heat surged through her as she led her father away before he caused himself more damage.

"Can I help in any way?" Luc asked.

"No," Renee said through her teeth.

They walked up the back steps, with Renee's hands on either side of her father.

"I'm not a child, Renee."

"Exactly. What were you thinking? You know you're limited with your back."

He grumbled, and Renee walked past him to the refrigerator. The upstairs landing was dark and Cait's voice floated down the stairs. The words were indecipherable but the tone to whoever she was speaking was clear. She wasn't over their conversation yet. Hunter let out a yap at their presence.

"Sit on the couch, Dad. I'm going to grab you some ice."

"It's fine, Renee." He let out another groan.

Renee grabbed all three of the cold packs from the freezer and positioned them against Marcus's side.

"This really is overkill."

"You're not as strong as you used to be, Dad. Leave this hard work to other people before you end up at the chiropractor again."

"If I say okay, will you leave me alone?"

"For now."

"Hand me that remote, will you?"

"I thought you didn't need my help?"

Marcus pulled a face. "Just this one time."

Renee smirked and tossed the remote on the couch.

"Where's Cait?"

Opening that conversation wasn't what she wanted. "We ate a lot at the venue, and I'm heading to the co-working space for a little while. How about I order you two pizza for dinner?"

"You're not joining us?" He glanced at the ceiling.

"I'll be back later."

"Sounds good." He settled against the cushion, and the crease in his brow smoothed a little as the pain seemed to seep out of him.

The moment Renee stepped out on the porch, she glanced at Luc's house. Now he knew what she had meant about not wanting Marcus to help with the renovations. The idea of her father getting hurt made her chest tighten. Renee didn't want to go to work; she wouldn't be able to concentrate. She needed to vent. The only person she could truly talk to about what was going on with her life was her best friend.

Chapter 10

With Sadie's husband, Ken, taking care of the kids, Sadie and Renee could have had the alone time they needed for Renee to unload about everything happening in her life. With the opportunity, they chose to go out to Johnny's, one of the local bars. The bar had an entrance off the main road down an alley between two shops downtown. Most tourists only made it there if they were lost or knew a local who had recommended it to them.

Renee hadn't been there for some time, but the darkened room and chipped wood-paneled walls embraced her like a warm hug. Sadie slid into a stool at the bar.

A petite, yet muscular woman with sleeves of tattoos walked over to them from behind the bar. "What can I get you?"

"A vodka cranberry and whatever light beer you have," Sadie said, ordering for the both of them.

"Thanks," Renee said, sliding into the seat next to her friend.

"Tell me more about Princess Cait," Sadie said. "I thought my lists would help you out."

"They did." Renee was grateful to her friend for helping her with the organizational tips she had needed to help plan the wedding with Cait. Little did she know at the time that Cait had a professional one phone call away. Simmering heat still lingered on the surface of Renee's skin, but it had lessened with the distance she had put between herself and her family.

"Then what is it?"

"It's not a big deal. I mean, I'm not sure why I said what I did."

"What did you say?"

Renee unloaded the events of the day after she had found out about Prudence's willingness to help Cait.

"Do you think it was too harsh?" Renee asked.

"Not at all."

The bartender returned with drinks. "I'm Viv, by the way. Are you eating here?"

Without asking Renee, Sadie ordered buffalo wings and French fries.

"I can't eat anything else today," Renee said.

"Of course you can. You're not the one getting married, and I haven't eaten out in forever."

"You and Ken don't go out?"

"Whenever we can get his parents to watch the kids, he has to work late. I take my nights out when I can."

Renee understood why she was so quick to leave the house earlier.

The door opened, and Renee spotted Luc as he strode inside. She whipped around to face the bar. The mirror behind the liquor bottles caught her expression.

So did Sadie. "What is it? Did Cait follow you here?" Sadie turned in her seat. The heavy silence from Sadie only lasted a few seconds. "Is that Luc?"

"Don't—"

"Luc!" Sadie called out.

Through the mirror, Sadie frantically waved to him.

Renee risked a look and spotted the confused tilt of his head. That was when his gaze slid to hers again.

"Why did you do that?" It would have been the perfect time for her stool to sink into the ground, letting it swallow her forever.

"He's coming over here."

Because you called him over! With the conversation about Cait, Renee had failed to mention Luc's involvement with her father's injury.

Luc squinted his eyes for a moment before he snapped his fingers. "Sadie, right?"

"That's me." Sadie pressed her hand against her chest. Her voice rose higher than Renee had heard before.

"Mind if I join you two?" Luc indicated the empty seat next to Sadie. At least there was a buffer between them in the form of her best friend.

"Not at all."

"You two were inseparable that summer I came to West Cove," Luc said.

"We are best friends!" Sadie chirped. It was almost too much. "Even after all these years. Crazy, right?"

Renee had wanted to spend the night with her friend. Now, Luc made three.

"What're you drinking?" Viv asked.

Luc ordered a beer, and Viv headed to the tap to pour it.

"So, Luc." Sadie swiveled her body to face him. "Renee told me you're in town for part of the summer, helping with the high school."

Renee bumped Sadie in the leg. She didn't want to make it seem as if she had gossiped about Luc behind his back.

"Well, she's right. I taught at a school in Cape Cod—"

"Do you not teach there anymore?" Sadie sipped from her tumbler, eyeing him over the top. Her gaze slid to Renee.

Renee pinched her friend's thigh, indicating for her to bring it down a notch.

Luc cleared his throat. "It's the summer." Viv dropped a pint glass in front of him and Luc took a long pull from it.

Sadie bopped her hand against the side of her head. "Duh!"

Duh? Renee pulled a face at her friend. She was acting like a teenager again. When Luc had first visited West Cove, Sadie was dating her high school boyfriend, Walt, and only had eyes for him. But even she couldn't escape how Luc had grown into his features.

"I bet all the girls have a crush on you."

"Sadie!" Renee couldn't hold back any longer.

Sadie shrugged. "If I had a teacher who looked like you, I would have a crush for sure."

Luc nearly choked on his beer.

"We're all adults here," Sadie said.

"Some more than others," Renee said under her breath.

Sadie played with the short straw in her drink, swirling the ice. "Are you married?"

Renee clenched her jaw, wishing she had stayed home.

"I almost was once," he said.

Renee sat up. "To Claire?" She wasn't sure why she cared to get the details.

Sadie narrowed her eyes at Renee. Those slits demanded more details when Luc wasn't around.

"Years ago," he said. "I was twenty-five. I met Claire at school, and we were together for a while. I would have married her if she hadn't fallen in love with someone else."

"Ouch," Sadie said.

Luc traced a line across the condensation forming on the glass in front of him. "It's ancient history. We're good friends now."

Renee wondered if he really meant that. Marcus had been a wreck after Isla divorced him for another man. Luc hadn't married Claire, but Renee suspected it was similar, especially since he hadn't been the one to break them up. Engagements were almost the same without all the paperwork and the expensive wedding. Yet another reason she didn't believe in marriage. No broken heart or messy breakups for her.

"I'm not friends with any of my ex's," Sadie said.

Luc shrugged. "How about you?"

Sadie lifted her phone and unlocked it. "Married with three kids." She showed pictures and videos from the barbecue of her kids playing in the pool.

"I always wanted a big family," Luc said. "Only child here. You're lucky."

"I know I am." Sadie stared lovingly at her family before blurting out, "Renee is single."

Renee balked, and Luc chuckled. "I knew that already."

Sadie let out a gasp, which nearly knocked Renee out of her chair. She was about to ask Sadie if she was okay when her friend blurted out, "Renee does need a plus-one to her sister's wedding." Sadie waggled her eyebrows at Renee. "She can't ask any locals since it would be a proper scandal. But a tourist like you would be perfect. You already know each other, so what do you say?"

"I don't need to go with anyone." Renee wished she could stop her friend's flapping lips. She loved Sadie like a sister, but sometimes her pushiness was too much. Especially when Renee was the focus.

"When is Cait's wedding again?" Luc asked.

Sadie dropped her jaw as if to say, "*See, he's interested!*"

Renee had to rescue herself from this conversation instead of Sadie guilting Luc to attend Cait's wedding with her. "The Fourth. I'm going with Marcus."

"Doesn't he have a plus-one?" Sadie asked.

"Who would he take?" Renee turned back to Luc. "Sometimes, Sadie can't stop controlling the people around her."

Sadie shrugged and leaned back in her chair before sipping from her glass. "Having three kids does that to you. They wouldn't know what to do without me telling them."

A shrill feedback sound filled the air, and everyone turned toward the back of the room. Four men stood behind their instruments. Renee hadn't even paid much attention to them since they had come in. Sadie had required a lot of her attention, so she didn't go too far into pushing Renee and Luc together. *Too late for that.*

"Hello, everyone," a bearded guy said into the mic. Renee recalled seeing the band once before at Johnny's. They had been good. Though the singer was new. Renee turned in her chair to face them. "We hope you enjoy our set and feel free to get outta your seats and dance if you feel the rhythm."

They started with a fast-paced number, loud enough to shake the rafters. The other patrons watched while trying to keep their conversations going.

The music had come at the perfect time, as Sadie wouldn't be able to coerce Luc into any commitment to the wedding. Spending time alone with Luc on the beach was one thing, but Sadie had steered the conversation into dangerous territory. Renee and Luc had only spent a total of two months of their lives together. They never connected when social media became more accessible and other than knowing his career choice, it didn't mean she wanted to lead him on over the summer just because she didn't want to show up to her sister's wedding alone.

It wasn't until the third song when Sadie jumped out of her chair and pulled Renee into an empty spot in front of the band. There were already two other couples dancing alongside a group of women who looked to be in their fifties and stood in a line, swaying to the music. Their husbands stood by the bar bobbing their heads along.

It took a few minutes for Renee to feed off Sadie's energy and start dancing. She rocked her hips to the beat of the song and found her thoughts about her family drifting away.

"Come on, Luc!" Sadie called.

Luc waved her off and remained at the bar. Renee spotted his amused grin and couldn't help noticing how his eyes never left hers. She spun and glanced at him again. His gaze hadn't wavered.

The movements made her warm with exertion, but part of the rippling heat licking across her body was from Luc's stare.

They played a silent game of hide-and-seek with their eyes. Luc seemed to be good at the game she made up in her head. Renee wondered what had brought him to the bar. Was it a coincidence, just like him coming back to West Cove?

Renee wasn't sure how many songs they danced to. Each one flowed into the next, and the energy never wavered. Between her movements and the resurgence of the crackling electricity between her and Luc, she was more comfortable than she'd been in a long time. She thought of Luc and herself over that summer together. Admitting to herself that the connection they had shared together hadn't completely gone away.

It wasn't until the final notes of the music ran out that Renee snapped back to the present.

"We're going to take a little break," the lead singer said into the mic.

Renee licked her dry lips and floated to the bar to order water. Her legs didn't feel like her own.

Luc wasn't at his chair. His drink was empty, yet there wasn't any money on the bar. Had he paid and left at some point?

Renee lifted her phone and noticed it was quarter to nine, and she didn't feel an ounce of fatigue. She wasn't sure how long that would keep up.

"He's in the bathroom," Sadie said as she wiped the sweat from her forehead with the bottom of her tank top.

"Who is?"

"Don't pretend you weren't panicked when you noticed Luc wasn't at the bar."

"I wasn't panicking."

"Sure, you weren't."

Viv dropped two glasses of water in front of their chairs. She grinned. "They're good, right?"

"So good," Sadie said before guzzling half the glass.

"My cousin is the bassist," Viv said. "He got me this job over the summer."

The conversations around them picked up again, creating a dull roar in the bar.

Luc reappeared behind them. "I picked up the tab. I'm headed out. I have an early morning tomorrow."

"Thanks," Renee said.

Sadie stretched her arms over her head. "I should get going. I'd love to stay out later, but the kids keep waking up at six like it's the school year. I can't win."

"Do you need a ride?" Luc asked.

Sadie pulled out her keys. "I drove, but would you mind taking Renee home?"

Renee's insides twisted. Even after all the fun they'd had, Sadie was back to this?

"I mean, you are neighbors."

Luc cleared his throat. "I'm parked in the back lot."

Sadie kissed Renee's cheek and spoke close to her ear. "Loosen up a bit. You usually do in the summer. Besides, it's not forever."

The trio walked out together and separated once they reached the alley. Sadie had parked on the main road, the opposite way from Luc. Renee peered after her friend, wondering once more if fate had done this to her. Outside, the air hadn't cooled much, even with the sun already down for the night. Heat rolled off Luc, and she tried to convince herself that it wasn't part of the reason her body temperature was higher than usual.

Renee tried to let Luc lead the way to his truck, but he slowed his pace to walk with her. "The band was good."

"They were."

"You looked as if you were having fun."

"I don't get out much."

Luc laughed, and Renee couldn't help joining him. She spotted the truck in the center of the lot. There weren't many cars, so it wasn't hard to miss.

"I understand not getting out," he said. "During the school year, I'm booked with grading papers, coaching, and other school events."

The Luc she knew always had his nose in a book. "I never saw you as the activity kind of guy."

"In high school, I wasn't. But it comes with the job of being a teacher."

A moment of silence held fast to the air around them. Luc opened the passenger side for her, and she climbed inside. He closed the door, sealing her in. She inhaled deeply. Even with the windows cracked open, the scent of Luc surrounded her. She briefly wondered what her teen self would have thought if she knew they would reunite years later.

Luc hopped into his side and started the truck. It rumbled to life under her. The familiar sound that she'd heard every day since Luc had moved into the house next door eased her. Sadie's words echoed in her mind.

It's not forever.

Renee had let her previous relationship with Luc dictate how she felt about him now. There was no pressure to rehash any of that. They were neighbors for a little while. Sure, he was handsome, charming, and he loved teaching kids. He was a catch for any woman who liked that. Renee wasn't completely oblivious to any of it, but as Luc had distracted her from her family tonight, there was no reason he couldn't do the same for the rest of the time Cait was living with her.

Luc pulled out of the lot and onto the main road. "Sorry about your dad today."

"What's that?" Without the music blocking out her life, she'd fallen back into her thoughts about the day.

"I, uh, promised he wouldn't get hurt, and on the first day, I broke that. I did tell him the box was heavy, but he insisted. Us guys are stupid and stubborn sometimes."

Renee smiled into her hand. Had Luc thought about apologizing to her the whole night? "He is stubborn. But there's no need to apologize to me."

"You seemed upset earlier."

"That had nothing to do with you or him." *Well, not entirely.* Her dad getting hurt only added to the stress of the argument between her and Cait.

Luc watched the road for a few seconds before speaking again. "Do you want to talk about it?"

No. Though Luc had interrupted her time with Sadie. He was objective to the discussion and could give some insight. "Cait and I argued about her wedding. Then I came home to Dad hurt like that, which is why I went out tonight with Sadie. I needed to talk to someone outside of my family."

"I see," he said with a sigh. "Well, I'm not happy about your fight, but I didn't want you upset with me. It's why I came out tonight too."

"What do you mean?"

"I, uh, asked your dad where you might have gone."

"You came to Johnny's looking for me?"

Luc glanced at her and then back to the road. "Yeah."

Renee turned to the window, failing to hide a smile. No wonder he had looked at her the way he had while she danced. He had come there to see her. Had he hoped for the opportunity to bring her home, or would he have waited until another time when they were alone to apologize?

Her thoughts of him shifted slightly.

"When we knew each other. Over that summer. You were quiet and thoughtful. I remember the conversations we had about your mother and all the stuff you had to deal with. I always wondered why you kept it inside. I thought you were doing the same with me this time too. Keeping your anger in."

Renee opened her mouth and closed it again. Luc had remembered much more about their time together than she'd realized. She had unloaded to him more than once that summer. Their connection had been strong, and like with Sadie, she wanted to open herself up to someone. Little did she know that he had kept her secrets all this time.

"I'm not that person anymore."

"I still see her in you. We all carry pieces of our youth with us."

As much as she wanted to dig in further, a snake coiled in her stomach at the thought of admitting how much it had meant to her to have him that summer. It was the first time she had wanted a relationship and believed that there was someone out there for her. Living without her mother made those possibilities come to light until Luc had left and didn't leave a trace in his wake.

"Well, I'm over the drama with my mother. And I'm not upset with you." Renee had avoided rehashing the argument with Cait, but Luc pushing her to talk about her past had brought those uncomfortable feelings out again.

"Sounds like it," Luc said, locking eyes with her. The red light in front of them lit up his face.

"Are we going to push this?"

"Not if you don't want to," he said. "I just wanted to be sure we were good."

"Why does it matter to you?" Renee hadn't intended for the question to come out that sharp.

Before she could take it back, Luc spoke. "Because you gave me an unforgettable summer all those years ago. I would hate to spend the rest of this one with you upset with me."

Renee twisted her fingers in her lap as she tried to ignore the lightness in her stomach. She wanted to know why it mattered to him so much, but she wasn't going to ruin the moment after him telling her she had been unforgettable to him. Little did he know that she had started to feel the same.

Chapter 11

The ride home with Luc ended like any friend dropping another friend home after a night out. They waved goodbye and Renee thanked him again. The words *unforgettable summer* clung to her mind as she entered the house. His admission of his feelings had surprised her.

The lightness within her helped her drift to sleep. But reality slammed into her the next morning when Cait's hard footfalls paced the room above her. They moved down the stairs and into the kitchen. Cait didn't even look into the living room before she let Hunter out. She stared at her phone, and the moment Hunter finished, she raced up the stairs again. The door to Renee's bedroom slammed.

Renee rolled onto her back and rubbed her hands over her face. There were no apologies from Cait—there never were—and every time they both fell back into the same place where they always ended up as sisters. Eventually.

That didn't mean Renee couldn't prepare herself for the inevitability of Cait bringing the subject up again. Renee wasn't going to back down but would wait until it became an issue to do so.

To limit their interaction and the possibility of cracking open that argument again, Renee drifted to the co-working space for most of the morning on Friday and Saturday. Once Renee caught up with current projects, she moved on with her advertisements and potential clients.

The end of the month was in her sights. After the wedding and sending Cait and Jorden off, her life would return to normal. Renee focused on filling slots for late July and August. The best and worst thing about freelancing was that there wasn't a break unless you intended on not getting paid for a certain amount of time. Since she loved West Cove for all the seasons, there wasn't much of a reason for a vacation to get in the way of work.

When Renee returned home on Saturday afternoon, Marcus's car was gone. Yet Renee spotted him in the backyard weeding the small patch of flowers in the beds, which spanned the length of the house.

Brandy sunbathed next to him with her paws up in the air. Hunter yapped from inside the house at the window closest to where they worked.

"Where's Cait?"

"She mentioned going into town," Marcus said without looking up.

Renee couldn't ignore the clench in her jaw. She checked her phone. Cait hadn't bothered to let her know about a trip to town. She would have happily gone with her.

"She asked me to ask you to take Hunter out for a walk."

At the word *walk*, Brandy perked up. She rolled over and shimmied into a standing position. Even though Brandy didn't take walks much anymore, it seemed as if Hunter's energy had gotten to her.

"That's fine, I've been sitting all morning anyway." *Anything to keep the bride happy.*

As Renee wandered into the house she couldn't help wondering what emergency drew Cait into town that she couldn't take her own dog for a walk. Renee buried the feeling as Brandy bumped her hand with her wet nose. "All right, girl."

Hunter bounced on his feet as if springs lived under his fur. It took a few seconds of Hunter jumping around before she could grab his collar and hook him up. He darted under her skirt, and the leash tangled around her legs.

Brandy glued herself to Renee's left side while she held the leash for Hunter in her right. It was as if she silently promised never to run away again as long as Renee didn't hook her up like Hunter. It took a moment for Renee to calm Hunter down enough to not tug on the leash. They formed a rhythm after a few minutes.

The walk was uneventful—a welcome reprieve from most of her summer—but when they returned home, Hunter's stride was a little sluggish, and his tongue lolled out of his mouth. The heat hadn't given up, and the reflection from the water and the radiating sand didn't help ease it away.

Luc was outside, digging through the tool bag propped in the bed of his truck. Renee smoothed her hair down. Normally, she didn't purposefully dress to impress anyone, but she was glad she'd chosen the sundress. The floral pattern was a shock of pinks and yellows and hugged her in all the right places.

Hunter snapped at Brandy, and the bigger dog sneezed in Hunter's face. Renee lifted Hunter and tucked him against her side.

Luc turned and waved at her. "It seems you have your hands full today."

"Just with this one." Renee hefted Hunter higher in her grip. His legs kicked out as if he were running in mid-air.

"Where's Cait?"

The mystery of the day. "She's out."

He clicked his tongue, and a shimmering sensation skittered up her arms. Luc's observations of Renee had been spot-on the other night and she wanted to know more of what he thought of her and their time together all those years ago. "Do you have a few minutes? I need a hand with something."

"Sure." Renee placed Hunter down in the living room and

unhooked him from the leash. Brandy flopped on her pillow and closed her eyes.

Renee stood by the open window where Marcus was still weeding. "Don't do this all day. You're going to be sore."

"Yeah, yeah."

Renee shook her head and sighed. As many times as she tried to get her father to slow down, she wasn't sure if it would ever work until he ended up in the hospital. She crossed her fingers, hoping that wouldn't be the case anytime soon.

She crossed the room, stopping at the bathroom to make sure the walk hadn't made her look too disheveled. A smirk twisted her lips, and she tried to shake away the pops of excitement coursing through her.

* * *

The back door to Luc's house was open. Slabs of wood, tools, and other materials covered the kitchen table. In the sink, dirty dishes balanced on top of each other. The dishwasher door was open, but the racks were missing. He had taken the renovation seriously, and it all seemed as if it would take more than the time he was in town. "Luc?"

"Up here!"

Renee walked through the living room and rounded the stairs. Luc stood at the top landing, opening a ladder. "I know you didn't want your father working here."

"I didn't say that." Renee climbed the steps.

"This job isn't great for someone with injuries. In case this thing breaks."

"If you think it's going to break, why are you using it?"

"I'm sure it's okay." He put pressure on the ladder. It wobbled slightly. "I just don't know how long Audrey's had this. And I don't trust it entirely. I need you to help keep it steady so I can change a few bulbs." Luc tucked a bulb in his back pocket and climbed the ladder. It strained under his weight.

Renee gripped the metal tight enough to press lines into her palm. Luc stood on the third rung and reached up to unscrew the burned-out one. He reached down and lifted the bulb from his pocket.

"Can you take this one?"

Renee held one of her hands out, putting more pressure on her other hand. It wasn't the most well cared for piece of equipment. It was rusted in some spots and leaned with Luc's weight. Their fingers brushed as she took the old bulb. She clamped down on her lip to keep the surprise from her face, or the fact that touching his hand brought back a wave of memories of the last time his hands were on her.

There were three bulbs in the hallway, and then they moved into the first bedroom. Renee recalled that one to be Audrey's. It was mostly the same as she remembered. The cream-colored walls used to be white, and scratch marks cut through the paint. The bed had a worn duvet with frayed edges halfway tucked under the mattress. The tall dresser with the shell-filled lamp brought back a wave of memories. Audrey used to comb the beach for them and decorate whatever part of the house she could with the authenticity of the town. The wall of windows facing the beach was probably the view that would sell the house. Renee almost didn't want to step inside the space, wishing to keep the memory the same before someone else bought it. How much would Luc update for the sale?

"Are all of them out?" Renee asked.

"No, I'm replacing them with energy-efficient bulbs. It's the most I can do for now. There's no point in completely rewiring everything."

No point if Audrey was selling the house. Would the new owner purchase it as a rental property for tourists? It wouldn't be any different than it had been for years, but there was something about knowing the owner of the home.

They moved into the next room. A set of twin beds were pushed against the back of the room. Those windows faced the back of the house. The floors creaked, and dust clung to the windowsill. The walls were the same paneling as the living room, making the space appear darker than it could have been.

The rooms appeared to absorb the light much more than she recalled. Inside the Hardy house, time seemed to stand still. While Luc cleared out the house and improved it as much as he could over the summer, maybe the next owner would renovate it to the current decade. Though, in that case, it might lose its charm.

Luc quickly replaced the bulbs in that room while Renee leaned against the doorframe, watching him, the memories flipping through her mind. Luc folded the ladder and leaned it against the wall.

"What about that one?" Renee pointed at the closed door across the hallway.

"I've already changed the bulbs in there."

Renee couldn't ignore the twinge of disappointment at not seeing inside his room. She tore her gaze from the door. It was his private place and none of her business.

Luc sighed and crossed his arms. "Do you have anything else to do today?"

"Do you need more help?"

"I was hoping to organize the sunroom so I can put more junk in there to dispose of."

Renee hesitated. There were other things she could be doing while Cait was gone. But Cait had left without explanation. When she was around Luc, everything seemed a little less overwhelming. "I can do that."

Luc unleashed a brilliant smile, and Renee had to turn away from it. Sadie's comment the other day about his students having a crush on him popped into her mind. She wholeheartedly agreed with her best friend that he was easy to like and attractive. "I need to eat first. Do you want a sandwich?"

"As long as it's not as bad as that lemonade."

Luc's lips quirked to the side. "I have to make my lunch every day for school, and not to brag, but I'm one hell of a sandwich stacker."

"I'd like to see that."

* * *

Renee and Luc spent the afternoon sorting through the back sunroom, loading rusted beach equipment, and other accumulated junk left from Audrey and her renters into the bed of his truck for disposal. Most properties had cleaning crews come through after each renter, but some—like Audrey's—relied on the renters to clean up after themselves. From the disintegrated paper plates and napkins in one corner of the room, it seemed most of the junk had come from a while ago.

They worked on filling black plastic bags with garbage. Luc played music from a portable speaker. His tastes had changed from classic rock to more popular music.

"It's all the kids listen to. It's hard to ignore when they're going on about the latest Snapchat celebrity. And slightly addictive."

"You're addicted to Snapchat?"

"No, uh, I mean the music."

Renee briefly imagined Luc with one of those filters, which made dog ears spring from his head, with a little black nose. She smiled to herself.

"Has your choice in music changed?"

"I don't listen to a lot of music. Mostly podcasts now." Marcus rarely allowed anyone, including Renee, to turn off his radio stations. For years, their only arguments had been about the choice of music played at home. During her summers in West Cove, she had pushed hard rock. Throughout college, it was hip-hop as her roommate blasted the music at the parties they had held in their dorm room.

"So, you're boring now?"

Renee snorted and tossed the nearest item in Luc's direction—an old straw sun hat. Luc caught it against his chest then plopped it on his head.

"How did you know I needed this?"

"Make sure no bugs are living in there."

Luc flicked the hat off his head. "You're still not great at throwing."

"It's not like I have a reason to practice."

Luc licked his lips. "Remember that time we tried to play Frisbee on the beach?"

Renee had to think about that one.

"Come on. You kept throwing into the water no matter how far I moved. That woman's dog kept running after it in the surf?"

The memory rose to the surface. It was the day she and Luc officially met. She knew Audrey's nephew was staying in West Cove for the summer and they were around the same age. Her father had asked Renee to take Audrey's nephew to the beach for the day. Neither were excited to be pushed together. It had been only a few days since Renee had arrived. Marcus must have realized how much Renee had missed Cait and had tried to get her to hang out with someone her age.

To appease Marcus and Audrey, Renee had brought Luc to the beach. Luc was lanky and hunched over when he walked as if he needed to appear as small as possible. Throughout the rest of the summer—as they got to know each other—she recalled that he stood at least a few inches taller.

"I found the Frisbee by the barrier." Renee relived the memory.

They were both unenthusiastic about the game at first, but then Luc gained the ability to aim, while Renee stayed the same: bad. Eventually, one of the renter's dogs who was bounding through the surf thought Renee wanted to play since she had thrown it in the water more times than not.

"I remember you ran after the dog," Renee said. "He was so fast."

Luc moved two beach chairs to the empty end of the sunroom,

leaning them against the wall. "I figured if he left with it, then you wouldn't want to spend any more time with me."

"You didn't need to torture yourself over that. I would have hung out with you."

Luc chuckled. "Your scowling face said otherwise. I mean, I would have been happy to sit on the beach all day, reading."

As they came to find out, that was an activity they had in common.

"It was fun, though," he said. "It was a start to an amazing summer." He returned to shoving a takeout container into the black bag.

Luc left that sentiment hanging in the air. For the first time since he had returned, there wasn't any awkwardness twisting her stomach. It had been stripped away by his confidence and how comfortable she felt around him. Almost as she had that summer. With the awkwardness gone, only the rippling tension in her gut remained. She couldn't deny it anymore; she wanted to get to know the adult Luc and work on getting back to the point where they had left off. They were already well on their way, and Renee could no longer ignore the stirring inside of her with each new meeting.

* * *

After another hour of clearing out the sunroom, it had enough space to house all of Luc's tools for further renovations. Renee returned home, experiencing the beginning effects of soreness creeping into places she wasn't sure could be sore. No wonder Dad had hurt himself helping Luc. It was a testament to Luc's physical shape that he didn't seem to mind. Maybe his conditioned body from playing beach volleyball helped. She'd seen the competitions at the Olympics. Those athletes were in great shape.

"Hey," Cait said from the porch.

Renee jumped back, startled. "When did you get back?"

Cait chewed on her lip. "A little while ago. What were you doing?"

"Helping Luc."

Renee waited for the quip from her sister about them being together . . .alone. But it never came.

"I'm sorry for not letting Prudence do the wedding." Cait's voice cracked. "I didn't realize that you would be so busy, and this would be an inconvenience."

"It's not an inconvenience."

"Don't lie to me, Renee. Every time I mention the wedding plans you're sharp with me and demanding. I know I'm the worst bride ever."

"You're not, Cait. Stop." Their argument seemed like an eternity ago, but Renee could let go of these things. Cait probably had stewed on it all day. "I'm sorry for acting the way I did. I had everything in place for work this month. The rearranging for your wedding plans was a little stressful, and I could have used some notice."

"You like your routine. I get it."

Renee walked up the steps and took her sister's hands. "Exactly. It wasn't about you. More about me. If you can let this go, I already have."

"Promise?"

"Promise."

Cait wrapped her arms around Renee and squeezed her. Renee nearly fell over from the strength of the embrace. Hunter barked madly from behind the screen door as if he thought someone was attacking his mom.

After Cait let her go, she skipped over to the rocking chair, lifting a small white bag from the floor. "I bought these for you today. As an apology."

"You didn't need to do that." Renee plucked a thick black glasses case from the bag.

"Well, you needed new sunglasses anyway. Yours are hideous."

Renee let out a snort. She was due for a new pair.

Cait hugged her again and sighed loudly. "I'm glad that's over. I stayed away as long as I could. I hate it when we fight."

It didn't happen often. "You never have to do that, Cait. My house is always yours, and no matter what happens between us, I'll always love you."

"You too." In front of her eyes, Cait's frown morphed into a devious smile. "You have to tell me all about your time with Luc."

Renee opened her mouth to deny it, but there wasn't a point. "I like spending time with him. Somehow, I'm still comfortable with him, even after all these years. Is that strange?"

"I don't think so. Luc was your first, and that holds a lot of meaning. Especially since you are still single."

Renee didn't have any doubt in that regard. Luc was there for the summer and the summer only. They both shared a connection. It would be harder to deny it. With the end date of him leaving weeks away, there was no reason for her to worry about the future, only the present.

Chapter 12

The volleyball clinic started earlier in the morning than Renee had anticipated. When she came downstairs after a shower, excited voices floated up from the beach through the open front windows of the house. The light from the sun was a thin sliver across the sky while the girls jogged up the sand from the public side.

From what Luc had told her, he worked with three groups throughout the day, based on the girls' ages and level of training. The program lasted three weeks. While she didn't mind since she woke early, she wondered what the other renters and locals would think. A program led by the high school was a worthy one and she doubted anyone would care as much as she had at the start.

Renee tried to remember that whatever Luc did wasn't her problem. Her feet seemed to think otherwise as she drifted over to the windows. She spotted him by the net. Two people stood by the pole watching the girls practice bumping and setting on both sides. One was Luc.

As her hand touched the windowsill, Luc turned in her direction. In a moment of panic, she stood there and waved.

Waved!

He waved back and leaned close to the other person before walking toward the house.

Renee's heart raced. From what Luc saw, it appeared as if she had been watching him from the window: stalker style. It had only been a day since she had helped him at the house, but the effect he had on her continued to linger, forcing tingles across her skin.

Brandy lifted her head as Luc approached, and her tail thumped on the wooden floors, but otherwise, she didn't move from her spot.

Before Hunter could sense another person nearby to bark at, Renee walked onto the porch to meet Luc.

He stood by the curb, stopping almost suddenly. "Hey, I hope we didn't wake you."

"Not at all."

Luc stepped onto the stairs. The sunlight behind him illuminated his outline. Even though it wasn't that hot out yet, he wore shorts and a tank top with a baseball cap on his head. A long cord with a whistle attached to the end dangled around his neck. "I, uh, wasn't sure if you were going to be around this week."

"I'm always around. Do you need more help with the house?"

Luc let out a sound between a cough and a laugh. "That house is always going to need help. That's not why I came over here. Are you— Do you want to come out with me this week? Thursday? Or Friday?"

Her instinct was to refuse, but the sentiment caught in her throat.

"There's this sushi place I saw in the next town over. I don't know if it's any good, but I'm craving it, and I thought we'd have a good time."

Under the brim of his cap, his eyes were dark and unreadable.

"Sushi, huh?" Renee tried to keep the disgust from her voice.

"Do you like sushi?"

Slimy raw fish in my mouth? No thanks. The thought of ingesting it made her empty stomach heave. But he'd put himself in a vulnerable place. Her mind still reeled from him asking her out.

"Do you want to come with me?"

The conversations with Cait and Sadie came to mind. Luc was only here for the summer, but a date? It wasn't as if he were a tourist and she'd never see him again. They were next-door neighbors until July. She'd have no distance from him if their date went sour.

"Renee?"

"What?" she asked, finding it hard to pull out of her thoughts.

His chest heaved, and his gaze lowered to the rocking chair behind her. "Never mind. It was just an idea. I should get back to it. See you."

Renee shook her head, still unable to form words.

He jogged across the street and bounded over the barrier. His feet sunk into the sand, appearing as heavy as her heart.

Renee stood there for way too long, imagining a date with Luc. It was something she didn't think she wanted. Refusing him seemed like the only option. Spending time at his house was fine. Even the flirty banter worked for her. Sealing her fondness for him with a date would only lead him on.

Renee couldn't make up her mind about Luc, and it frustrated her to no end. His attention didn't waver from the girls and standing on the porch watching him wasn't going to help her stick to the refusal.

She wandered back into the house, making her way to the coffee machine to start it. A heaviness pooled in her stomach, tugging at it with a strength she hadn't experienced in a while. Maybe not since after the summer she shared with Luc. Through her years in college with her therapist, Renee learned so much about herself and the damaging relationship with her mother. A determination to never be like Isla flowed through her with each new romantic relationship, which was why they never lasted long. She couldn't put her heart out there. Not like Isla did. Isla fell into relationships like diving under the surface of the water, quick and effortless. Her mother had destroyed lives that way. Renee had seen enough destruction to harden her heart sufficiently to not jump into relationships lasting longer than a summer.

Luc was more complicated since the stirrings from their summer together were still there.

But, it was better this way.

* * *

Over the next few days, Renee acted like the pre-Luc teenager she had been all those years ago. Her avoidance of the house unnerved her to no end, but it was necessary. Each morning, she left for the co-working space by sneaking into her car before he spotted her. She made sure to come home around noon when the volleyball groups were having lunch at the public beach, far enough from the house that he couldn't spot her.

Renee did everything to avoid the beach and the front porch, even though those had been *her* spots for years. She watched Luc from afar, well not that far, but he continued his renovations on the house without any sign that her refusal had bothered him.

It wasn't until Friday that he came to her house again after the camp had ended for the day. He surprised her when he appeared at the door. Hunter and Brandy rushed over to him, and he gave them lots of scratches.

Renee and Cait were in the middle of some reality show that Cait insisted Renee watch.

"Hey," Renee said, standing from the couch. She couldn't bear to look at Cait for fear of her pushing her and Luc together. Renee hadn't told anyone other than Sadie about refusing his offer for a date.

Luc's stare captured hers. "Marcus said I could take some topsoil you had. I thought he was here."

Renee shook her head. Her father hadn't mentioned that conversation. "Did he say where he left it?"

"Uh, no."

Renee figured it was in the backyard since there was no way Marcus's tidy tendencies would allow soil into the house. She halted when she spotted tiny brown paw prints scattered across the kitchen floor. The trail led upstairs. Renee closed her eyes briefly, knowing what was coming next. The empty bag of soil was on the back landing, but on its side. Hunter-sized paw prints dipped in brown littered the area around the bag.

The pile of the remainder of the topsoil was in the backyard, soaking into the grass. "That's unfortunate," she said.

Luc rubbed the back of his neck. "I'll need more than that anyway. I, uh, should head to the store."

Renee glared at Hunter. Luc was already sweating from the amount of time he had spent outside that week. His skin had darkened to a golden tan. He looked as if he belonged at the beach. At her beach.

The refusal of the date formed a thick cloud between them. Was this how it would be between them forever? It had been her fault entirely, but with the passing days, she had come to realize her mistake. Renee had to fix their relationship and keep it friendly. Luc had only been kind to her, and she wasn't treating him as she should.

"I'll come with you."

Luc's eyebrows rose. "Are you sure?"

Renee had expected him to turn her invitation down after she'd done the same to him. It would only be fair, but she had to make it up to him somehow. Even with just an apology. "Yes. I have to head into town anyway."

"Great," he said.

Renee didn't want to hear anything from Cait about going

with Luc, so she grabbed her purse from the kitchen table and left with Luc out through the back door.

"I'm going into town. Be back soon! Can you clean up after Hunter, please?"

"Wait!" Cait said, but Renee closed the door on her sister.

Nothing would deter Cait, though. Renee's phone pinged three times in a row before she silenced it. Cait knocked on the window facing the driveway, and Renee waved her off. Her sister's lips moved and pointed to her phone. Reading Cait's texts would only get in her head about what she was doing with Luc.

Luc got into his truck, and the engine roared to life. Renee hesitated by the door, led by the feelings she had when she turned down his date. She inhaled deeply and got inside. Luc was just a friend. There was no reason she needed to feel awkward around him. Once they were completely alone, Luc could ask about her refusal. Or he could make it more awkward by making small talk about it. Renee had made a point to go with him, so she couldn't back down now. There were no hard feelings from her, and they could still get along as neighbors.

Renee left her fate up to whoever decided it. If Luc asked about the date, then she would have to be honest with him about where to keep their friendship.

"Do you have a preference for music?" he asked, then nodded. "Oh yeah, you're a podcast woman." Luc's serious expression cracked with a smile.

Renee's shoulders relaxed, and she melted against the seat. "Your choice."

He hooked his phone to the radio and turned on a classic rock playlist. Renee stared out the window, trying not to smile. She wondered how much of an influence she'd had after she had teased him the other day.

Luc turned the corner, leaving the beach behind them. "What did you have to do in town?"

"Huh?"

"You said you had to go into town?"

Renee couldn't admit she'd lied. But the topsoil issue had partly been her fault. Hunter's presence hadn't been missed, but she should have known he was getting into trouble. "Oh, I need to make sure the bridesmaids' dresses have arrived for the wedding. The girls want physical evidence. I think to post them online." It was half true. Renee knew the dresses were already there since they checked earlier in the week. Most of the bridal party had agreed that shipping them ahead of time would avoid risking them getting lost during their travel to West Cove.

"Cait's still making you do all the wedding stuff for her?"

"I don't mind." Renee knew enough about Luc's kind nature that he didn't intend to bring up a sore subject between her and Cait. But she was also lying through her teeth about why she had ended up in the car with him. She had two choices to make: admit her lying, or lie more.

"As long as you don't mind." Luc glanced at her as he slowed at a stop sign. "Thanks for tagging along with me. It's nice to have adult company after hanging out with teens all week."

"Don't you do that every day?"

"Sure, in a classroom setting where I'm the boss. And there are other teachers and administrators around. But Dale—the assistant coach—isn't one to hang out after work."

"Are you liking it?"

"I love it."

"Even with the renovations?"

"They're for a good cause. Audrey has been talking about getting that place off her back for years. She needs the money to pay for the nursing home, and I'm glad to help."

Renee almost wished Luc wasn't such a good guy. The more she thought about it, the more she believed that turning him down had been a mistake. Had she momentarily lost her mind? Sadie hadn't let it go either. Her best friend didn't see any harm in going out with him. The worry about the fallout when it was time for him to leave flew to the front of her mind. There was a chance they could fall into the same rhythm as they had all those summers ago.

She'd glimpsed it during the time they'd spent together cleaning the house. Would he have the urge to want to continue long-distance? She couldn't do that to either of them. Her forever home was in West Cove. If they remained friends, then maybe they would like each other's pictures on Facebook, but at least she wouldn't have to worry about hurting him if he thought she was interested in more. Though, not accepting the date didn't sit right in her gut. It twisted and turned as if she had eaten rotting food. It overwhelmed her enough that she didn't realize she was speaking until she had blurted out, "I'm sorry about the date."

"What date?"

"The one you asked me on."

"Oh." Luc's hands clutched the wheel a little tighter. "Why are you sorry?"

"I didn't want to lead you on." Renee's face flushed enough that she turned the vents blasting air conditioning directly at her cheeks. "I mean, I didn't want you to think I wanted more from you. I like hanging out. But I wasn't sure how much you were looking for."

His silence was worse than anything he could have said to her at that moment.

"Say something," she urged.

"You could have just said that." Luc pulled the truck into the lot of the hardware store. "I didn't mean for you to get in your head about it. But I'm going to be honest with you. I still want to go on a date. I like being around you, Renee. No matter what happens after." Luc parked the car, unbuckled his seat, and shifted to face her. "You make me feel as if no time has passed since that summer we were together. Having the girls around makes me want to embrace that summer excitement again. I'm not looking for forever, if that's what you're worried about. I thought it would be fun to take you out for the night." He chuckled to himself. "We never got to since we were broke that summer."

Renee shook her head, remembering how hard it had been to get away from Marcus and Audrey's prying eyes. "Neither of us had a car either."

"Exactly." He spoke around a broad smile, melting the weight in her gut. "I'm okay with being your neighbor too."

"You are?"

"Of course. I'm sorry for making you feel awkward. That was never my intention." He scratched his head, fluffing his hair to one side. "I feel like an ass now."

"Don't," she said, touching his arm.

It tensed under her hand, and she pulled away. "Sorry."

"Can we move on from this? Go back to friends?"

"Sure."

Luc smiled and hopped out of the truck. Renee turned her tingling hand over and wondered if she was protesting too much when it came to him. Summers were supposed to be about fun, and so far, she had been a killjoy about most activities with Cait and Luc as they had pushed their way into her life in the last few weeks.

Renee wished she could let the awkwardness go as easily as Luc did. He was a good influence on her, and maybe she could learn from him.

* * *

They stopped at the hardware store first. Luc moved around the store as if he owned the place. He quickly strode down the aisle with the gardening supplies. Along the way, several locals stopped them four separate times. Three out of the four mentioned they knew he was helping at Audrey's house. That was the thing about small towns. No one could walk through any of the stores without knowing at least the person at the register by their first name and identifying one or more of their relatives.

Since they were in a hardware store, there weren't many of the gossiping older women who made a point to remind Renee of her single status. But she was sure their husbands would comment on who they had seen Renee Clarke with at the store.

That was another reason Renee had chosen to spend her summers with tourists and avoided any invitations from locals setting her up with their sons, nephews, or cousins.

Everyone considered Audrey a local, even though she hadn't been to the house in years. So, by default, was Luc. Renee with a local was unheard of, and she wanted to limit the gossip as much as possible when Luc finally went home.

Renee could hear the comments now, which would plague her forever.

How's Luc?

Do you stay in touch?

You let a good one go there.

If you keep refusing to date, you'll never get married.

After they checked out of the store, Renee was finally able to breathe under the imaginary pressure she had put herself under. Normally, she didn't care much about what people thought, but that was the way of West Cove. It was unavoidable, so she evaded the fallout when she could.

"Where's the dress shop?" Luc stacked the two bags in the bed of the truck.

"The what? Oh!" Renee had been so wrapped up in convincing the locals that she and Luc were only friends that she'd forgotten the lie that had brought her to town. "It's down the street."

"Let's go, then," he said.

"You don't have to come. It will only take a few minutes."

"It's okay. You went with me in there and battled against accusations of our involvement."

Renee winced. "Did you notice that?"

Luc laughed, as if it wasn't a big deal, even though Renee's cheeks flamed. "Anytime I go to my hometown, all of my parents' friends ask the same questions. Especially since Claire. They seem to think I can't function without a woman in my life."

The tension in her chest deflated. "It's sad, right? They don't realize how stressful it can be to get pressure from strangers. It's like they want you to be unhappy."

Luc pulled a face. "What do you mean . . . unhappy?"

Renee opened her mouth and closed it again. Luc had eased her mind and she had presumed she was free to express hers. To anyone who didn't know her family situation, Renee might have seemed cynical. He must not have remembered as much as she thought. "You don't need to be with someone to be content."

"Sure, but when you find that someone, it's almost like an extra dose."

"I guess." Renee started forward and Luc glued himself to her side. "It's not that I have a problem with dating. But not everyone has to get married, you know?"

"You don't want to get married?"

Renee shook her head. "Not after growing up with my mother."

"But, you're planning your sister's wedding."

"Cait already planned most of it." Another lie, but she wasn't giving in to his bait. "And that doesn't mean I want to."

Luc scratched his head. "Huh."

"You think I'm strange, right?"

"No, I get it."

"You do?"

"Sure. My parents divorced when I was eighteen, and that was tough. I can't imagine being so young and seeing your parents like that."

Renee eyed him for a moment until he indicated for them

126

to cross the street. She concentrated on the WALK signal, not wanting to witness his disappointment in her. "I just don't think it's for me. I watched my dad live his life alone after my mother left. Cait's father was alone until he passed." It seemed as if marriage brought disaster. Why would she ever associate herself with the institution?

"That makes sense, but I wonder if you ever thought that if you found the right person you would consider it."

"You aren't the first person to suggest it."

"I had to try."

"Is this going to be a thing?"

"Not if you don't want it to be."

"I don't."

"Noted."

They walked into Unveiled Bridal, and their conversation played on repeat in her mind. They were inside of a store where weddings were the literal theme. She thought of his wedding to his ex and wondered how far he and his fiancée had gone before the breakup. Renee didn't want to dive into her feelings surrounding weddings and marriage, so she didn't ask about his.

As they walked through the store, a sliver of a vision pierced her mind and she couldn't help imagining what her wedding would look like if she ever took that dive. It would involve the beach, for sure. Her immediate family and friends, locals from town. Small and simple. Maybe even a reception at a restaurant. She wouldn't go as far as the country club.

Luc cleared his throat, and Renee blinked. She stood by the glass case of wedding jewelry, completely dazed.

Nadia stood next to Luc, her lips pursed. Renee wondered if she was a fan of lemons or chose to greet people in that way.

"Oh, hi. I was checking on the bridesmaids' dresses. Have they arrived?"

"Yes," Nadia said curtly. She looked Renee up and down. "Is that all?"

"I— The girls wanted me to take pictures of them."

"Didn't your sister do that the other day?" Nadia's thin eyebrows rose almost to her hairline.

Luc was right behind her and Renee's entire body tingled. "She did? Oh, great. I'll see you later, then."

Nadia muttered something under her breath as Renee fled from the store, hoping that Luc was unable to see the flush in her cheeks.

Chapter 13

With the awkwardness of Renee's refusal gone, she and Luc fell into the same neighborly nature as they had right before. He was with the high school girls for most of the day at the beach, while Renee chose to stay home more than travel to her co-working space. Whether it was Cait's complaining that she "never saw her sister" or wanting to be able to peek at Luc at any time, she wasn't sure or willing to admit that was the case.

Like she had when they first had met all those years ago, seeing Luc through her window sent a flurry of excitement through her each time she caught him peering at her house.

Luc hadn't denied wanting to be around Renee in a more private way, but she continued to hesitate, even with the insistence from both Cait and Sadie to take a chance on him. They could blame it on her needing a plus-one to Cait's wedding, but she wasn't sure that she wanted photographic evidence of her summer fling in Cait's wedding album. She could almost hear the pinging of her cell phone each time Cait looked at it, asking if Renee had spoken to Luc. It was up there with the locals asking about him too. If she made that leap, there was no backing down from it.

Renee didn't know why everyone had to push her into a relationship. Nothing between them could ever go further than the summer. Luc seemed to be the type that whoever he dated, marriage was the eventual goal. His breakup from Claire hadn't deterred him one bit, while Renee's past with Isla dictated her future entirely.

Renee's phone blared, and she glanced at an unknown number with an Arizona area code. An icy hand clamped around her heart and squeezed. There was no way her mother would call her. She hadn't in years.

"Aren't you going to get that?" Cait asked from the couch. "I can't hear my show."

Renee had set up her laptop at the dining room table in the seat, giving her a picturesque view of the beach—and the volleyball court.

"It's an unknown number."

"From where?" Cait asked.

"Arizona."

"That's probably Blair."

"Blair? Why is she calling me?" Cait's best friend and maid of honor had always been a young hurricane of excitement and trouble ever since they met in kindergarten. Cait's laissez-faire nature complemented her friend.

"I don't know. She said she needed to talk to you, and that was it. I gave her your number. Pick it up or else she's just going to keep calling."

Renee's phone rang again with the same number. She picked it up that time, hoping the universe hadn't tricked her into thinking it wasn't her mother. "Hello?"

Hunter chose that minute to jump up from Cait's lap and bark at the joggers passing by the house.

"Renee?" Blair's nasally voice was barely audible over Hunter's incessant barking. Renee knew enough about the dog not to bother with him when he went on these tangents.

"One second," Renee said, standing from the chair.

"Tell her I said hi!" Cait trilled from the couch. She turned the television to deafening volume with the equally shrill reality show characters.

"Is this better?" Renee asked after walking outside.

"I could hear you before?" Blair tended to sound like all her statements were questions.

Scratching paws scraped down the door. Hunter continued to bark from inside, so she knew it wasn't the pest-dog. Renee opened the door for Brandy, and she trotted down the steps to the grassy area.

"What's going on?" Renee asked.

"Is Cait around?"

"She's inside."

"I need a favor?"

"Sure." Renee leaned against the railing, wondering if Blair would ever get to the point.

"The bachelorette party is next weekend?"

"I'm aware."

Blair paused. "If I Venmo you some money, will you buy all of the stuff for us?"

"What do you need?"

"Have you ever been to one of these before?"

As many weddings as she had been to, there were fewer invites to bachelorette parties. Sadie's was in the city, but that was years ago. "I have."

"I'll send you a list of what I'm looking for? This is important, and we need it done, right?"

"Can't you order online and ship it here?"

"No? This stuff needs to be vetted and bought in person? Thanks, Renee?"

The phone line clicked off, and less than a second later, a text popped onto her screen. The amount of times that vulgar words had ever crossed her phone screen was nothing compared to the barrage of penis paraphernalia on Blair's list.

"She's got to be kidding."

* * *

131

After a conversation with Sadie, involving lots of laughter, they found an adult store that catered to a particular crowd, including those attending and hosting bachelor and bachelorette parties.

The store was a town over, behind one of the shopping centers. Renee nearly cracked her neck as she whipped her attention back and forth both sides of the street. If she saw anyone she knew, she wasn't ever going to live it down. She had the excuse of Cait's wedding, but she couldn't imagine if she ran into anyone from town in or around that place.

Sweetest Valentine seemed as if it could be a wholesome type of shop, as the front sign showed Cupid shooting an arrow at the heart-shaped dot above the I.

Renee tightened the grip on her purse and shoved open the door.

"Renee!" Sadie had insisted on coming with her, but Renee hadn't expected her to be there already, gripping a massive dildo.

"Put that down," Renee hissed.

Instead of listening to her, Sadie wiggled it around a few more times before Renee knocked it out of her hands. "I shouldn't have said anything to you."

"Have some fun. Don't you remember mine?"

Sadie had been twenty-five when she married Ken, and Renee barely recalled the night of her best friend's bachelorette party when they attended a nightclub filled with men who were more interested in each other than the group of women in the middle of the dance floor. It was one of the most fun nights of her life and had included a smaller amount of a similar variety of items.

"This is for my kid sister," Renee said, pulling out her list.

"Can I help you find something?" Renee turned. The woman's cleavage spilled from her purple V-neck shirt. Glittery pink eyeshadow sparkled around Instagram-worthy perfect winged eyeliner. Her lips were plump with a glossy red lipstick.

Renee thrust her phone at the woman. "I need these things."

The woman took the phone and turned on her oversized heels.

Renee watched her thin legs balance on the platform shoes as she walked through the store.

Sadie made her way to the lingerie section with no shortage of fluffy fabric attached to the skimpy outfits.

"What do you think of this one?" Sadie held up a black number with what looked like a purple boa attached to the bra.

Renee waved her off as the employee dropped several packs of straws labeled as "Party Willies" into the basket looped in her arm.

"Do you think Luc would like this color?" Sadie held out another one.

"I'm not listening to you," Renee said through her teeth.

"Any news with that?"

"We're neighbors." Renee abandoned the employee who already had her list and headed over to Sadie. There was no reason for her to be involved in a private conversation about Luc. "That's all."

"Did you tell him you were an idiot for turning him down?"

"Not exactly. We did discuss it though. He's fine with it."

"He can't be fine with it. You refused him!"

"I don't want to go into this."

"Come on, Renee. You know you like him. Your infatuation with him those next two summers after you left proved that. Remember when you made Marcus call Audrey to see if you could get Luc's number?"

"That was years ago."

"And you didn't even call him."

"Like I said, years ago." Renee had been a little obsessed with Luc, which was until she went to college and forgot about him entirely. He knew where she lived and never returned.

As Sadie pointed out more lewd merchandise, Renee fell into her thoughts about Luc. He had said his parents divorced when he was eighteen. Maybe if Renee had called him, they could have kept in touch. She wouldn't have minded it. They could have helped each other, or at least she could have helped him cope with his parents' divorce. She had experience. The more she thought about her regrets, the more her stomach roiled.

Ten minutes later, Sadie and Renee walked out of the shop with two massive black bags, displaying the logo of the store.

Renee curled her hand around the logo as she walked, not wanting anyone to know where she had shopped.

"You read the book club book yet?" Sadie asked.

"Almost done."

"Ugh, it's so boring. Give me the synopsis, and I'll pretend I read it."

Renee laughed and shook her head. "I'm not bailing you out again."

"If we can pick something I like, I might read it."

"If you ever suggest a book you might like, then we can vote on it."

"With all the time I have?" Sadie checked her phone. "Speaking of, I need to head back to the house to make lunch. Thanks for giving me some adult time."

"Sure."

Sadie opened her car door. "Now, go get some adult time with Luc, huh?"

"Bye!" Renee said.

"You can ignore me now, but I know where you live." Sadie's laugh was loud enough to hear from inside Renee's stuffy car. But she refused to open the window until she was far enough away from her friend. While she loved Sadie like a sister, she hated the way her friend had weaseled her way into her mind about Luc, and the possibility that she had made a mistake about refusing his offer for a date.

* * *

When Renee arrived home, she tucked the bags against her body to hide them from Cait. Renee had the perfect spot in the pantry, and she just had to make it into the house without Cait noticing.

From the window, she spotted the top of Cait and Marcus's heads poking out over the back of the couch. Hunter must have heard the car door slam and was already barking at the front door. For once, he was helping her by becoming a distraction instead of a nuisance.

Renee was midway up the back steps when Luc called out to her. She whirled around, grasping for the railing as one of the bags slipped from her grip slightly. Her fingers curled around the bag, keeping the items concealed.

"Hey!" she said a little too loud.

Luc noticed and cocked his head to the side. "You all right?"

"Yes, yup. What's going on?"

"I'm finished for the week and wanted to grill tonight for dinner. Did you all want to join me?"

"S-sure," she said, needing to get inside to unload the bags before Cait noticed.

"Great, you can come by anytime after seven." Luc stepped forward and leaned over to pick something up off the ground. When he stood, he held one of the red straws up to her. The tip was a small penis.

As her body temperature spiked to molten level, Luc pressed his lips together. He wasn't doing a good job of concealing his amusement as he walked away.

An explanation about the bachelorette party died on her tongue as she ran into the house.

* * *

Around six-thirty, Renee and Marcus stood next to each other by the countertop, chopping vegetables on separate cutting boards. They were part of a crop-share for the summer, hosted by a farm several towns over from West Cove, and always had an influx of fresh vegetables over the summer months. Cait barely ate unless they went out in town, so having the opportunity to feed four was enough of an excuse to make a massive salad with fresh romaine, tomatoes, carrots, and peppers. Partnered with Marcus's vinaigrette, it was the consistent summery meal they had shared for years.

"Should I bring Hunter?" Cait asked. He was in her lap, and she was rubbing his chin as his nose snuffled the air.

"No," Renee and Marcus said at the same time.

"They don't mean that," Cait said in a cutesy voice to Hunter.

"There's construction equipment all over the place," Renee said. "You wouldn't want a nail in his paw."

Cait shook her head violently. "Hunt, you stay here."

Renee was the last out of the back door, and she made sure the cabinet with the treats was closed.

Unlike Hunter, Brandy was welcome at Luc's house. She had already made herself at home the first day he'd moved in. With her tail held high, she led the group to the house before disappearing into the living room.

As Marcus and Cait put away the white wine and salad in the refrigerator, Renee popped into the living room and found Luc scratching behind Brandy's ears. The dog was snuggled on the couch in the smallest ball possible and her tongue lolled from her mouth.

"Hey, make yourself at home, girl," Luc said to her.

For once, there weren't tools and renovation equipment all over every surface. Renee hadn't been inside the house in over a week, and Luc had undoubtedly done a lot. The surfaces weren't covered in dust or debris and the cobwebs were missing from the corners of the ceilings. The bookshelf was filled to the brim with books instead of random dusty trinkets.

"Where did you get all these?" Renee asked, thumbing through the titles. They were a mix of classics, contemporary fiction, and everything in between. Luc read a lot, but these books didn't seem like his taste.

136

"I went to the used bookstore in town. I don't like an empty bookshelf."

"I can see that."

"Feel free to borrow anything," he said. "Maybe something on the second shelf might interest you."

Renee eyed him before taking the bait. None of the titles seemed that special until she spotted one, and a small gasp escaped her lips.

A thin, black book called to her. It was *The Giver* by Lois Lowry. Her favorite book. She had read it at least once a year—sometimes more—from sixth to twelfth grade. In her many moves with her mother, she had lost her copy. Blaming Isla, she hadn't repurchased it for fear of the memory spoiling her experience. But she still loved the story. It was the first book she ever remembered loving so completely.

Heat surged behind her eyes. "You remembered."

"You were the one to show it to me. I thought it was a special keepsake to have in this house."

Renee heaved a sigh. "You constantly surprise me with how much you remember."

Luc stared at the bookshelf as he spoke, as if the words from his heart were dropping from the pages. His finger touched the top of the book—her book—and pulled it out, cradling it in his hands. "I liked disappearing into books, but that summer was the first time I could look up and see something more than just my parents fighting."

"Luc," she choked out his name.

His hand brushed over her shoulder. The movement of her hair tingled the top of her head. A breath caught in her throat as her eyes lifted to his.

"Anyone need a drink?" Cait's voice floated into the room.

Luc had turned around quick enough to appear as if nothing was happening between them at all. That crack of electricity lingered in the air, but Renee knew precisely where to hide it.

Renee tore away from Luc, not wanting to give her sister any more fuel to tease her with when it came to him. Mostly because she was sure there was more growing between them by the second.

The air in the kitchen seemed to have dropped ten degrees. Or moving away from Luc had removed his searing body heat from inches away from her.

Luc entered the kitchen, and his hair was tucked behind his ears as if he had needed a minute to compose himself too. He looked at her and gave her a secret smile, which made her toes curl.

Cait poured wine for everyone in mismatched glasses with various vineyards and slogans etched into the sides. "Quite a collection here, Luc."

"I guess that's what happens when you leave glass around for renters. These used to at least have pairs."

"You two have a pair," Cait said, pointing at Renee and Luc's glasses.

"Will you look at that," Marcus mused.

"Thanks for inviting us," Renee said, clinking glasses with Luc.

"It's my pleasure," he said, and for some reason, it seemed as if he were only speaking to her.

* * *

Luc and Marcus took care of cooking on the grill. Somehow it seemed like a friendly competition between the two of them as they disagreed about the length of time for steak to cook. Renee and Cait set the table, salad, and fixings for the four large aluminum-foil-wrapped potatoes cooking in the corner of the grill.

Cait retrieved the bottle of wine and filled up everyone's glasses. "So, Luc. You've been here a few weeks, but I feel like I know nothing about you. Other than what Renee has told us, of course."

Renee shot her sister a look. Both of them had had two glasses of wine, but Cait seemed like she was the only one who had loosened up.

Luc moved away from the grill and sipped from the glass. "Not sure what you want to know."

"You're a teacher," Cait helped.

"Yeah."

"Why did you want to become a teacher?"

"It's selfish, really," Luc said, rubbing a hand over his neck. "I love to read, and when I found a job where I could do that all the time, I went for it."

"What's your favorite book?" Cait asked.

"*The Lion, the Witch, and the Wardrobe*," Renee answered for him.

Luc blinked in surprise. "Yes. It was a book my grandfather read to me. It's the only memory I have of him."

Cait opened her mouth with mock-shock at Renee.

"Audrey had the books here," Renee said as if that were the explanation for how she knew his favorite book. "You were rereading them that summer we met."

"I was a little too old for the series, but somehow they took me back to a simpler time—before my parents got divorced. Besides, what kid wouldn't want to escape through a magical portal?"

"Sorry to hear that," Cait said. "My parents divorced when I was young too."

Renee tried not to look at Marcus. She rarely discussed Isla in front of him, and even less the divorce which had separated them years ago. It was a time in her life she wanted to forget, and Marcus never pushed her to talk about it.

Luc took another sip from the wine and placed his glass down on the wooden table. "Anyway. That was a long time ago."

"Isn't it crazy how you two reunited after all these years?"

Renee shot her sister another look. She was moving away from subtle really quickly.

Luc chuckled as if he suspected Cait's interest.

"It's sad that I'm getting married before you two," Cait said.

Renee decided to get it in the open before Cait pushed Luc too hard. "He was engaged once."

"What happened?" Cait asked. Renee could have sworn she had mentioned it to Cait, but her sister seemed dumbstruck. Did she think talking about it would make Renee change her mind about him? Renee took another sip from her glass to conceal her annoyance.

"It wasn't meant to be," said Luc. "We were young when we got together. It was right after my parents' divorce."

Renee's drink caught in her throat, and it took all her effort to swallow it. She hadn't heard that part before.

Maybe because you didn't ask.

Luc shook his head. "I don't want to bring down the mood—"

"No," Cait said. "We're getting to know you. Unless it's too personal?"

As if that ever stopped her before.

"Not at all," he said. "It was a long time ago. Long story short, we were both in weird places in our lives, but we were there for each other. Through college, we went through a rough patch but came out mostly unscathed. The next step seemed to be marriage, but as we started to nail down the details, such as where we wanted to live, how many kids to have, even wedding details, it didn't seem like we would work for the long haul. It's a happy ending, though, since Claire is married and has a kid already."

"It's not happy for you," Cait said.

"I'm happy right now." Luc glanced at Renee for a second too long. Her pulse spiked, and she rubbed a hand over her arms to stop the rush of goose bumps. "With all of you. Everything happens for a reason, and it all worked out in the end."

"At least you've held on to a positive attitude." Marcus glanced at the grill. "I think it's time to flip those."

Luc and Marcus walked over to the grill.

Cait moved to the other side of the table and sat across from Renee.

"What are you doing?" Renee mouthed.

Cait winked. "Trust me."

Luc helped Marcus plate the steaks and the potatoes on a platter. Marcus sat next to Cait, and Luc slid into the seat next to Renee. Brandy glued herself to Marcus's side—her normal spot whenever he ate.

Luc passed the platter around and they all took the food.

Renee was aware of how close Luc was to her, though he seemed as comfortable as ever.

"This looks good," Cait said, dipping her knife into the side of the potato. Steam rose up from it.

"Cait, tell me all about your wedding," Luc said.

"Renee didn't talk to you about it?" Cait asked.

Renee shrugged. "It hasn't come up."

Luc accidently bumped her arm. "Sorry."

Cait glanced between the two of them before speaking. "Well, she's been a big help. I'm not the organized type."

"You did fine," Renee said, cutting into the steak.

"Renee is the best part of this place," Cait said. "I don't know what I would do without her."

"Back 'atcha," Renee said, squeezing her sister's arm again.

The conversation had taken a turn away from Luc toward Cait as she detailed the décor and events of the wedding. Renee dreaded the inevitable moment where Cait would bring up Renee's plus-one, but it never happened.

Renee focused on it so much that it stuck in her mind as a possibility. Luc was in town until at least the Fourth. From the way that he had pressed her about going on a date, she had a feeling he would say yes. But was that what she wanted from him?

A part of her wanted to see him dressed in a suit and pressed against her while they danced. Local gossip be damned.

Renee caught his eye more than a few times during their dinner. Each moment dragged on until it was as if the two of them shared their own silent language. She started to realize that shaking off Luc wasn't going to be easy. And she wasn't sure if she wanted to at all.

Chapter 14

Over the next week, Renee was in touch with Blair about the rest of the plans for the bachelorette party. Blair seemed like a professional party planner compared to Cait. But that didn't count for much. All she had done was secure six rooms at the casino upstate.

When Cait and Renee picked Blair up from the airport, Renee felt as if she had entered a vortex and had fallen back in time to when she had driven them to activities together when they were seventeen. Their excited squeals were the same, along with the inside jokes. They'd mutter a few incoherent words through their giggles before bursting into laughter.

Cait had made a point to Blair that Renee's house was too small for all the girls to stay, so they booked several rooms at the West Cove Inn. It seemed to be enough for Blair, and the other girls who had come in throughout the day, but they wanted beach time. Their squeals of excitement over Cait's wedding boosted Renee's mood.

When they headed for the private beach, Cait seemed happier than she had all week.

Five of Cait's friends came on the Friday before the bachelorette party, while the rest would head straight for the casino the next day. Renee could appreciate some of the girls not wanting to take off work for the event, as they had to fly in again in less than two weeks for the wedding.

A few times, Renee was tempted to ask Cait about why she scheduled her wedding and bachelorette party so close together and both in West Cove. The wedding planning was out of her hands, and she didn't want Cait to think too hard about her upcoming nuptials, so she didn't say anything. Renee was going to use the time away from Cait and her friends to get more work done on her projects, but Cait insisted that she take a day off to be at the beach with them. Granted, she then immediately asked Renee to make lunches for all the girls, complete with dietary restrictions. Renee shoved aside her instinct to ask them to make their own lunches, and instead doted on her sister and fulfilled her requests.

While she and Luc had moved past any awkwardness between them, Renee had avoided the beach during his working hours. She didn't want to lead him on in any way. Her mixed-up feelings for him were already confusing enough. She didn't want to add any signs that could be misinterpreted by either of them.

As Renee walked across the street, it took all of her effort to keep her eyes on Cait and her friends and not the group playing volleyball yards away from them. She held a cooler in one hand, with several towels under her other, and her e-reader. The sun was burning exceptionally bright, and she was already sweating. Marcus had helped the girls set up several beach umbrellas, and she hoped there was room or else she was going to burn.

"Renee!" Luc called as she crossed the barrier.

The light from the sun blinked out as a white ball smashed against her hands. Renee fumbled the cooler and dropped two of the four towels on the sand. They unrolled in front of her.

A teen girl almost a foot taller than Renee sprinted over, ricocheting a wave of sand around her feet. "Sorry about that." She picked up the towels from the ground and handed the heap over.

"It's fine," Renee said.

"Willa's trying to show off for Coach," one of the other girls called. "She needs to stay in her lane."

"And keep her ball on the court," another said.

"I know, right?"

Willa's face fell before she apologized again.

"It's not a big deal. Really."

Willa sprinted back to the court. Her shoulders were hunched over as she trudged back.

Blair and Cait walked over to Renee.

"You okay?" Cait asked.

Renee didn't need any more unnecessary attention from anyone. "Yeah, just grab those towels for me."

"Sure thing?" Blair reached down and picked the corner of one up with two fingers as if it were crawling with sand fleas.

Renee carried on, pulling the cooler against the sand. Her attention went to the girls playing. They had resumed the game, but instead of Luc watching them, he watched her. So intently that a delicious shiver rolled down her spine. Renee stood straighter as she walked over to the other girls. She had avoided wearing a bikini around him, but she'd never felt more confident than she did at that moment.

Even after pulling her gaze from him, she had a feeling he was still watching.

Renee settled into an empty chair on the edge of the group. Cait and her friends gossiped about their relationships with the guys and girls in their lives. Renee didn't have much to offer, but a swell of pride moved through her as her sister laughed along with her friends. Cait talked about Jorden with the same giggling smile she always had. Renee couldn't help understanding how a mother would feel as she watched a daughter grow into an independent and strong woman. Sure, Cait relied on Jorden for a lot of things, but Jorden also was blessed with a fiancée who adored him as much as he did her.

144

It was around two o'clock when the camp wrapped up for the day. Cait's friend Emma stood up and glanced at the net. She was the tallest of the girls and had the glossiest black pixie cut, which complimented her heart-shaped face. "Can we play for a bit?"

"That's Luc's net," Cait said, sliding a look at Renee. "Renee, can you check with him?"

All the girls looked at Renee.

To keep Cait's grin from getting wider or spilling any imaginary relationship between Luc and Renee, she got up and walked over to the net. Luc was still with the assistant coach and they were rolling up the boundary line. The closer she got to him, the more her body heated up. Her gaze raked over his bronzed body until his eyes met hers.

"Hey," he said. "Hope we didn't interrupt your beach day."

"Not at all," Renee said. "The girls want to play and wondered if they could use the court."

"Sure."

The assistant coach—Dale Leary—grunted as she started to unroll the boundary line again. She stood eye to eye with Luc. Renee had seen her slam spikes into the sand numerous times while coaching the girls. Renee didn't want to be on the other side of that glare.

"That's not necessary," Renee said to her. "It's just for fun. I'll clean up when they're done." Renee couldn't imagine the girls playing for too long in the hot sun. They had already been out there for almost two hours, and a few had discussed going back to the inn to relax in their rooms.

Luc nodded at Dale. "I'll stick around and finish that."

Dale handed off the boundary line and slogged toward the barrier.

"She's not a fan of the sun," Luc said.

"Then why help coach beach volleyball?"

"She's making sure I don't steal her spot as an indoor coach."

"Why would you steal her spot?" He was leaving at the end of the summer.

145

"Exactly."

Renee glanced at the girls, all of them still staring at her. Cait made a make-out gesture at Renee, and she immediately snapped her attention to Luc. He was busy with the boundary line and he hadn't noticed. Renee regretted waving them over, wondering how much Cait had told the girls in Renee's absence about Luc.

"I'm going to go in the water?" Blair said when they arrived. "I feel like I'm on the surface of the sun?"

"We're uneven then," Dee whined.

"I'll play," Luc offered.

"You don't have to," Renee said. "You've been out here all day."

"I'd hate for you to be uneven." A sly smile crossed his lips.

"Okay," Renee said, a little out of breath.

Cait took it upon herself to separate the group into teams, leaving Renee and Luc with Dee. Dee and Emma had played high school volleyball at competing schools.

No one mentioned that it was unfair for two experienced players to be on the same side, but Renee understood that Cait wanted her and Luc to be together. She wasn't sneaky about it, but Renee knew if she ignored the ploy to get them together, maybe it would cool Cait down a little.

"Luc, you should start," Cait said, rolling the ball to him. It stopped in front of Renee instead, and she tossed it to him.

"Take it easy on us!" Fiona adjusted the too-small bikini top over her chest, and Renee wasn't sure if she caught an exaggerated wink under her sunglasses. From their conversation before, Fiona didn't prefer one sex over the other, and had broken up with her girlfriend a week prior. Cait and the other girls had spent a good ten minutes trying to figure out who else was single at the wedding that she could hook up with for the night. She was young, but Renee imagined Luc would have to be blind not to think she was gorgeous.

A flare of jealousy reared its head. Before she could wrestle it down, Luc served the ball over the net. Cait raised both of her hands in the air and tossed it back over the net. Luc moved forward and bumped it to Dee. She expertly set it in front of Renee. She bumped it over and it grazed the top of the net, losing momentum and falling right in front of Fiona. She bumped it, but without enough force for it to get over the net again.

"Nice!" Dee said, raising her hand for a high five from Luc.

"I'll give you that one," Emma said with a curl of her lip. She gathered her team, and they huddled together for a moment before breaking apart. Cait had a wicked grin on her face, not unlike every time she tried to get more feelings out of Renee about their temporary neighbor.

"She's a sore loser," Dee said. "Always has been."

"This is supposed to be fun, right?" Renee asked, trying to smooth out the tension between the girls.

"That's what losers say," Fiona remarked.

Renee had come into the game thinking it was going to be a friendly one, but with the next few matches, she wasn't so sure. It became apparent that she was the weakest link on her team, and Dee spent more time trying to get Luc to pass to her, even when it wasn't her place.

In his coaching ways, he instructed and encouraged both teams with positive and helpful tips. Dee grumbled each time the other side scored on them from Luc's instruction. None of the girls said anything to him, as each of them wanted to appear their best selves around the attractive man living next door to Cait. She understood how they felt as she tried to improve her game as well.

When it was Emma's turn to serve, Renee's team backed up. Luc had already removed the boundary line, but her serves were consistently hitting the corner of the court on their side. There had been enough arguments of what was "in", that moving toward her sweet spot offered them the ability to get the point instead of into a heated argument.

Fiona served, and the ball soared over the net in Renee's direction. It moved quickly toward her, falling with each second. She took several steps back to line up her shot when Luc's hands clutched her waist, holding her steady against him. Her heart scrambled up her throat, lodging itself in there.

"You have this."

Luc's hands slid away from her as she bumped her arms against the ball. It sailed over to Dee, and she jumped up and spiked it onto the other side. It landed with a *thump* in the sand at Cait's feet.

A lightness burst through her, and she turned to Luc. He raised his hand for a high five as she wrapped her arms around him. A second later, his arms enveloped her into a tight embrace. Renee lifted on her toes and rested her chin against his shoulder.

"That was awesome," Dee said, coming over to them.

Renee realized that she was skin-to-skin with Luc and untangled herself as quickly as possible. The moment between them was over, but the prickling heat from his body danced across her skin.

Dee fist-bumped them and went over to the net to mock her friends. It was all in good fun, but Emma and Fiona stormed off toward the water to join Blair.

"Come on," Cait called out to her friends.

"I think that's the game," Luc said.

The girls went into the water, standing knee-deep before they were far enough away, leaving Luc and Renee alone together. For once, she wasn't itching to go home. His touch had awakened something inside of her, and she wanted more of it.

"Thanks for letting us play."

"It's my pleasure. As much as I'm out here, there's not a lot of time for me to play for fun. Between coaching and the house, this summer is going by a lot quicker than I realized."

It was true. There were only two more weeks until the camp was over. Renee had no idea if he would stick around longer to work on the house or not. A tightness settled in her throat as they walked over to the other side of the net to retrieve the two balls he had left behind.

"You're leaving tomorrow?" Luc rolled one of the volleyballs between his hands.

Renee had the other. "Just for the night." While she wasn't looking forward to corralling Cait's drunk friends all over the casino, she looked forward to it even less as she wouldn't see Luc. It was preposterous that she should have thought that way since they weren't in any way a couple, but the regret was there.

"I hope you have fun and relax a little."

"I'm relaxed."

He tucked the ball under his arm and touched both of her shoulders, pressing them downward. She allowed the tension to leave her body.

"I see what you mean."

"I didn't notice it before, but there was a difference when you were playing, versus before and after. Is Cait bogging you down with wedding plans again?"

"Not at all," she said quickly. Then, the list of upcoming activities between the bachelorette party and last-minute preparations flitted through her mind. "I want to be sure everything goes smoothly tomorrow. It's the last big event before the wedding."

"Well, enjoy it. If the bride doesn't have a care in the world, then you shouldn't either."

It was Renee's planning that helped Cait not to care. But she didn't want to dig into that with Luc and ruin the effect of the time she'd spent with him that afternoon. She preferred to preserve the memory of the feel of his hands on her instead. At least that would put her in a good mood whenever she needed it.

Chapter 15

While Renee wanted to get on the road before noon on Saturday, the girls staying at the inn decided to make the party bus wait an extra hour before they were ready. They piled out of their rooms in skyscraper heels and wedges with dresses hugging all of their curves. As opposed to the relaxing day before at the beach, these girls were done up to impress. Even Cait had taken a little extra time that morning getting ready, while Renee had spent most of it on her laptop finishing two days' worth of client work before responding to emails.

When Renee came home on Sunday, she'd be able to recover from whatever shenanigans the girls decided to come up with at the casino.

Admittedly, she looked forward to a night out. The last one she had was with Sadie and Luc, and before that—she couldn't remember. It was a nice escape from her life, and she had no idea when it would happen with Cait again.

While Renee waited inside the air-conditioned bus, with the driver who was enamored by his phone, she thought of Luc and the day before at the beach. The girls had stayed at the house for dinner and well after, but Renee hadn't seen Luc other than his shadow moving around the house when she had returned from bringing the girls back to the inn.

That morning, his truck was gone by the time she had woken up. From the bus, she sat on the side facing the road, looking for him. There was no way he'd know she was inside, but at least knowing that he was headed home or getting a glimpse of him would have eased her mind a little.

Everything had changed at the beach. The way he had treated Cait and her friends and his gentle touch against her skin threw her back in time to when it was just her and Luc together as teens. Their legs tangled up together in the sand as they read books together or sunbathed.

The bus rocked, propelling Renee from her thoughts. The girls whooped and cheered as they strode down the aisle, taking their seats. There was enough room for at least twenty people, but the girls paired up with each other.

Blair glanced at Renee, and she indicated where the supplies were. Renee pointed at the overhead storage and Blair nodded at her. Her serious expression didn't waver as she took her seat next to Cait.

The bus roared to life and turned onto the main road. Renee's gut twisted as the moment finally came for her to leave West Cove for the night, something she hadn't done in a while. Partly, she worried for Marcus, but mostly she wasn't sure she'd be able to get Luc out of her mind.

* * *

The half-hour trip to the casino offered a reprieve from Renee's thoughts as she acted like a server, getting drinks and snacks for all the girls. As much as they had complained about their weight and dieting for the wedding the day before at the beach, with the sugary spiked drinks they were garbage disposals for the salty snacks Renee had insisted on bringing.

They checked into the hotel first. The other girls itched to get onto the casino floor. Renee offered to bring the bags to the rooms since most of them doubled up on their luggage as it was just for the night.

On the way up the elevator toward the rooms, she texted Sadie and Marcus to let them know they'd arrived. Renee scrolled through her phone and clicked on Luc's name. She debated on texting him but wanted to show him how much she could relax. Renee removed all the bags from her shoulders, snapped a selfie, and sent it before she'd lost her nerve. Before closing out of the message, the three dots appeared at the bottom of the screen before Luc sent a picture in return.

His skin shone with sweat as his crooked smile stared back at her. A smidge of primer paint cut across his cheek. Behind him, the guest bedroom was empty with blue painter's tape outlining the trim in the room.

Enjoy yourself for once.

Feel free to send more pictures too.

The elevator stopped at the twelfth floor, and Renee floated off down the hall. While all their rooms were on the same level, they were in different locations. She hoped none of the girls would mind getting their bags at another time because Renee wanted to start enjoying herself, as Luc had said.

Renee left the bags inside the entrance to her and Cait's room. She glanced at her jean shorts and tank top in the full-length mirror attached to the closet door. She had put in thick waves with a curling iron and wore her favorite necklace and earrings, but compared to the other girls, she looked plain.

Unzipping her bag, she thanked the Renee who that morning packed one of her most comfortable and flattering dresses and wedge heels. She slipped both on and found a new person standing in front of her in the mirror. It would be too much to send Luc another picture, but her fingers itched to do it. She resisted and left the room with the thought that he would approve.

* * *

Renee found the girls surrounding a blackjack table on the main floor. The air was tinged with cigarette smoke, and those around her gave no mind to those who didn't want to clog their lungs with cancer. The singing slot machines faded as she weaved through the tables toward the group.

Cait spotted her first and waved her hand in the air.

Fiona's hard expression stared at the table in front of her as Renee sidled up to Cait.

"You look amazing," Cait said. "I knew that dress was a good idea."

"Yeah, well, we don't need to make a big deal of it."

"It's my party, and I'll do what I want," Cait said with a grin. She adjusted the white sash across her body, which read BRIDE across it in glittery gold lettering. One of the girls must have brought it with them since that hadn't been on Renee's list from Blair. A tiara sat atop her head reflecting the distant lights of the slot machines in front of them.

"Fiona is a gambler?" Cait's friend played with the stack of chips in front of her. It was double the amount any of the other players had.

"She has it down to a science," Cait said. "She's going to fund the entire night with only two games."

"Are you serious?"

"Oh yeah. When we went on that cruise several years ago, she had paid for the entire trip in a day. Watch."

The serious-looking man behind the table dealt the cards to the four players seated around the table. Fiona seemed unimpressed and knocked on the table for the dealer to "hit". He did and, with that, Fiona had beat the table with twenty-one. The dealer slid a pile of chips in her direction. Fiona scooped them up and dropped them into Cait's hands. "Let's have the best night we'll ever forget."

* * *

153

The winnings amounted to eight hundred dollars. Cait handed the cash to Renee. "We don't have any pockets." She grinned sheepishly as Renee tucked the money into her purse. With that amount in her bag, she felt more vulnerable than ever, but at least the girls wouldn't have to worry about it.

Tonight wasn't about Renee. Yet the fun she was hoping to have faded away as she turned into the babysitter for the group.

It was only the afternoon, but the dim lights of the casino made it feel like midnight. Dee suggested a bar she'd researched before coming.

The Black Dahlia was a gothic-themed bar with blood-red curtains billowing at the entrance. The dark-stained wood of the walls, bar, and tables and chairs added to the creepy feel of the place. The smoke smell had faded since they were off the casino floor, but Renee's throat was already scratchy from the time they had spent there.

After the girls ordered their drinks, Renee put her credit card down as a tab. She wasn't comfortable flashing the money yet.

They found a spot at the front of the bar with a full view of the restaurant and the walkway outside. Everyone except for Cait and Renee were on the prowl, or at least seemed that way. Their eyes flitted to the group of guys facing a television at the back of the room with a football game on. It wasn't the theme of the bar, but most restaurants wanted to make their customers happy.

Everyone who walked by their group spotted Cait right away. Most congratulated her, and she soaked up the attention like a dry sponge. Renee made all the girls happy enough that they practically skipped to their dinner reservation at the famous steakhouse. The walkway overlooked the floor below them, where all the people walked toward the slot machines. The girls shouted to everyone who passed that Cait was a bride-to-be, stopping more people in their tracks to congratulate her.

* * *

Two hours later, they reached the club and Cait and her friends were more wired than ever. Renee had put a brave face on during dinner when the girls chugged drinks, but she was exhausted. She had an idea of how Sadie felt after wrangling her kids all day.

Outside the entrance to the club, the girls bopped to the music while the bouncer checked IDs. He wasn't impressed that Cait was a future bride and made them wait. Cait's friends heckled him until they finally let them inside. Cait raced to the front of the group and led the girls to the dance floor. They squeezed between other dancers toward the DJ elevated at the front of the room. The bass rattled Renee's chest as she made her way to the bar. She ordered bottled water for all the girls as she watched their group head toward the center of the room. Between their hoots of celebration, they caught a lot of attention from the men around them. Most of the girls paired up but remained diligent around Cait. Fiona shoved several guys away from the group who were overly friendly toward the girls.

"You with them?" a guy at the bar shouted at her. He wore a suit as if he had just come from a business meeting. His narrowed eyes squinted against the blinding blue, purple, and pink lights spiraling around them. He was handsome, but even his perfectly square jaw had nothing on Luc.

"Yes," she shouted over the music.

"Why aren't you dancing?" He licked his lips, and Renee moved away from him. He seemed harmless and slightly drunk, but she wasn't taking any chances. She knew well enough about men at clubs, even before seeing the packs of them surround Cait's party.

"I don't dance," she lied.

"Neither do I." His gaze fell to her chest. "I prefer to watch."

"Have a good night!" Renee said, gathering up her bottles of water.

The guy touched her waist, and she skittered away from him toward the dance floor. He shouted after her, but thankfully the music was too loud to hear any of his words. A crawling sensation rolled up her spine, and her teeth chattered. Even the heat from the dozens of bodies pulsing against her didn't take away from the chill moving through her.

Renee heard her name over the music and turned to find Dee and Blair at a round table near the edge of the dance floor. Renee dropped the waters there, and Dee downed one of them before she spoke again.

"Where is your drink?" Fiona asked.

"I'm fine."

"You have my money." Fiona glanced at Dee. "Use it. Loosen up a bit."

Renee frowned. "I'm loose."

Dee cackled. "Cait asked us to make sure you have fun too."

Renee glanced at her sister. They locked eyes, and Cait waved to Renee as she bounced in time with the music. "I don't need to drink to have fun."

"But you do need to loosen up. Go out there and dance. We'll protect your water," Fiona said.

Renee wasn't going to be a downer, and since Fiona and Dee were already on her case, appeasing them could make the rest of the night easier on her. She didn't want Cait to think she wasn't having fun. Renee preferred the role of mother in the group, but if Cait's friends had noticed, then Cait surely would eventually.

Squeezing through the crush of people, Renee found Cait.

"Nay!" Cait said, wrapping her in a sweaty embrace. "Dance with me!"

Cait seemed oblivious to the leering men behind her. Renee twisted her body, so she was on the outside of the group while Cait was on the inside. Even though she'd already been touched that night, and was not asking for more, she wanted to keep the leering guys at bay and away from her sister.

Cait was oblivious as usual. Her attention soared between the

DJ and the swinging lights above them. She gyrated her hips to the music and sang along.

It took several songs before Renee heard one that she recognized. Cait's eyes widened, and she grabbed Renee's hands and they swung each other around the space. Cait was unsteady on her feet so they bumped into more people than not, but they were giggling by the time the song was over.

"I wish Jorden was here," Cait shouted in Renee's ear. "I miss him so much. I want him here."

"At your bachelorette party? That's not really the point."

Cait pulled her phone from the front of her dress. She opened it to a long text chain between them that had taken place throughout the entire day. "These parties aren't really for the bride and groom. It's for our friends."

Renee glanced at the other girls who seemed to be having the time of their lives. "Well, you've accomplished that."

"Jorden dances well," she said. "I can't wait for our first dance." She grinned to herself and twisted around as if it were Jorden with her instead of her sister.

The bliss across Cait's face punched Renee in the chest, enough for her to lose her breath. Luc snapped into her mind, and she too wondered what it would have been like to have him there. Logic didn't play into it at all. That guy at the bar had touched her the way that Luc had the other day at the beach, yet they were different experiences. For a moment, she allowed herself to fall into a fantasy of Luc there with them and couldn't help smiling herself. He would have claimed her so that no other man would have touched her in that way. A warmth moved through her at that idea.

Luc clung to her thoughts as she danced the night away with Cait. The next opportunity for dancing like that would be at Cait's wedding.

It could be with Luc.

It was a stretch, especially since she had turned him down for an innocent date between two friends. But the idea stuck with her even as the night turned hazier with a mix of colorful lights and tinkling slot machines eventually leading her path back to the hotel.

Chapter 16

The next morning was rough for everyone, including the bride-to-be. Between the dry mouth and the general prune-like feeling of dehydration, peeling themselves off the beds, and some off the floors, proved more difficult than anticipated. Renee and Cait had shared a room, but somehow Blair ended up curled at the end of Renee's bed in a fetal position.

Renee made it to the bathroom and downed several cups of water. Her appearance in the mirror was closer to a horror show. Mascara and eyeliner smeared under her eyes, making her appear ghoulish. Spotty memories of the night before clouded her mind as she washed her face.

Despite her fuzzy brain, Renee still had the urge to get home as soon as possible to see Luc. She'd made up her mind the night before to reverse her decision about the date and ask him to be her plus-one to the wedding. Fiona and Dee's voices echoed in her head for her to loosen up, and Luc was the perfect excuse. He liked her, and she liked him. It didn't have to be any more complicated than that. Luc had asked her out, knowing he was leaving, so why not sign up for a little fun? Renee could treat him like any other tourist, and they had the added bonus of already skipping over the awkward 'getting to know you' stage.

The plan formed in her mind as they took the somewhat rocky ride home. Or maybe it seemed that way as she guzzled water to stay ahead of the twisting in her gut and the deep ache in her head.

The overcast clouds turned darker and more ominous as they made their way back to town.

The ride was unbearably silent as most of the girls had fallen asleep. Cait leaned on Renee's shoulder, which prevented her from moving an inch at the chance of waking her sister. Instead, she pressed her forehead against the window and anticipated the conversation with Luc.

He had to say yes. Luc had flirted with her and even touched her after her awkward refusal. He was still interested, and he knew about her hesitation with relationships.

The closer they moved toward West Cove, the more doubt seeped into her body. Renee had all the confidence in the world until she had to confront him. Would he give her a taste of how he'd felt when she turned him down?

The bus dropped them all at the inn, and Renee drove Cait home after twenty minutes of her friends standing outside their rooms and retelling the night before with fits of giggles. The rest in the bus seemed to help boost their mood, but Renee kept checking the road, wanting to talk to Luc.

As Renee passed Luc's house, her stomach plummeted. Luc's truck wasn't in the driveway next door. After parking, she glanced at her phone, wondering if she should call him or not. She decided not to as she didn't want to appear desperate.

Drops of rain plopped onto the windshield, and a rumble of thunder rolled in the distance. Renee wasn't going to get caught in the rain, so she pushed out of the car. She could wait until she got inside to compose the perfect text.

When they reached the porch, Hunter started yapping. He wasn't supposed to be on the couch, but there he was on two legs and digging his claws into the screens of the windows.

Renee rapped on the window, but he wasn't deterred.

"Hunty, shh," Cait said weakly. She pulled at the slider handle, but it didn't budge. "Isn't Papa Marcus here?"

"His car is."

"Maybe he's taking a nap or something. I'm headed up to do the same."

Renee slipped her key into the door and pulled it open. "I'm spending the rest of the day on the couch."

"Why did we drink so much?"

"Beats me. Did you have fun?"

"Of course!" Cait walked over to Hunter, and Renee had to grab his collar before he ran outside. Renee wasn't about to chase after him in the pouring rain. The skies had opened up, and the cool breeze whipping across the water filtered into the stuffy room. The window unit air conditioners were turned off, and Renee opened the windows facing the ocean so she could circulate the air through the house.

Brandy shuffled up to her and bopped her nose against Renee's hand. She scratched her floppy ears before calling out for Marcus.

"He's not up here," Cait said from upstairs.

Hunter went on the prowl looking for his owner. He raced up the stairs, giving Renee a momentary reprieve.

Renee peered through the window facing Luc's house. Had Marcus gone with Luc to the store for supplies? Renee texted him, and seconds later heard a familiar ping from the kitchen table. His phone was behind the bowl of fruit. She lifted his phone and her messages filled the screen from last night when Renee had checked in with him after they arrived at the casino and this morning on the ride home. Marcus was sparse with his responses, but he rarely forgot his phone whenever he left the house. Having her texts go unanswered for an entire night formed a knot in her stomach.

With Luc gone, there was only one other neighbor who might know where he would have gone.

Renee grabbed her thin gray raincoat and lifted the hood over

161

her hair. She headed outside toward Olivia's house. The lights were on in the kitchen and she hoped that her neighbor would have some idea where Marcus had gone. She took the front steps two at a time until she reached the porch.

Renee pressed the doorbell and peered inside. Half of the front door was made of glass and she expected to see Olivia alone in there. But she wasn't.

Two people peered at Renee from the couch. Their legs were tangled together under a blanket as the light from the television illuminated their surprised expressions.

Renee cupped her hands against the window, making sure she wasn't seeing things. "Dad?"

Marcus moved the blanket off his body, revealing his socked feet. Renee walked away from the door, feeling the full force of her hangover. The dizziness overwhelmed her, and she drew in deep breaths.

The door opened, and Marcus stood there with no expression on his face. "Are you just going to stand out there?"

"I'm trying to figure out what's going on."

"Don't be so dramatic. We're all adults."

Olivia stood too, wrapping her arms around her chest. She was a petite woman with stark white hair. It was cut close to her head and styled once a week downtown. Renee had seen her more than once there, knitting various items of clothes in that chair as she waited. For someone who lived on the beach, her skin was mostly wrinkle-free and pale. Lines creased her otherwise perfect forehead as her hands twined in front of her.

Marcus closed the door, sealing them inside.

"Hi, Renee." Olivia glanced at Marcus. Clearly, she had barged in on a moment between them.

"Hi. I was looking for Dad."

"You found me," Dad said gruffly.

Renee glanced at Olivia, feeling more like a kid in front of an adult who was about to scold her. "Here?"

162

"Let's get this over with," Marcus said. "Olivia and I have been seeing each other."

Seeing each other. It sounded preposterous, like they were teenagers in love. Renee wasn't sure how to feel. A thickness squeezed her throat as if she had been the one caught with a boy under a blanket instead of her father and their neighbor. "How long?"

"About a year," Marcus said, glancing at Olivia for confirmation.

"Officially, yes," she added.

"There was an unofficial time?"

"Well, we've been neighbors for a long time," Marcus said.

"And friends, too. After George passed, I needed more help than I thought."

Marcus cleared his throat. "We weren't sure how to tell you."

Renee recalled the dinners that they'd had together over the last few years. They weren't often but enough. How had she missed it? Renee's earlier mortification bubbled out into a release of laughter.

"What's so funny?" Marcus said.

"You two sneaking around. Hiding from me."

"I told you she wouldn't mind," Olivia said, swatting at Marcus.

Marcus narrowed his gaze at Renee. "You sure you're fine with this?"

"Of course," Renee said as a swell moved within her. All this time, she thought that Marcus needed her to stick around at home for him when in fact, with Olivia there, he hadn't needed her at all.

Headlights flashed into the window, and Renee spun around to see Luc pulling into his driveway.

"Do you want to stay for dinner tonight?" Olivia asked. "Cait is welcome too."

"Sure," Renee said. "But I have to do something first."

* * *

163

Renee's heated cheeks cooled against the rain that was smattering against her skin. The slam of the car door added an extra spring in her step. She needed to get to Luc so she could end the weekend as she had started it.

He wasn't by his truck, so she sprinted to the back door and burst into the sunroom. With the gloomy weather all around, the room was much darker and less airy. Shadows curved in the corners before another flash of lightning illuminated the space.

Renee stopped halfway through the room. What was she doing? She couldn't just burst into his house without knocking. What if he said no? What if her chance was gone? This was a bad idea. She turned around and headed for the door.

"Hello?" Luc called from inside. His footfalls were quicker and becoming louder. Renee had already committed to walking inside the house. She couldn't back down even though she wished she had thought through barging into his space.

The idea of him refusing her now made her friendly smile a bit shakier. "Hey, it's me . . . Renee."

Luc came into view. Droplets of water fell from his hair, and he was shirtless. A clump of wet fabric was wrapped around his hands. Her gaze strained not to trail along his chest down to the edge of his waistband. "Oh, hey. I didn't know you were back so soon. Do you want to come inside?"

"Sure," she said, losing her nerve with each step.

He dropped his shirt in the corner of the room by the doors for the pantry with the washer and dryer. He moved papers scattered over the kitchen table and stacked them on the counter. "Sit down. Tell me about last night."

Luc opened the refrigerator and grabbed the filtered pitcher of water. "Want some?"

"Sure." The dry mouth from the hangover intensified.

Luc poured two glasses. "Sorry, I'm a bit of a mess." He sat next to her, bumping her leg with his. "How did it go?"

The confidence from the night before slinked away. She felt

ashamed, and afraid. "It was fun. We danced and most of the girls were in rough shape this morning, but they had a good time."

"Did you?"

"Yes," she said, sipping the water. It cooled her throat and reminded her why she had come over to begin with. The feelings for him were still there, so why couldn't she get them out?

"Good," he said and pulled a face.

"What is it?"

He shook his head. "You seem off? Drink a little too much?" He waggled his eyebrows and smirked. "Do you need some aspirin? I have a new bottle. I wouldn't trust any of the bottles that Audrey kept. They probably expired years ago."

"That's not why I came over."

Luc leaned closer to her. "Oh, okay."

With him so near, she was reminded of the volleyball game from the other day, and his hands on her waist. And last night how she wanted that to happen again. Over and over again.

"I wanted to ask you something."

"Sure."

If only she hadn't stopped at Olivia's and witnessed the unthinkable with Marcus. Though, if her father could find his happiness after Isla, Renee could too, even if it was only for a little while.

"I wanted to ask you out."

Luc sat back in his chair. He scrubbed a hand over his face.

"Say something," she prompted.

"You didn't want to go out before."

"I said that. But I changed my mind."

His hand dropped to hers, and his warm touch sent a shiver through her. "Name the time and place."

Chapter 17

Renee wasn't sure why she had chosen Thursday for their date. The four days between were spent trying not to watch Luc practicing on the beach and imagining how their date was going to go.

The wedding was a little over a week away, and the threat of that time made Cait into the most harried version of herself that Renee had ever seen. Cait double- and triple-checked the already laid plans with each of the vendors. Enough that Renee had to field a few courtesy phone calls from them wondering if Renee had wanted changes or if they were dealing with a bridezilla.

As calmly as she could, Renee repeatedly explained that her sister wasn't one of those types of brides. But that statement proved harder to keep as Cait pushed Renee to make all last-minute appointments that week instead of the next.

"I'm not going to have any time!" Cait said Wednesday morning, pacing around the kitchen. "Jorden is coming Monday, and he's not going to want to sit around while I get my hair done for the wedding."

"Do you want me to squeeze us in for this week?"

"Can you?" Cait asked, her eyes wide and hopeful.

"I can try." Counting down the days until Jorden arrived didn't give them much time. Renee could try and bargain her way into the salon for the two of them. It would be nice to get a blowout of her hair for her date with Luc. Cait wanted to touch up her roots in the process, so she called Salon Fresh right away and squeezed them in on the day of her date with Luc around noon. It took a promise to revamp the salon's website, but it was worth it. At least she wouldn't have to figure out how to tame her hair in the humidity.

* * *

On the morning of the date, Renee kept her mind occupied, working at the co-working space until ten. Seeing Luc on the beach would only distract her from work, and she had plenty of time to see him that night. Scenarios of their date and how she was going to manage pretending to eat sushi distracted her from work. She'd chosen the same place Luc had originally asked for their first date. He wanted to go there, and she had a lot to make up for with him. It was only one date, and after everything she'd gone through so far that month with Cait, she could handle raw fish for one night. As long as Luc was there.

A quick drive home around eleven-thirty had Cait and Renee on time for a twelve-o'clock appointment at the salon. Cait hadn't bothered to shower or wash her hair ahead of time. It was the most disheveled she'd seen her sister since her arrival. Darkness colored the thickness under her eyes, and Renee couldn't help asking how she was sleeping.

"I keep having these nightmares about the wedding," Cait said, rubbing her eyes. "The vendors don't show up. There's a tornado . . ."

"That's normal."

"A tornado?"

Renee snorted. "No, the nightmares. I experience bad dreams all the time before an important event or meeting. Especially if I'm looking forward to it."

"I don't know. This doesn't feel right."

Renee hesitated but had to ask. "Are you having second thoughts?"

"No," Cait said firmly. "I haven't been this far away from Jorden in so long, and I miss him. He's usually there to talk me down from all this."

"Have you spoken to him?"

"He has a lot going on with work. I don't want to bother him."

"He's going to be your husband."

"I want to be confident about what I've been doing. He can't see me like this."

"Aren't you taking too much of this on? Shouldn't you share the good and bad together?" Renee waited for Cait to go off on her and say she had no experience with long-term relationships, so she had no idea what she was talking about.

But Cait bobbed her head instead. "We do. I oversold that I was able to handle this. Which is why I enlisted you to help me."

Renee thought about that for a minute as a crawling sensation rolled up her arms. The same stickiness clung to her insides at the idea that Cait had assumed her sister would take care of everything. But she was past it. Which was why she left the subject alone as she pulled into the lot across the street from the salon.

* * *

Renee had gone to Salon Fresh since she was a little girl. The same mother and daughter duo ran the place with other hairstylists renting chairs throughout the years. Ginger, the owner, was a woman in her sixties who sported the newest fashion hairstyle each time Renee had gone in for a simple trim. Today she had purple extensions in her hair, which glimmered off the fluorescent light above them. The woman moved her hips to the music playing over the speakers. The floors gleamed white as Ginger had insisted on keeping a tidy working space. She spotted Renee the moment she stepped through the door.

"There's the Clarke girl who's going to put me on the map." Ginger waved her scissors and comb in the air around her as she leaned in for a cheek kiss.

Her daughter, Helen, peered around the corner. "Websites don't exactly do that, Ma." She walked into the main space from the area where they washed hair, holding a plastic bowl in one hand while stirring the brush inside with another. "We have a loyal customer base." Helen was the more laidback of the two and less open to changing her hair as much as her mother, although she was always the one experimenting with her regulars. They were both the same height yet didn't resemble each other except for their round pale blue eyes.

"It's always good to branch out." Ginger went back to the older woman in her chair.

Helen tapped her finger on the black swiveling chair next to her. "Cait, plop your tush here, and I'll be right with you." She handed off the dye to one of the other stylists, a young girl who looked fresh out of school. "Let it set for no less than thirty-five."

Cait sat, and Helen played with her hair as they chattered away about the wedding. Renee picked a chair in the waiting area and grabbed a magazine. Helen would wash and blow out her hair in between Cait's waiting sessions for her coloring. It was the only way they were able to get the appointment.

Helen was a good listener, and probably knew most of the gossip around town before it reached the inner circles of the older crowd. Once it hit them, it was like wildfire.

"Renee has a date tonight," Cait said.

"Really?" Renee looked up from her magazine. "Why are we talking about me?"

"Because this is a monumental occasion," Ginger said.

For once, Helen agreed with her mother. "Who's the lucky tourist?"

They knew Renee too well.

"Our next-door renter," Renee offered.

"Who she lost her virginity to," Cait said.

Heat pulsed through Renee as the other women in the salon whooped with glee. Even the older woman in Ginger's chair seemed more interested in the conversation after that tidbit of information.

"All right, that's enough."

"Audrey's nephew?" Ginger asked. Her memory was better than most.

"Yeah," Renee said, wondering where she was going with that.

"Sweet boy. He used to bring her here weekly over that summer."

Renee's cheeks burned, mostly because Cait was grinning at her like the Cheshire cat.

"So, he's not a tourist?" Helen's thin eyebrows arched.

"He is," Renee insisted. Any idea that their dating would continue after the summer made her stomach flutter.

"Technically not," Cait added unhelpfully.

"He's only here to help with the volleyball camp." And get the house into a saleable condition. There was no reason for him to return to West Cove after that. A quickening gripped her stomach. *This is what you wanted. A fleeting summer moment with an old flame.*

The conversation shifted to talking about summer romances. They didn't directly address Renee, but she couldn't help connecting the experiences to her own. Instead of easing her mind, the women made her feel even more self-conscious. She didn't talk much, even when she was in Helen's chair; the others' conversation was enough that she didn't need to, but that meant her mind was on overdrive. As Helen transformed her hair from a frizzy mess to smooth and tame, she thought about the date with Luc. She wasn't excited about the food, but she couldn't go back on her word about how much she loved sushi. Renee flipped through her phone, searching articles for the best food to order if you didn't want raw fish on your plate. It was all she could do to distract herself from thinking of Luc and how their night would unravel.

* * *

After the salon, they stopped by the local deli for sandwiches. Renee made sure to order a large one, so she wasn't starving for the date. The less she exposed herself to the sushi, the better.

Cait's earlier excitement faded as they made their way back to the house. It seemed the women at the salon had zapped her energy out as much as it had ramped up Renee's.

Her attention was sharp, keeping an eye on the influx of tourists walking the sidewalks. A familiar truck sat in the parking lot of the real estate office, and Renee eased off the gas pedal to practically a crawl to get a better look. Luc wasn't inside of his truck. The impending sale of the house weighed on her. It wasn't as if it would go that quickly, but he was probably updating the listing with all the changes that he'd made. Renee imagined seeing Audrey's house listing and the repairs and cleaning she and Marcus had helped with in the photographs on the realtor website.

Renee reached for the radio dial and turned up the volume of the current station. She'd never thought about any future with any of the tourists she'd dated. With Luc, everything was different. She was different. Her views on relationships had shifted. They had both returned to a simpler time, and they reached for it with all of their strength. And that scared her more than the sushi.

* * *

When they arrived at the house, Cait excused herself to go upstairs and rest. Hunter bounced at her feet, but she ignored him entirely. No one was more surprised than the demon dog himself.

"Want a walk?" Renee asked the dogs.

Brandy stood up from the couch and lumbered over to Renee while Hunter spun in circles around her. When she finally clasped the leash on the little collar, she tugged them out of the house to give Cait some privacy.

The walk gave her nothing but time to think about the night ahead. While she kept the deeper thoughts of what would happen after the Fourth out of her mind, she thought of what to wear. She wanted to be comfortable—as that was the top priority of any of her outfits—but enjoyed the way he had looked at her that day on the beach. Renee hoped for a look like that with whatever dress she chose.

The nights weren't as cool as she would have expected for late June, so she had a few options for spaghetti strap dresses. It would also allow Luc to comfort her if she was cold.

The grin on her face didn't diminish, even as Hunter tugged at the leash in search of a spot on the beach to do his business. Renee led him to a patch of grass behind the barrier, which was dog-friendly, near the public beach complete with a complimentary biodegradable bag dispenser.

Normally, Renee didn't walk to the public areas, but she wanted the first opportunity to spot Luc returning home. The entire evening was devoted to them spending time together, but she liked having him nearby, and not planning for his imminent escape from West Cove.

The walk was longer than usual, as she wanted to tucker out Hunter for Cait's sake. Wandering away from the beach, they took to the narrow streets between the rental properties. There were even fewer residents closer to the public beach, and families of all sizes walked back and forth, rolling their coolers, and shouldering stuffed bags, umbrellas, and beach chairs.

Renee smiled at everyone, greeting those who wanted to get a better look at the dogs. Hunter barked at everyone while Brandy's tail ticked like a metronome at every drop of attention, especially from the kids. The spaces between the houses widened the further Renee walked from the beach. She weaved through the streets until even Hunter had slowed and stopped pulling the leash.

Looping around, Renee picked up her pace, hoping to run into Luc when she arrived home.

But, instead of his truck greeting her in the driveway, it was still empty.

Renee trudged inside, and both Hunter and Brandy shuffled toward their water bowls before jumping on the couch. Hunter dug his nails into the cushions before twirling twice and lying flat. His belly bounced up and down with his heavy breathing while Brandy's eyes slid shut.

With the house calmer than it had been all summer, Renee walked into the kitchen for some water. Her reflection in the microwave door stopped her. Her hair had held up from the walk but prickling sweat clung to her neck. She adjusted a chunk of it behind her ear.

That wasn't going to do.

Chapter 18

The knock on the door came at six-thirty exactly. Cait and Marcus had left for dinner around six, which gave Renee the last half-hour to pace around her room, the kitchen, and then the living room where Hunter thought it was a fun game of Follow the Leader as she waited for Luc to cross the driveway. Then, Renee started to doubt herself and wondered if she should have gone over to his place since she was ready first. But ultimately she decided to wait. Renee didn't want to show her hand on how ready she was for the date to begin.

Since the screen door was the only thing between the two of them, Renee got a full view of Luc walking up to the house before he spotted her.

Hunter raced for the door, barking wildly. The house had been quiet for the last half-hour, but he turned up the volume ten notches.

"Sorry," Luc said through the door.

"It's fine," Renee said, pushing by Hunter, who was looking for head scratches. Cait hadn't rolled out of Renee's room until dinner when Marcus bribed her with a local barbecue, which meant she hadn't pampered Hunter as much as usual. He was desperate for attention.

Luc stepped backward as Renee walked outside, keeping her foot out to block Hunter.

Brandy harrumphed from her bed while Hunter carried on.

"Is he going to be all right in there?" Luc asked.

Renee waved him off. "He'll calm down in a minute."

With the sun still blazing against the horizon, Renee got a better look at Luc. He wore gray jeans with a white button-down top. His hair was slightly damp at the roots, making it appear darker than usual. His cologne had a rich scent that Renee committed to memory.

"You look great." The black dress fit her well, but under his scrutiny, she almost felt naked. Shivers moved through her, and she wondered if she should have brought a small sweater to cover the goose bumps across her arms.

Renee enjoyed the way he looked at her. "Thanks, you too."

"This old thing?" he said with a grin.

Little did he know how old her dress was. But it did the job.

Luc held the truck door for her. The night at the bar flew to the front of her mind. How different she had felt about him then. That seemed to be the night her feelings for him had shifted. Over her shoulder, he rounded the truck and moved along his side of the truck. He looked up, and their eyes met.

When he opened the door, a fresh wave of his scent filled the small space. He turned to her, and his eyes narrowed.

"What is it?"

"You did something to your hair."

"I did." Renee smoothed her hand over her tresses.

"It looks good." He reached over and pinched a chunk between two fingers. "The way the light is hitting it right now makes it shimmer."

The slight tug against her scalp traveled through her until her toes tingled.

Luc's hand rested on the edge of her seat as he focused on the road and backed out of the driveway.

It brushed over her hair again when he navigated down the street.

The space was too silent. Renee couldn't stay in her head much longer. "What did you do today?"

"I, uh, worked with the camp, and then headed into town."

Renee waited for him to expand on that, but he didn't. She debated on delving deeper but thought better of it. She knew the house was going on the market eventually, so he might not have thought it was pertinent to give her more information.

"Any new last-minute items for the wedding?"

"Cait touched up her hair today. Jorden, her fiancé, is coming into town Monday."

"So, you'll be off the hook Monday?"

"I'm not holding my breath. I'm sure there will be last-minute additions."

"You could always say no. There's not much that could happen in this short amount of time."

"I could. But I don't mind." Her flat, broken record was back. The only reason was to keep Luc from opening more conversations like that one. He forced her to confront her feelings about her family and life, and right now, she only wanted to concentrate on them. Thinking about life outside of Luc would make his leaving a reality.

It was too much to think about on their first date. Renee channeled Sadie and Cait, thinking of how they were going to want her to explain every second of the date. Boring them with details about how she couldn't get out of her own head wouldn't do.

"As long as you're happy with what you're contributing, that's all that matters."

Renee was glad he finally understood. "How did the practices go today?"

Luc beamed and started in with a play-by-play of all three groups. He excitedly played out the big moments as much as he could without taking his hands off the wheel too often.

"You love to coach, huh?"

Luc sighed. "I do. It's my passion. Passing on what I know to these kids is just, uh, indescribable."

Renee tried to swallow against the lump forming in her throat. She'd never remotely felt what he had for her job. It was enjoyable, sure. Exciting? Never. The closest she felt to that was when she was around Cait. Having a hand in her turning out the way she did was most likely her best achievement. It wasn't the worst thing she could accomplish.

Luc pulled into the parking lot for the sushi restaurant. It was its own building, set a street over from the main road. It was about double the size of her house, which made it seem less like a full restaurant, and rather like a small house to drive by and leave in her rearview mirror.

The lot was almost full, but Luc found a spot near the back of the building.

Inside, they squeezed into the small waiting area. Renee bumped her nose against his shoulder and inhaled deeply. Glass walls took up two sides of the space as a petite woman wearing black pants and a button-up long-sleeve shirt came up to her. She pulled a stylus from her high bun and posed it against a tablet, which fit into the palm of her hand.

"Do you have a reservation?"

Renee shook her head as Luc said, "Yes. Under 'Hardy'."

The woman slid the stylus over the screen and then nodded. "This way, please."

"I didn't know you needed a reservation to come here," Renee said to Luc.

He cocked his head to the side. "I thought you liked sushi? This is the only place around."

"I-I haven't had it for a while."

"I got one just in case. And I'm glad I did." He slowed his steps, and his hand rested against her waist. Heat radiated from his hand and seared her skin. Walking behind her, he couldn't see the slow smile spreading across her lips.

The woman stopped at a table by a window. It was set for two and rather close to the ones next to it. Luc and Renee had to squeeze by the couple at the next table, almost brushing against them.

"Your server will be with you shortly." The woman dropped two menus in front of them and scurried away.

Luc folded himself into the chair and scooted back as far as he could without hitting the wall behind him.

"Do you have enough room?" Renee dropped the strap of her purse on the back of her chair.

"I did ask for a window seat."

"If the windows were open, we could have a patio seat."

He glanced outside. "You're not kidding."

Their server passed waters over the table next to them. The couple curled their lips in annoyance but said nothing to the large man with his belly nearly in their soup.

"Do you want wine?" Luc asked, peering up from the drink menu.

"Yes. You choose."

He eyed her for a few seconds before looking at the menu again. What was it about Luc that made her want to say yes to everything he asked? Was it fear of missing the short time they had together? Renee wasn't at all sure. Her agreement had brought her to this place, but she would want to be with him anywhere. She bit down on her lip, wondering where that idea had come from.

The waiter came back and took their drink order before flitting off toward the bar area of the restaurant.

"What are you thinking for sushi? I prefer the hand rolls, but I could go all in if you want."

She certainly did not want to go all in. "Rolls are fine."

"Any preference?"

Renee almost wished he was a pushy date and chose the food for her. She studied the menu, harder than she had for most tests in her college years. The ingredients were listed, and the only option without seafood was the California roll. She couldn't be much of a sushi lover if she went the easy route. The couple next to them were eating off the same plate with several colorful options. "How about we get a bunch to split?"

"Great idea," he said, opening the package of chopsticks. He rubbed the edges together. She lifted hers and copied his actions.

"What made you change your mind about tonight?" Luc asked.

It certainly wasn't the food choice. Renee hadn't anticipated him questioning her after he had accepted so easily. It was a valid question. Her need to keep her heart closed off to him warred against honesty. Though they were in a place she didn't want to be, she wanted to be with him. The longer she didn't answer, the more Luc would question her response.

"Sometimes, my past has kept me from doing the things I wanted. It was a reflex to say no to go out with someone I had a history with."

"We haven't seen each other in years. Does that still count?" Luc's knee bumped against hers. She wanted to believe it was an accident but also wanted it to not be from the way her body scooted closer to him.

With her ability to recall most days they had spent together as youths, it did. "It does."

"So, when did you realize that?"

Renee shrugged. Could she tell him that when she was dancing at the club all she wanted was his hands on her body? And every accidental touch set fire to her? "It just came to me. Over the time we spent together."

The server came over, and Renee exhaled a deep breath. It was a lot to explain her motives to him, but she hadn't revealed much, had she? It wasn't comfortable hiding around Luc as it was to any other stranger. He knew her. Well, the teen her, and a part of the adult Renee.

Luc ordered four different hand rolls. None of them the California variety.

When the wine came, she gulped a hefty swig. The warm, sweet red wine coiled in her stomach and spread itself through her.

It didn't take long for the food to arrive, only ten minutes of keeping to neutral topics. Renee could barely concentrate on the conversation as the idea of eating the rolls made her stomach churn.

The platter dropped on the table, filled with colorful cylinders with various sauces on top. The stench of raw fish filled her nose, and she inhaled another gulp of wine before setting down her glass.

"This looks great," Luc said. "I have been craving this since I've been here. The best place to get fish is near the shore, am I right?"

"Yeah," she said quickly.

Luc used his chopsticks to lift one into his mouth. He popped it inside and started to chew, while Renee tried to figure out which one wouldn't make her gag.

Jutting her chopsticks at the smallest one, she had trouble getting the balance right. She stabbed the roll and got it into her mouth before it started to unroll.

The texture wasn't as she expected. It was firmer, and the flavors exploded in her mouth. She barely registered the fishy taste as the warmth from the sauce spread across her tongue.

"That one is good," she said, stabbing another one.

Luc didn't comment on her chopsticks skills. Instead, he grabbed one too.

"You're right about that."

After she ate that roll, Renee plotted to find another, which was equally tasty. Unfortunately, she didn't have quite the same luck.

For every three or four Luc ate, Renee grimaced through one. The greatest relief swelled within her as Luc scraped a bit of wasabi onto the last roll. When he finished chewing, he sipped from his wine and placed it in front of him. He sighed heavily as if he was about to reveal his darkest secret. "You don't really like sushi, do you?"

Renee's hands tightened in her lap. "The meal was good."

"Was it? I'm sure you ate four total. I've seen you put away a steak."

The least she owed him was an explanation. "To be honest, I never had the urge to try it." She wasn't sure if it was the sweet wine lubricating the conversation or the fact that he had caught her in the lie. The weight of her fibs ballooned away.

"We could have gone anywhere."

"I just wanted to be with you."

Luc smiled, but he still eyed her with wariness. "I feel like I need to question you more about these things. You're always putting yourself second."

"Did you have a good time?"

His hand dropped onto the table, brushing against hers. "Of course, I did. But, you're probably starving. How about dessert?"

"As long as it's not fish, I'll have anything."

Luc's hand rested on hers and didn't move until the banana and ice cream tempura landed on the table.

* * *

The ride home was much shorter than the charged one to the restaurant, and the spaces between their conversation lengthened. The end of the date neared, yet she wasn't ready. Renee wasn't much of a mind-reader, but she could tell Luc didn't want it to end either. She caught the not so subtle bob of Luc's Adam's apple. Four times in thirty seconds. Why was she counting them?

When he pulled into the driveway, he sighed. "Do you want to take a walk?"

"Yes," she said a little too quickly.

The light in Renee's room was still on, and the flickering of the television screen illuminated the living room. All the shades were drawn, but Renee felt as if she were blasted into the past to that summer with Luc. They were adults now, but she couldn't help the giddiness within her at sneaking to the beach with Luc in tow.

With the moon shining down on them, and the cool sand under her toes, Renee was more at home than ever. All of her nervous energy transformed into comfort at her happy place. Luc's hand brushed against hers as they walked far enough from the surf not to get their feet wet but still feel the spray of the water.

Luc broke the silence between them. "Now that we've established you don't like sushi, what would be your perfect date?"

"Here," she breathed. The salty air fueled her lungs.

"I had a feeling," he said, rubbing the back of his neck.

"I had a great time tonight." It was the most honest thing she'd said all day.

"Me too."

Thoughts swirled through her mind about Luc—about their past. There was a time clock on all of it, and she had no idea what would happen when Luc finally drove away from the house. A sense of urgency filled her chest, creating pressure so powerful it stole her breath.

"I'm glad you changed your mind." Luc's steps slowed. "I think this visit has turned out better than I expected."

Renee stopped to face him. "What do you mean?"

"When Audrey asked me to help with the house, I decided to for purely selfish reasons. I wanted to travel the same path as I had all those years ago. I never thought you would be in West Cove, or even next door. I had hoped that we could reconnect, though."

Luc's divulging of what was on his mind was unexpected. As she focused on his words, her peripheral turned inky black.

"You wanted to see me again?"

Luc trapped his lip under his teeth. "You were a big part of it."

"That's um—"

"Creepy?" He chuckled and raked a hand through his hair. "I'm starting to think it sounds that way."

"No, not at all." The moment she'd seen Luc again, all those feelings had rushed back to her. Renee hadn't realized how much she had wanted him in her life too. Now, it seemed as if letting him go might be harder than she anticipated. Especially with his admission for how he felt about her.

"If I did find you, I wanted to see if that . . . spark still existed between us. That it wasn't some fluke. That these situations could happen. After Claire, I wasn't sure anymore. Both my parents seem content without each other, but I've never forgotten how I felt that summer. As if the world was different than what it had showed me." He inhaled sharply. "Wow. Sorry, that's a lot. Around you, I feel like I can blurt out whatever I want without judgment."

Renee understood that, probably more than he realized. Which was why she stepped closer to him and twined her fingers with his. His shoulders relaxed, even though he had to twist his neck to look down at her. "I don't know what to say." She knew enough from the swirling tendrils of wanting, which tightened with each breath. Her hands untangled from his and slid up his shirt to rest on his shoulders. Lifting on her toes, she pressed her lips against his. His mouth parted slightly, and he drew a breath, snaking his hands around her waist. Heat bloomed at his touch and moved lower.

Luc's mouth was softer than she remembered, but the movements were the same. It was as if they had pressed pause on their summer together and restarted at that moment. His fingers splayed across her back, digging in to bring her closer to him. Renee deepened the kiss, reveling in the pleasure rippling through her body.

This is right.

They held each other for what seemed like hours with the waves crashing against the shore behind them, though it had only been a few minutes.

Renee broke the kiss, her lips swollen and warm. Luc's eyes opened lazily.

"What—?"

With a touch of her finger to his lips, she silenced him. "I want this." Her gaze slid to the other houses on the street. "But we should go inside."

Luc's eyebrows twitched. She knew what he was thinking and planned to give him what he anticipated. What she had wanted from the moment she had spotted him again.

Their hands wove together as they sprinted for his house. The sand kicked out around them as they navigated the moving surface below them.

At the front door, Luc struggled for the key as Renee itched to have her hands on him again. She glanced at her house before tumbling inside with Luc's strong hands around her waist once more.

* * *

Crashing waves outside the window woke Renee with a start. She sat up and a breeze skittered over her bare skin. She lifted the unfamiliar sheet, as the room tilted slightly. It was strange at first until the night washed over her. Luc's hands and mouth lingering against every inch of her body, her memorizing all of his.

The door opened, and Luc appeared in his boxers, holding two steaming mugs. His hair was disheveled. She recalled tugging her hands through it as they explored each other for hours the night before. "Good morning."

"Morning." Her lips were dry, and she licked the moisture back into them as she reached for the coffee. The sheet slipped away from her body, and she struggled to tug it against her while balancing the hot cup in her hands.

The curtains surrounding the bay windows were wide open, but the bed was far enough back that no one outside could see in. It was a better view of the beach than her room. She melted into the pillow as Luc sat next to her. The room smelled of fresh paint, making her slightly dizzy. Or maybe it was the man next to her.

184

He planted a kiss on her shoulder before settling in with his coffee. "You sleep okay?"

"Yes, thanks."

If at all possible, she wanted to avoid that awkward morning-after conversation. It only shadowed the perfect evening they'd had the night before. If this wasn't going to last forever, she wanted to burn him into her memory, so it did.

Renee placed the mug on the side table and turned to him. She lifted his from his hands and did the same. Then, she allowed the sheet to fall away from her body. Luc's pupils widened as she straddled him before dipping lower to kiss him. He pulled her close, and they melted into the sheets together with the sound of the waves and gulls as their music.

Chapter 19

Renee regretted nothing about her night with Luc, though she dreaded going home. Not just because she didn't want to leave Luc's warm embrace, but she wasn't prepared for the amount of questions both Cait and Sadie would demand once she was away from him. She and Luc had discussed her going home eventually but pushed it back several times as they continued to distract each other away from their adult obligations. Their time together away from the magical cover of the night hadn't deterred them from being together twice more.

Luc's schedule with the camp propelled Renee from the bed. He told her she could stay, but if Cait caught Luc across the street at the beach without Renee returning home, she wasn't sure if her sister's imagination would run wild. It was better to stay ahead of those thoughts.

After five minutes of goodbye kissing, Renee trudged across the gravel. Once she reached the top of the back stairs, she peered over the railing to find Marcus's car still in the driveway.

She groaned.

Hunter announced her arrival before she had the door open. He attacked her ankles the moment she stepped through the back door. He slid around the room in circles, begging for attention, or treats.

"Shh!" she hissed and scratched his back.

He continued to yap and twirl around for her fingers to find the right spot to scratch.

"Look at you!" Cait trilled, as she came down the stairs.

Renee craned her neck into the living room, looking out for Marcus.

"Hush," Renee chided her sister.

It didn't deter the massive grin on her sister's face. "I'm assuming the date went well." Cait made a lewd gesture, and Renee swatted at her. "Oh, stop. Papa Marcus isn't here."

"He's not?"

Cait leaned against the doorframe. "Ever since you discovered him and Olivia, he's not hiding anymore."

Renee opened her mouth and closed it. The way Cait said that forced a question through her lips. "Did you know about them?"

"Of course." Cait flipped her hair over her shoulder and opened the cabinet. She lifted the bag with Hunter's treats and sat at the table.

"They've been at it for some time, Nay." The tone of the nickname wasn't cutesy as usual but threatening. "I'm surprised you haven't noticed."

Renee thought about all the nights Marcus went to the club. Was he at Olivia's? Was he meeting her for dinner? How had no one in town said anything to her?

"He hid it from me. I did nothing wrong."

"I didn't realize your repulsion with relationships involved not seeing one right in front of you."

"Can we move on from this?"

"Sure." Cait held a treat out for Hunter, making him sit for it. Then she dropped it. He was talented at catching them. Eating was the only time he was quiet. "I'm assuming you had lots of sex last night."

Renee groaned and trudged up the stairs.

"You're not disagreeing with me, so it must be a yes!"

"That's not how that works."

"Of course it is."

"I'm going to take a shower now."

"Good, you smell like him." Cait's laughter followed her up the stairs.

Renee wasn't one to kiss and tell, but she couldn't help smiling to the bathroom and into the shower.

* * *

Renee had no urge to face her father that afternoon, so she treated Cait to a late lunch and shopping around town. Between all the wedding plans, they hadn't spent much time browsing the shops. Though, Cait did pick out gifts for her bridesmaids. It was another check off her dwindling list of wedding plans.

As they walked through the streets, Renee made a note of everyone walking by. Luc hadn't contacted her since the morning, but it would be a welcome surprise to see him in town.

By the evening, Renee was successful enough in deterring Cait from any innuendos about Luc that there was hardly a discussion about him over dinner with Marcus.

It seemed as if she and her father had a silent truce about not delving into each other's personal lives, and that was okay with her.

* * *

Renee was never the type to show off any of her flings around town but jumped at the opportunity to assist Luc at the hardware store over the weekend. She was aware of the time clock on whatever they were doing and wanted to be with him as much as she could.

Unlike the first time they had gone together, she wasn't annoyed with the stares in their direction. Especially when Luc took her hand in his as they walked. She floated through the weekend with Luc inches from her at all times, even at night when they decided their new routine was to walk the beach together under the moonlight. It took time for the sun to go down, so they filled that space taking the dogs out for longer walks than they were used to and tumbling onto his bed together before making love.

When Monday came, Renee tucked herself under an umbrella and sat on the edge of her Wi-Fi zone so she could work from her laptop. If she at all thought Luc wanted his space, his constant gaze in her direction would have told her otherwise. Neither of them could staunch their grins at each other until they were at the point where the girls and Dale started to notice.

Luc made his way toward her. Renee had packed them both sandwiches, while Luc handed off money to his assistant coach to pay for the girls to eat from the food trucks at the public beach. Neither seemed interested in tasting anything but each other until Renee's phone rang a third time in a row.

"Should you get that?" Luc dragged his fingers across her shoulders. A wave of ripples moved through her at his touch.

"It's Cait." She turned in her seat. Cait stood at the porch, pointing to her phone. "She could come over here." Instead of arguing or yelling across the street, she called her back.

Luc opened the cooler and lifted a sandwich from the plastic container.

"What is it?" Renee asked.

"We're supposed to get Jorden at the airport. Remember? He's landing in like an hour!"

Renee stood from her chair, smashing her head against the umbrella. "Ow! Why didn't you remind me?"

"I thought you were going to remind *me*!" Cait's voice screeched in her ear as she stomped her foot against the patio.

Cait hung up, and Renee heard an audible huff from across the street.

"Luc, I have to go. I have to pick up Jorden at the airport and bring them to the hotel. I totally forgot."

189

"Can I keep this sandwich?"

"Of course." She leaned over to kiss him. "I'll be back later." She slid her laptop into her bag and placed it on the chair.

"Dinner at my place. I'm making burgers. I need to clear them from my refrigerator before they go bad."

"Well, I can't refuse that offer." Renee lifted her chair from the sand.

"Leave your things. I'll bring them over in a few minutes." He stood and wiped the sand from his shorts.

"Thanks." She kissed him again. This one lingered until Hunter started barking.

Renee moved away from Luc, spotting Cait antagonizing her dog from outside. No doubt that was her plan to get Renee's attention.

Renee pulled a sarong over her bathing suit as she crossed the street.

"We're going to be late." Cait dragged her rolling suitcases down the front steps. They skidded to a stop at her feet.

"It's not my fault." Renee lifted Cait's bag from the porch and swung it over her shoulder.

Cait stood by the trunk, tapping her foot. "You're the one driving me."

"All right, can we drop this? It takes at least an hour to get there, and he has baggage, right?"

"Duh!"

Renee ground her teeth together, opening the trunk. Cait stormed over to the passenger side, leaving the packing to Renee. "Text him and let him know we're on the way. The luggage carousel will take at least twenty minutes. Worst case, he can wait a few minutes."

Cait got inside and slammed her door. "He's going to think I forgot about him."

"That's a little dramatic."

"For weeks, I've been here. And we couldn't even get there in time."

There was no getting through to Cait when she was in a mood. They spotted Luc as they drove by. He stood by the barrier, finishing the last bite of the turkey sandwich. Renee's stomach grumbled. Between all the exercise they were getting at the beach and in the bedroom, she had looked forward to a leisurely lunch with him. No such luck.

He waved, and she returned it. Too bad he wasn't in the car with her to defuse the situation.

Over the last few days, Cait seemed more agitated when Renee and Luc were together. But Renee only had a few more hours with her sister, and she was to blame for Cait's mood. Normally, she was organized and on top of all the details of her life. Even her phone had reminded her of when they should have left for the airport. It was early enough in the day that there shouldn't be too much traffic, but Cait was right that she should have paid more attention.

Cait was silent for most of the ride through town. A few minutes onto the highway, her crossed arms melted into a stiff posture. Renee sensed the shift in her mood. "You can take care of Hunter this week, right?"

Renee focused on the road. "You're not bringing him to the hotel?"

"I'm not sure they allow dogs. Besides, I wanted to take Jorden around. Show him the town. Take a few day trips."

"There are five days until your wedding."

"Yeah, which is why I don't have time for Hunter."

If she didn't have time for him, she should have left him home. From the way the month had gone on, Renee and Marcus had cared for the little menace more than Cait.

"Please, Nay. It's the last thing I'll ask of you. I promise. We're taking him to a dog resort while we're on the honeymoon, and he's going to miss us so much."

It seemed as if she'd had everything planned. Just like she had when she sprung the wedding plans on Renee. If she agreed, Cait couldn't be mad at her for being late to the airport. Besides, it wasn't as if Renee wasn't going to be home or twenty feet away from Hunter the rest of the week. A heavy weight settled in her stomach as she agreed to the idea. "Fine."

"You're the best."

Just like that, Renee was forgiven. She settled in her seat while Cait grabbed the cord for the music and plugged her phone in. Upbeat music from the speakers flowed throughout the car at deafening levels as Renee concentrated on the road ahead. It wasn't her particular brand of music, but as long as it got them to the airport without any more fighting, it was worth it.

* * *

The reunion between Cait and Jorden was both dramatic and romantic, as if it were plucked from a movie. Cait raced for the door as Jorden came out with his suitcases. He dropped them as Cait rushed into his arms. They spun around three times before he let her down. Their kiss was enough to make Renee blush, and she turned away to give them privacy. The airport attendant walked up to her car and rapped on the window.

"You can't idle in the pickup zone," the rather grumpy-looking guy said. He seemed too young for that type of attitude. He had to be no more than twenty-five.

"He's right there," Renee said, pointing at Jorden.

Jorden spotted him and disengaged from Cait. Her lipstick was smeared across his mouth, staining it red. They came over to the car, and Renee popped the trunk. From the way the attendant eyed the vehicle, she wasn't about to step out of it.

"Hey!" Jorden folded his tall frame into the car. He sat in the back seat behind the passenger side, leaving it open for Cait. Instead, she slid in next to him in the back seat.

"How was your flight?" Cait's knee jutted against the back of Renee's seat. Now she was a cab driver?

For the first thirty minutes, Cait shared all the details of the wedding with Jorden. Renee eyed him through the rearview mirror. His attention never wavered, and she wondered if Cait had overreacted about him and how she struggled with the wedding. From the caring attention he offered to all the details, he seemed as if he could have been helpful in the process.

Renee stopped herself from focusing on it too hard. Everything was set in place, and there wasn't much to do other than the rehearsal dinner. At least nothing to plan. The bridesmaids were coming in throughout the week and they had pedicures and manicures planned as a group. They would distract Cait enough that Renee could finally relax and enjoy all the hard work she had done with Cait.

* * *

Jorden had secured the bridal suite for the entire week as a mini-retreat before their wedding. West Cove Country Club had a beachside resort on the property, close to the water. For almost a week, Cait would be immersed in the location where she'd get married. The smile on her face was picture-perfect enough that Renee could forget she was in charge of Hunter without Cait as a buffer until after the wedding.

After dropping Cait off with Jorden at the main building at the country club, Renee drove away as a weight floated off her shoulders. It continued to lessen even as she drove onto her street toward the house. Her chair, umbrella, and cooler were gone from the beach, and she hoped that Luc had brought them to his place so she would have an excuse to go over there and retrieve them.

Marcus's car wasn't in the driveway. The divide between them widened in his absence. Cait's words from the other day repeated in her mind. As much as she didn't want to know about the more personal details of his and Olivia's relationship, Renee didn't want her relationship with her father to suffer. When all was said and done with the wedding, Cait—and Luc—would be gone, leaving her with Marcus and Olivia.

The more she thought about it, the more her shoulders started to creep upward toward her ears again. She inhaled and let it go before texting her father to see where he was.

Hunter and Brady both barked from inside the house, but she wanted to see Luc first. Maybe he would take a walk with them.

Her phone pinged with a text from Marcus.

Out picking up dress for Cait's wedding.

Renee stopped in her tracks before another one came through.

With Olivia. I'm not wearing a dress.

She laughed at her father's text. Of course Cait would allow 'Papa Marcus' to bring a plus-one to the wedding as she had with Renee. She looked up, peering at Luc's house. The night at the club, she had wanted to dance with Luc. Now was her opportunity.

Worry snaked through her, but Renee promptly pushed it down and out of her body. She'd live a day at a time, especially when it came to Luc. Denial was the only way she'd get through without questioning her life.

Luc was around the back of the house, setting up the grill.

"Hey," he said, putting down the brush and strolling over to her.

They kissed, and Renee forgot entirely what she was going to say to him. His hands rested at her waist and a shiver rolled down her spine.

"How was the trip?" he asked.

"Uneventful."

"Cait gone?"

"Yeah, she and Jorden are staying at the club."

"With Hunter?"

Renee twined her fingers together. "We're watching him until after the wedding."

Luc chuckled and shook his head. "Still a pushover."

She swatted at him. "I'm not."

"I brought all of your things inside. Marcus was still here earlier."

"Thanks." Renee rocked on her heels, wondering why the words weren't coming out. That fear of rejection haunted her as before she asked him on their date. That turned out better than she imagined, so asking him to come to the wedding with her couldn't be that bad. Could it?

"Am I in trouble?" Luc asked.

Renee snapped out of her thoughts. "Not at all, why?"

"You look as if you want to say something important."

He always seemed one step ahead of her. "I do."

Luc adjusted his stance and crossed his arms. "Don't hold me in suspense."

"Do you want to come to Cait's wedding with me? She let me have a plus-one, even though I've been single forever, but I thought it would be nice to go with you. But you don't have any obligation to go. I don't even know if you dance, or if you'd want to . . ." She trailed off, her cheeks burning with embarrassment at her rambling.

Luc let out a toothy grin.

"What?"

He reached out and cupped her cheek in his hand. "I'd love to go. But there is a problem."

"What's that?"

He held her against him, his lips brushing hers. "I need to know what color your dress is so I can match."

Chapter 20

With Luc as her plus-one, the pressure was on for Renee. Before inviting him, she only had Cait's needs in mind. Now, she wanted to make it a special night for both of them. It was one, if not the last night they would have together. What happened after that was anyone's guess, but Renee had an idea it would involve Luc leaving West Cove for good.

Like any thoughts of Isla, Renee pushed away those creeping ideas. Luc didn't seem bothered by their imminent end-of-June goodbye.

With Cait already spending her days with Jorden, the only thing that Renee had left to think about was what delicious dish she would cook up for West Cove's annual fireworks potluck.

It was a tradition, well loved by the local residents on their part of the beach, and each year they would watch the fireworks over the water. As residents of the private beach, they had exclusive, non-crowded, front-row seats to the festivities, while the public beach tended to swarm with crowds that started gathering in the early afternoon.

Other than Cait's wedding, it was probably the most romantic evening Renee and Luc would share. Years ago, they attended together as teens, and it was the place where they'd shared their first kiss.

Memories of that time flooded her mind, and Renee couldn't stop the pops of excitement bursting within her in the days leading up to the wedding.

On Tuesday afternoon, Renee helped Luc take down the volleyball net, making space for the family members of the residents. They left the equipment in the newly cleared sunroom and started on the slow cooker chili for the potluck. Luc had found the recipe for Audrey's famous fireworks potluck dish while cleaning the kitchen cabinets.

Since it was the summer of reminiscing about the past, Renee insisted that they make the dish.

The potluck started around six and all the families gathered at Olivia's house. She was the only one with a driveway large enough to contain the long tables and number of people.

When Renee and Luc arrived, there were already about fifty people in attendance, with more in the distance walking toward them.

Luc held the slow cooker and placed it next to the other hot dishes. The group around them converged on the chili after only brief pleasantries to the new couple.

"Let's give them some space." Renee locked hands with Luc and moved away from the tables. As much as she was hungry, there was no getting between anyone and Aunt Audrey's chili.

"Aren't you two the cutest!" Cait's voice shrilled over the group. She and Jorden strode up the driveway as their Uber drove off down the street behind them.

Renee tried to tug her hand from Luc's, but he held it tighter. "I'm not letting you go that easy."

Renee tried to smile, but a heat wave surged throughout her body. "Can you not, Cait?"

Hunter started barking from the house, and Cait lifted on her toes to spot him in the window.

"Denny, will you mind getting Hunter? I miss him so much!" Cait kissed Jorden on the cheek and he loped away toward the house.

Cait wrapped her arms around both Luc and Renee. "I'm so excited that Denny is here for the fireworks. We were hoping they would be the night of the wedding, but this is okay too."

Every year the surrounding towns rotated the days of the fireworks. Throughout most nights during that week, a fireworks display went off in the distance. Renee would have been a little bummed to miss the potluck if it was the night of Cait's wedding. The tradition had always been one of her favorites as it celebrated both the residents of her neighborhood and the beach she loved.

"I'm glad we can have you both for the night." Renee glanced over the fence for Jorden. "How are you two doing?"

"Great," Cait said. "He loved the downtown, and the views from our room are amazing. It's the perfect start to our marriage, don't you think?"

Hunter's barking carried over to them. Denny had the dog on a leash and Brandy sauntered behind them.

Cait lifted the dog and snuggled her nose against his fur. "I missed you, Hunty!"

Marcus shuffled over to the group and shook Jorden's hand. "Nice to see you."

Jorden swallowed hard. "You two, Mr. Clarke." Even though Marcus wasn't Cait's father, Jorden seemed nervous all the same. A swell of pride filled Renee's chest. With Jacob gone, Marcus was the only father figure to Cait. Jorden knew that and showed his respect.

Renee's father squeezed a hand on Luc's shoulder. "You better get some grub before it's all gone."

* * *

While eating and weaving her way through the crowd of neighbors to introduce Luc, Renee stepped out of her body several times as if she were watching someone else live her life. It was the same ease she had when she'd kissed him on the beach after their first date. As much as she tried to fault Cait for marrying a man she'd known forever, it seemed as if she and Luc were doing the same thing. Distance and circumstance had separated them, yet they'd come back together as if no time had passed at all.

A hollowing sensation carved out her middle, but she blinked and shoved it away. Renee had to live in the moment, and she intended to do that. She focused on the conversations with her neighbors, the feel of Luc's body next to hers, and having Cait and Jorden nearby. All her favorite people were in the same place on the most memorable day of the summer. It was almost perfect.

When the sky darkened enough, everyone gathered their food items to bring home before making their way to the beach. Luc and Jorden insisted on helping Marcus, which left Cait, Renee, and Olivia to set up the blankets on the sand.

Renee had pulled out four massive beach blankets. They were worn with age, but the soft fabric invoked memories from years past. She recalled sitting with Luc on the blue patchwork one that had been Audrey's but somehow ended up at their house. It was a blanket that reminded her of Luc over the years, and tonight was no different.

Olivia and Cait walked back to the house together, while Renee walked down to the surf. The heat from the day quickly dissipated, but she hadn't been able to shake Luc's warmth, even when he wasn't nearby.

The cool water surged over her feet before pulling the sand from under her on its path back to the larger ocean. The barge where the fireworks took off faded into the inky black night. The descent of the sun moved quicker, just like her time left with Luc.

Renee shivered and stepped back, connecting with another person.

"Oh!" Renee whirled around.

Luc's hands rested on her waist. "I didn't mean to scare you."

Renee shook her head. "You didn't."

Luc's grin faltered slightly. "Are you all right?"

"Yeah." Renee blinked and a hot tear rolled down her face. She wiped it away. "Sand got in my eye, I guess."

"As long as that's all. You've been a little quiet. I just wanted to make sure everything was okay."

Renee pressed herself against him. As long as she was with him, everything was fine. She'd worry about the rest when she needed to.

Luc lowered his chin and kissed her, long and slow. The waves continued to pool around their feet and the sound blocked out the people around them. This was where Renee wanted to stay for as long as possible.

The sounds of splashing feet grew closer and Renee pulled away from Luc as three teenagers sprinted down the sand. One of them backpedaled toward them, and Luc gripped Renee and moved her out of the way as the teen jumped up and caught a football mid-air.

Without a look at them, he whooped and chased after his friends from where they came.

"Do you want to sit?" Renee asked.

"We might as well. These waters are getting dangerous." A smile quirked his lips and his fingers twined with hers.

Marcus and Olivia were already lying on the red and white checkered blanket when they arrived. Luc sat first, tugging Renee down against him. She plopped into his lap and tried to move away until his arms snaked around hers. "This is the perfect seat."

That warmth moved through her again, even as a slightly cooler breeze whipped from the water.

"Where are Cait and Jorden?" Renee asked.

"Taking Hunter for a walk," Olivia said. "She thinks he's not going to like the fireworks."

Renee chewed on her lip. She hadn't even thought of the poor dog and the loud display about to happen. Hunter had made a lot of noise in his time at the house, but he had no understanding of what fireworks were.

"I'm sure she can handle it," Luc said softly against her shoulder. He kissed the spot twice and leaned back.

Renee fell along with him until they were lying side by side. There wasn't an inch between them.

"What are you thinking about?"

Renee turned her head. She was nose to nose with Luc. Without the blazing sun or any of the streetlights around, his face started to become a shadowed version of itself. "Nothing."

"Really?"

Turning to the sky, she nodded. "Yes. For once. I'm not looking ahead to anything. I'm just here."

"How do you feel about that?"

"Good."

"Good."

"I feel like there's more to that question."

Luc shook his head. "Not at all."

Renee sighed, taking in every detail of their moment together. The soft blanket on the sand. The smell of Audrey's chili lingering in her nose. The feel of Luc's hand in hers. If forever was something she wanted, it would look and feel like this.

A distant *thump* across the water signaled the start of the fireworks. A light shot into the sky and exploded in white dots. People around them cheered for more, but Renee's attention was pulled toward the house instead. *Where is Cait?* The windows were dark, and she didn't hear Hunter's barking. Renee didn't see Cait nor Jorden on the front porch. "I should check on Cait."

"Stay here and be in the present, remember?"

Renee snapped out of her thoughts. Luc was right. She lay back down and watched two more fireworks shoot into the sky. The red and purple explosion caused the crowd to go wild once more.

They watched the fireworks for a few minutes before Cait and Jorden slid onto the blanket together. Renee itched to ask them where they'd been, but Luc's reminder repeated over again in her mind. She settled against him, once again accepting the flow of peace throughout her body at how right everything seemed.

"Every year I watch the fireworks at home," Luc said, drawing her attention away from the sky. "I wanted to be sure I wasn't making this up."

"Making what up?"

"About these and the ones from that summer. They were the best I'd ever seen. It wasn't the actual display since most are pretty much the same. It's you, Renee. I wasn't sure until this moment."

Luc's hand slipped over her cheek and tilted her mouth toward his. She covered it with hers and the fireworks exploded overhead. A smile crossed her lips at the irony before she deepened the kiss.

Her chest ached as if she couldn't fully inhale. She imagined watching Luc's truck drive out of town. How he'd take her heart with him.

Was this what love felt like?

How could she have those feelings for Luc when—

A cacophony crackled throughout the sky. Luc broke the kiss and the inevitable thoughts from her mind. She gripped his arm, holding him as close as possible. Holding on to every precious moment with him before they slipped away.

Chapter 21

The last group activity for the wedding party before the rehearsal dinner was manicures and pedicures. Blair had seen a Pinterest board with various nail art designs and had convinced Cait that they were picture-perfect for the photographer to take of the girls holding bouquets.

Renee didn't recall the last time she'd been at the nail salon. With her constant computer work, she couldn't keep any manicure without chipping her nails almost immediately after getting them done. The beach was a natural pumice stone for her feet, and she preferred to keep her toenails bare.

Between the wedding photos and the open-toed shoes at the wedding, there was no reason she couldn't treat herself. She got the full pedicure package with leg massage and back massage while her nails were drying. With all the girls vying for Cait's attention, Renee relaxed more than she had in some time with Cait around. The feel of the masseuse working the muscles in her back reminded her of Luc and his hands all over her earlier that morning. The countdown clock tried to ring its alarm at her, but she'd had enough practice over the years to shut it down.

* * *

After the salon, Cait invited everyone to The Coffee Pot for lunch.

Renee pulled Cait aside from the group for fear of being the practical one. "We might need to call ahead. It's the lunch rush."

Cait waved her off. "It's taken care of."

Renee watched her sister move to the front of the group and wondered if her tendencies of planning had rubbed off on Cait at all.

Her phone pinged, and it was a text from Luc.

How did they turn out?

As she was typing, a text came through from Sadie. Renee swiped it away and snapped a picture of her fingernails with the shimmery French-tip style with tiny flowers on the ring fingers and sent it to Luc.

A phone call came in from Sadie, but she denied it as they were already at the restaurant. She knew it was going to be loud in there, so she'd call Sadie later. But Sadie called again. A quiver in her chest forced her to pick up the phone.

"What's wrong?" Renee asked.

"Did you read my text? Don't go into The Coffee Pot."

Renee looked around the waiting area, expecting to find something on fire. "Are you here? What's wrong?"

"Greer called me the minute she found out who was there."

"Who's here?" Her question caught in her throat as she spotted a ghost from her past—more like a poltergeist—kissing Cait on the cheek before hugging her tightly against her.

"You saw her, didn't you?"

"What is my mother doing here?" Renee hissed into the phone.

"It was inevitable, right? Because of the wedding? Do you want me to come down there for moral support? Or a literal buffer?"

"I have to go."

"Call me later."

"Yeah." Renee hung up the phone as a buzzing sound vibrated in her ears. The floor sunk under her as she slunk toward the long table set up in the middle of the room. Cait hadn't planned the lunch; her mother had.

Cait turned as if she could read Renee's thoughts. Her mouth and eyes were wide in a "surprise!" expression.

It was a surprise, but not a welcome one. Renee had thought she had a few more days before seeing her mother again.

Stripping away the bottle-blonde hair—perfectly matching Cait's—and the pounds of makeup concealing her age, Renee wasn't fooled at all by the woman greeting all the girls with air-kisses and hugs.

Renee stood at the farthest chair from her mother. Her fingers curled over the chair back, blanching with the pressure. She caught a pitying look from Greer. Most locals in West Cove knew about Isla, as she had spent years as a local herself—only to run away with her child and new family without looking back. She was up there with Voldemort when it came to not speaking her name in Renee and Marcus's presence.

After Isla completed her round of Cait's friends, she put Renee in her sights. Cait watched both her mother and sister, and tears stung at Renee's eyes at her sister's betrayal.

Isla slinked over to Renee and draped an arm over her shoulder.

Renee slipped away from her mother's touch. "Hi."

It was all she could muster at the moment. She wanted to explode and leave the restaurant, but Cait's pleading expression held her in place.

"It's good to see you," Isla said.

Renee gave her a curt nod.

Isla clapped her hands together. "Let's all sit, shall we? I've ordered the best that this place has to offer, and the food should be out shortly."

It was just like her mother to order the food for everyone without asking. Just the same, showing up in West Cove without warning.

Isla ushered Cait to the head of the table, while Renee sat at the other. Isla sat next to Cait, preening, and complimenting her while Renee stewed. She wanted to pull out her phone and text

Sadie again with all her feelings, but that wouldn't keep Cait at the center of the lunch.

Cait had to know she'd messed up by surprising Renee, but they were adults, and Renee would never want to purposefully be the one to make her sister have a terrible time.

Renee grabbed on to whatever strength she had left inside of her and smiled and engaged with the women at the table—all except for Isla.

The food helped quell some of her anger—turning it down to a simmer. But it wasn't until it was time for the bill that it spiked again.

Isla held the check in her hand, glancing at the other girls with narrowed eyes. Most of them were enjoying their conversations until Isla cleared her throat, obnoxiously enough to catch their attention. She feigned innocence of course, after a few of the girls offered to pay.

"Oh, I couldn't force you to do that," Isla said, clutching at her necklace. "Unless you insist."

Renee had seen that before when men her mother had dated took Isla out on family dates to show how they were dad material. Even though Isla should have paid at least half, she always found a way to keep her money out of it.

The girls dug into their purses and handed over their shares.

Cait seemed blissfully unaware of the situation unfolding in front of her. The heat cranked up again in Renee's cheeks as she handed over more than her share down the line toward her mother. Isla didn't blink twice at the overpayment, but the corners of her eyes twinkled—probably with excitement that she wouldn't have to pay anything.

It was only when everyone was distracted that she pulled out her phone and texted Sadie.

She hasn't changed a bit.

* * *

After lunch, most of the girls wanted to explore the town. With Isla staying there, Cait willingly parted from her friends to hang out with their mother.

That left the three of them standing in the middle of the sidewalk together.

"Why are you so tense, Renee?" Isla asked.

Renee took a deep breath, smoothing out her attitude. There was something about Isla that turned her into a rebellious teenager again. She wanted to go against everything Isla said and did. But this was for Cait. She could last a few more days in her mother's presence without blemishing any part of Cait's wedding. "I'm thinking about work."

Cait rolled her eyes. "I thought you were off this week?"

Renee had always planned to take this week off to help Cait with her wedding, and she had, but it was an understandable excuse. "It's nothing. I'm going to head home so you two can catch up."

Isla reached out and circled her smooth—and cold—fingers around Renee's wrist. "I wondered if we could go to the house."

"What house?"

"Our—my old house."

It was enough having Isla in town, never mind intruding on her space. Even more so, Luc was there. It was a bubble she didn't want Isla to pop.

"I was thinking," Cait said. "We could all catch up. Maybe have a barbecue."

"I'll need to make sure Dad doesn't have anything going on between him and Olivia." It was petty to involve Marcus's new relationship, but the twitch in Isla's cheek satisfied Renee enough for now.

"He already knows," Cait said.

"Excuse me?"

"I called this morning and told him I was coming. He invited me over," Isla said. "Honestly, I don't know why you're like this, Renee."

"Like what?"

"Asking so many questions. I'm your mother, and I can handle organizing my day. I planned this entire lunch for all of you."

That we paid for!

"I've been married after your father. If you're worried about Olivia, then you shouldn't be."

"I'm not," Renee said.

"Good, now, who's driving? I remember how small the driveway is, and I'm not parking my rental at the beach for a tourist to dent. Do you know how much those places charge for even a small scratch?"

Renee swung her keys from her purse. "I guess I am."

* * *

Like the ride from the airport, Renee stayed quiet as Isla and Cait chattered—catching up on the wedding plans that she had missed, which was all of them. Isla mentioned her take on the event, curling her lip on various occasions with the choices for flowers, bridesmaids' dresses, and music. Cait assured her that it would all be great, but Renee spotted more than once through the rearview mirror that her sister second-guessed herself.

Isla wasn't going away, but Renee would do whatever she could to keep her sister smiling until she left West Cove for her honeymoon.

"The vendors in town know what they're doing, Mother," Renee said.

"You know I hate when you call me that," Isla said. "Mom is just fine."

Renee held back a smirk, feeling somewhat victorious. Though it faded as she turned onto their street and the ocean opened up against the horizon. Her heartbeat slowed as the invasion of her life widened like the sky above them.

"It's just as I remember," Isla said. "More tourists, though. I don't blame the homeowners for leaving in the summer. This place is teeming with strangers three months out of the year. Who would want to raise children here?"

"Plenty of people—" Renee said, as Cait said, "What was your favorite part about living here, Mom?"

Renee caught Cait's "cut it out" glare from the back seat. As much as Isla ignored the digs at her, Cait didn't. Renee took a breath and sunk into her seat even more. Cait was right, but that didn't mean Renee had to like it.

After they pulled into the driveway, Hunter started barking incessantly, as he always did when they got home.

"You brought Hunter?" Isla asked.

"I've been here for almost a month," Cait said, eyeing Renee.

"Thankfully, I'm not staying here. You know he makes me sneeze."

It was a good thing for everyone. If Isla had invited herself into her home as Cait had, she and Luc were getting a hotel room to get as far away from her as possible. Her thoughts snapped to Luc. She was so distracted by their mother that she hadn't seen him at the beach.

It was close to two in the afternoon, and the end of camp for the day. Luc coming to the house would be her worst nightmare. Cait wouldn't call out their relationship, but Isla would see it in a second. She was unaware of the damage she had caused in their lives and Renee had to protect Luc and her current relationship with him without making Isla aware.

There would be too much going on at the wedding for her to say much when it came to her and Luc, so keeping them separate before that day was a must.

When she reached the porch, Renee texted him quickly.

Don't come over.

Renee spotted him through the kitchen window. He reached for his phone and then he glanced at the house. His mouth moved, but she wasn't sure what he was saying.

Okay?

I'll explain later x

She hoped the "x" would be enough to show him that she wasn't upset with him, but not as an invitation over her house.

Isla's sharp voice stopped Renee in her tracks.

"Hunty!" Cait said, chasing after him. Renee had missed the confrontation, but from the way he trembled under the table she knew it wasn't a good one.

"Marcus, darling."

Marcus stood from the couch and hugged Isla. "It's been a while since you've been on the east coast, huh?"

"Years." Isla flitted her hands in the air around them. "This place is just as I remembered it."

"We've done a lot to fix it up," Renee said.

Isla sniffed. "Even the scent is like walking into a memory."

Renee bit back another remark. "Can I get you something to drink?"

"Sparkling water please," Isla said.

"Tap it is." Renee didn't wait for her mother's reaction as she walked into the kitchen.

Chapter 22

To help keep her sanity for the rest of the evening, Renee texted Luc, recapping the dinner with her mother. Marcus didn't seem bothered by having his girlfriend and his ex-wife in the house at the same time, while the boastful nature of her mother mortified Renee. She was newly single and didn't care that no one in the room wanted to know about her ten-years-younger ex who had pampered and adored her for six short months.

Another change was Cait's overall helpfulness around the house. Unlike the rest of the month, Cait was attentive to everyone's needs and even assisted with setting the table for dinner and cleaning up after. It was as if the world had turned upside down in a matter of hours.

"Mind putting the phone down?" Marcus asked when he and Renee were alone in the kitchen. They had eaten at the dining room table, where Isla insisted on sitting in his chair so she could face the windows with the view of the ocean.

"I'm talking to Luc. I need a distraction. I can't stand this. I can't stand her."

"I know, but she's a guest and your mother. Remember that. She hasn't changed her ways since I've known her."

"And you wonder why I left her as soon as I could? She's never been much of a mother to me."

"You can see Luc after," Marcus said. "You don't have to enjoy yourself but at least pretend. If she notices, she won't let it go."

Her mother rarely noticed anyone outside a five-inch radius of herself, so it was likely Renee wasn't even on her radar.

In the dining room, Isla poured another glass of pinot grigio from the bottle. She drained it all on her own, neglecting to offer it around the table.

The end of the night couldn't come quickly enough. Renee wanted to go next door and snuggle in bed with Luc, letting the waves outside his bedroom window wash away the day.

"Renee will bring us back to the resort," Isla said without asking.

"You're staying there too?" Renee asked.

"Jorden graciously offered to pay for a private bungalow by the beach. There are only a few of them available. I'm so lucky to have such a great son-in-law."

Jorden was certainly kind and gracious. But she also knew how much those bungalows cost per night and wondered how many times Isla had suggested it to Cait to get Jorden to pay for her stay.

It's not your problem. Renee tried to remind herself of that, but found the way that Isla manipulated people hard to stomach.

"Let's go then," Renee said, typing a message to Luc. She hoped that he was still up for meeting after her stiff text earlier, and she yearned to be around someone who would help her forget her dysfunctional family for a while. With a few days until the wedding, the end was in sight. Isla would be out of West Cove as soon as she could, and Renee's life could get back to normal.

However, that normal didn't include Cait or Luc. Renee stifled the growing sensation of anticipation in her gut, she knew in her heart that she didn't want either of them to leave.

"Cait, will you be a dear and grab my handbag?" Isla asked, breaking through her thoughts of Luc leaving.

Cait was already halfway into the back seat but hopped out to go back inside to retrieve the bag.

Renee hesitated before locking herself in a small space with her mother. She stood outside the car, silently begging for Cait to end her conversation with Marcus.

Isla's voice floated through the air from the other side of the car. "Renee, honey, can you turn on the car, I'm sweating."

Renee had the urge to ignore the request, but Marcus's words appeared in her mind. She opened the car door and sat before turning the engine over.

Isla flipped the vents in her direction and played with the dials. She somehow turned on the heat.

"I've got it," Renee said, turning down the air conditioning. "It needs a minute."

"Speaking of a minute, I'd like to talk to you about something. I've wanted to discuss it all day, but I couldn't find the time for us to be alone."

Renee glanced inside, and Cait was on her way. "What did you want to talk about?" Having Cait in on the conversation might make it less awkward.

"Alone," Isla said.

Cait hopped in the car, placing Isla's purse next to her. "Sorry about that."

Isla yawned. "How did you deal with this jet lag?"

"Oh," Cait said. "You try and stay awake for as long as possible."

Cait had suffered from jet lag for days after her arrival, but Renee wasn't going to dispute anything her sister said. All she could think about was the conversation awaiting her when Isla got her alone.

* * *

Renee parked close to the resort on the beach side of the club. A sprawling hotel with exclusive views made tourists pay whatever asking price the club set, and they did pay. Renee couldn't help wondering how much Jorden had dished out to pay for Isla. No doubt after her insistence.

No sound or movement her mother made gave any indication of what she wanted to talk about. It was as if she'd never made the request at all from the way she doted on Cait.

That didn't last long as they walked Cait to the entrance to the main building. It had at least twenty suites on two floors, reserved for only those who could afford the luxury amenities. Renee wasn't sure she made enough to clean a place like that.

"Your father would have loved this place," Isla said, her voice thick with emotion.

"I know," Cait agreed. "I feel him here—I know that sounds strange."

"Not at all," Renee said.

Cait watched her mother, her wide eyes pleading for agreement from Isla.

"I'm honored to walk you down the aisle."

Renee balked, but neither Cait nor Isla noticed or made a show of noticing. It was a detail that Renee hadn't thought of for the wedding. It made sense, but having Isla pry her way up from just mother of the bride to walking Cait down the aisle was enough to curl her hands into fists.

"Renee will walk me to my door," Isla said, air-kissing Cait.

When their mother turned to face Renee, Cait widened her eyes in a questioning look. Renee wanted to shrug her off, but now she was more than curious about what her mother had to say.

As they walked out of the building and toward the beach, Isla didn't say much other than commenting on the weather.

"I don't miss the sand everywhere, but I do miss the sound," Isla said. "It's incredibly soothing. It's why I bring a sound machine wherever I go. It helps me sleep."

The bungalows were on the edge of the private beach before the jetty. Beyond that lay the main road toward the stretch of houses where Marcus and Renee lived.

"I can't imagine living anywhere else."

"You did."

"Not by choice." Renee sensed the conversation was headed in that direction, so she didn't shy away from it anymore. There was no use denying the inevitable.

"You must know what I want to say then," Isla said, slowing her steps. She kicked off her heels and sank her feet into the sand, leveling her eyes with Renee.

"I have no idea what you want to say," Renee said honestly.

Isla could have screamed and shouted at Renee for anything, but it wouldn't have surprised her more than her mother leaning closer and wrapping her arms around her shoulders and pulling her close.

"W—what are you—?" Words escaped Renee as the full force of her mother's touch overwhelmed her senses. She could hardly breathe, and a buzzing in her ears overpowered the rush of the ocean behind her.

"I'm sorry, Renee. I'm so, so sorry. I know I was never the best mother to you." She held tight to Renee's shoulders and stared into her daughter's eyes. "I've been working on myself. This last year, in particular. I've been seeing a therapist. She suggested I try to reconcile with you. It was the best idea that I never thought of, but I wasn't sure of a time to do it. I knew I'd see you here, so I thought it would be perfect. I didn't say anything today. I knew you were upset to have me surprise you, but you wouldn't have wanted to see me on your own."

You're not wrong about that.

Isla had given her fair share of apologies in the past, but this one seemed different. Renee's hackles rose as a tear trailed down her mother's cheek. She was reluctant to trust Isla and risk her heart breaking all over again. Caution kept her safe.

"Okay." Allowing Isla to do what she needed to do, then get out of West Cove, and Renee's life, was the only plan that would satisfy them both.

"Okay?" Isla's thin eyebrows arched.

"What else do you want me to say?" The flare of annoyance spiked within her.

"Anything."

"Well, I'm an adult now. I'm over all of this."

"I guess Cait was right about you."

Renee didn't want to take the bait, but around her mother, she was transported back to a time with so many emotions. "What did Cait say?"

Isla shrugged as if she hadn't opened up the discussion with her own dig against Renee. Using her sister was low, but Renee needed to know what Cait had said about her to Isla. "She said you were a little selfish lately. You've been hanging out with that man next door. You forgot all about Jorden and picking him up from the airport."

Renee wanted to tell Isla about how she had planned most of the wedding last-minute. And had only been seeing Luc for barely a week—though, with their shared past, it seemed like a lifetime. But falling for her bait would only result in a fight. A fight would result in awkwardness during the rest of the wedding activities for the week.

"You wanted to talk to me, and all these questions aren't resulting in much of a conversation." Annoyance bubbled to the surface, soiling the beach she loved. Of course, her mother would do that to her. Nothing had changed. Her apology seemed even less sincere as the conversation progressed.

"Not that I wanted a fight from you, but I came here expecting one. That's why I wanted to be alone. Growing up with you, there weren't any lack of arguments. This passivity is a little unnerving."

"Do you want a fight?" Renee could supply one. There were numerous topics she could discuss with her mother.

"Not at all. But forgiveness might be nice."

A part of Renee snapped inside. It took most of her willpower not to react based on her emotions. "Forgiveness? Because of one apology?"

Isla shoved a chunk of hair out of her face. The breeze had picked up, and Renee wished it would carry her mother away. "I mean it, Renee. I'm sorry."

"For what?"

"Everything." Renee noted a hint of a question at the end of her statement.

Renee wanted a list of all the wrongs against her but knew Isla well enough to realize she'd never get one. Giving Renee receipts for her issues would be even more of a shock than Renee's calmness throughout the conversation.

"You know, you remind me of myself at your age."

Renee snorted. "I'm nothing like you."

Isla either ignored the acid in Renee's voice or was too wrapped up in her own mind to realize it.

"You're living in Boring Town USA. Remember, I lived here for years before and after I had you. Small-town gossip thrives here when there's a bigger world out there. I can see the boredom in your eyes."

"I'm not bored."

"I've heard you only date tourists."

Dammit, Cait! "So?"

"Well, falling for a tourist was how I got out of this place for a start."

"What?"

"Jacob was a tourist. He was in the area for a conference. I bumped into him at the beach while he was with his co-workers. He was the extra push I needed to figure out what I needed for myself to be happy."

Renee didn't know much about the relationship between Isla and Cait's father outside of living with him and his children after Isla won custody of Renee after the divorce. Knowing he was a tourist sent a punch against her gut. She had spent the majority of her life—more than half at this point—pushing away from her mother and any action that had to do with her. Renee promised herself she would never go to the extremes her mother did, like changing her personality, looks, and even politics at times depending on the man she was with.

Luc had done that to her. Well, he didn't, but she certainly did. The sushi place seemed like years ago instead of less than a week. She'd gone there with him on the pretense of liking it. She'd ignored the alarm on her phone when it was time to pick up Jorden, so that she could spend more time with him. They were small acts, but would they lead to a bigger similarity between her and Isla?

"I'm not a terrible person," Isla said. "You are my daughter. We're bound to have things in common." Her mother reached out for her, but Renee backed away with her hands between them.

"Don't ever compare us." The men in Renee's life were fleeting, just as they were in Isla's. Her commitment to never marry wasn't enough to separate herself from her mother. Unconsciously she had fallen into Isla's ways of dating, when she should have been trying to find a good relationship with stability.

"Renee, you turned out wonderful. I made some mistakes in my relationships, but I never stopped loving you. You and Cait are my world."

"I have to go." Renee was unable to listen to her lies anymore. She trudged up the beach, away from her mother, who called to her. As usual, she kept her back turned from her past and propelled toward a future without Isla.

Chapter 23

The more distance Renee put between herself and Isla, the better. The buzzing in her bones settled into a dull roar during the ride home.

From the moment Isla mentioned Renee's dating habits, Luc was on her mind. He wasn't the typical tourist, but whatever they were doing would end the same way, sometime after the wedding. Renee picked apart the time she and Luc had spent together. He had wrapped a rope around her heart and tugged it every step of the way. She'd put off her sister, work, and even her own wants to be around him. Just as Isla did with her relationships. Renee's past tourist relationships were the same. She had paid no mind to her life, knowing they had an expiration date.

Renee wanted Luc to be different, and she had dug herself a hole big enough that she wasn't sure she'd be able to climb out. She had chosen to ignore their expiration date, and now that it was right in front of her face, she didn't want it to end. The only way she could break the cycle was changing her habits for good.

What did that mean for her and Luc? Could she ride out the rest of the time he was in West Cove, anticipating the inevitable heartache she was going to face after he left? Breaking it off right away would put her back to where she had been—and make the next few days incredibly awkward.

Isla had weaseled her way into Renee's mind, and tugged on that already fragile rope holding her and Luc together. Her mother brought back all the feelings of insecurity and lack of hope for any future that involved love.

All Renee wanted to do was crawl into bed and only emerge once the wedding was over. But seconds after she pulled into the driveway, her phone buzzed with a text.

Renee prayed that it wasn't Luc until his message appeared.

Do you want to stop by?

Of course she did. But the conversation with Isla hovered over her like a gray cloud spoiling a summer day. She inhaled a sharp breath. This was Luc. He always calmed her. Most of the time they were together, the two of them was all she could think about. Talking to Luc might ease her mind about Isla's influence.

I'll be right over.

The lights in Renee's house were off. She peered over at Olivia's house, and the flash of the television blinked through the window.

At least Marcus wouldn't be home to ask Renee what had happened on the ride home with her sister and Isla. Not that she was sure she could tell him anyway. Their paths were inextricably linked and talking about her relationships with men as a comparison to her mother's would have crossed a line she wasn't willing to come close to.

Luc was already outside when she crossed her patio and onto his driveway. He sat on the edge of the open bed of his truck. He held two beers in his hands. "Thought you could use one."

Sharing a beer with him before a tumble in the sheets was an act she would have been all over a half-hour ago. Now, she wasn't sure what she wanted. A lead weight pressed against her stomach as she sat. She couldn't get closer to the edge of the seat, furthest from him.

"Cheers." He clinked his bottle against hers. "I'm assuming dinner was awkward?"

"I'd say it was awkward since lunch." Her fingernail picked at the label on the beer. "I can't believe Cait didn't tell me."

"You knew your mother was coming, though."

Renee glanced at him. His tone seemed a little accusatory. "Obviously. But I thought she would swoop into town on the day of the rehearsal dinner. At least I would have expected that."

"It's only a few more days, right? If you've made it this far, I'm sure it will all turn out fine."

It wouldn't, though. Not with any aspect of her life. Renee could deal with Cait and Isla leaving, but Luc? Where would that leave her and the status of her life? Was she a perpetual dater like her mother? How could she ever find peace in a place like this? Isla's thoughts crept into her mind, causing tendrils of doubt to spread across her body.

"Renee?" Luc's voice pushed through the jumbled thoughts.

"Yeah?"

"Do you want to take a walk?" Luc's hand slid closer to hers, and she lifted it away. He stared at the spot where her hand had been, then glanced up at her. "I'm sensing everything isn't okay."

Renee placed the beer down. She raked her hands through her hair several times as if the motion could remove what was bothering her. "Seeing my mother again, it brought back a lot of memories." *And how much we have in common.*

"That's understandable. You've been under a lot of stress with the wedding too."

"The wedding has nothing to do with it."

"Renee, come on. You've been planning the entire thing. Even when we're together, you pull away from me when you're thinking about it."

The interrogation felt the same as when her mother pushed her about how similar they were. The same urge to repel anything she said came out toward Luc. "I'm not distracted at all." That wasn't what was happening. How did she ever think being with Luc, even for a short amount of time, would be easy?

Luc took another pull from his beer and swiped a hand over his mouth. "Sorry if I misinterpreted you. I'm with teen girls all day and I can sense when they don't want to talk about something. It's given me a lot of insight into women over the years." He chuckled lightly.

A grimace tugged at her lips. "You're comparing me to a teen girl?" Renee understood that he was trying to make her feel better, but it wasn't working.

Luc chuckled. "No—"

"You know what?" Heat licked at her skin, and she had to distance herself. "It was a mistake to come here. I should get going."

Luc stood too. "I didn't mean to offend you."

"You didn't." Their argument was entirely Isla's fault. One conversation had made Renee question everything in her life, and she needed to go to the one place that would help her clear her head. "Thanks for the beer."

Renee hopped off the truck and strode across the driveway. Luc didn't call her back, and she wasn't sure if that made the situation worse or better. A small part of her wanted to talk to him, but the more substantial part yearned for solace. The only way she could piece her thoughts together was to distract herself.

When she got inside the house, Hunter weaved his way through her legs while barking. The sound was even more shrill in her ears.

"Walk?" Renee grabbed the leash, and Hunter stopped moving—all except for his wagging tail. "Brandy?" The large dog glanced at her with a tired expression and rolled on her back, closing her eyes again.

"Just the two of us, huh?" Renee locked the lead around

Hunter's collar, and they left the house. She glanced at Luc's place for fear of seeing him again. The prickling heat moved to a thick, slithery sensation pooling in her gut. The distance from him and their conversation eased her mind slightly, but it wasn't until she dug her bare feet in the sand that she was able to take a full breath.

Renee was relieved to find that her mother's conversation hadn't completely tainted her relationship with the beach. She wasn't sure anyone could. Though she avoided walking by the volleyball net and instead opted for the continued private beach toward the end of the street.

The moon shone over her like it had every night, throwing long shadows across the sand. The closer she got to the jetty at the end of the beach, the easier her steps became.

For once, Hunter seemed to sense that Renee wasn't in the mood for tug-of-war with him and padded in time with her stride.

The movement of her feet against the sand and the crashing waves had overpowered the angry thoughts in her mind. That was until she stopped moving. Renee turned to face the rest of the beach from where she had walked. Her house and Luc's seemed so far away, but the conversation between them slammed to the forefront of her mind.

The memory of Luc's confused and hurt expression lanced through her. It wasn't fair that he was caught up in her mess, and it was up to Renee to fix it.

The only way to break ties with any similarities between her and her mother was to take those scissors and cut through that thin thread linking them together. Isla had no shame in wrecking families at any whim. Renee would never be that destructive to herself or others. It was time to turn from the way she was acting toward a new life without any remnants of Isla.

* * *

The next morning, Renee woke with a pounding headache. Even without drinking much, hangover symptoms slammed into her as if she had partied all night instead of being confronted by her mother and Luc. Luc's downtrodden expression burned into her vision.

Hunter was curled up at the end of the bed. His eyes peeled open before his entire body started to shake.

"Shh," she said as he barked. He jumped up and launched off the bed toward the door. "I guess we're up."

Renee grabbed her phone from the charger. There were several texts from Cait, asking her to detail the conversation between her and Isla.

I saw you from my window. What were you talking about? A surprise for me? The celebration horn emojis filled the next line of the text.

Renee didn't have the energy to respond quite yet. Once she had peeled herself off her bed, she turned on her computer. The routine she had curated over the years quickly returned to her. She checked her email and responded to clients before heading downstairs.

The voice of a news reporter floated up the stairs to meet her.

Marcus sat on the couch with his cup of coffee, and both Brandy and Hunter snuggled up against him.

"Nice to have your couch back?" she asked while pouring a mug of coffee.

"Cait wasn't as big of an inconvenience as you think."

"It was a joke, Dad."

"Not as much as your mother, apparently."

Renee sat next to him, fitting into the seat where she had shared many nights with her father. It was almost molded to her body. "How could you tell?"

"I know you're not a fan of her, but your sister adores her. She wanted you two to get along for the wedding."

"How much more do I have to do for this wedding?" As the

words tumbled out of her mouth, she couldn't believe she'd said them. A lightness spread through her at the admission.

"Finally, the truth comes out."

"What are you talking about?"

"I love your sister, but she can be a handful at times. I don't think you remember all those summers where I was the adult in the house with her visiting."

"She made it hard on you?"

"At times, but I showed her who was the boss."

"I couldn't refuse to help her with her wedding."

"Couldn't you? I know you hate disappointing her, but that's life. Sometimes she needs to realize that."

Renee glanced at the window overlooking Luc's house. The conversation from last night swelled in her gut. He'd been trying to talk to her, but Isla had been on her mind enough that she acted the same way around him as she did her. Storming away from him hadn't been fair to do.

Wriggling up from the couch, she placed her coffee on the table. "I'll be right back."

It was early enough that the girls hadn't arrived for camp yet. Renee marched over to the back door and knocked. She waited, digging her hands against her waist. The shyness about what she wore was no longer there. Luc had seen her entire body unclothed; being without a bra wasn't going to embarrass her any more than she already was from the conversation the night before.

Luc came to the door with a toothbrush sticking out of his mouth. "Hey," he said around it. He hesitated and then waved her inside. "Do you want to come in?"

"Sure." Renee followed him inside. Several brand-new cardboard boxes leaned against the beach chairs. They were still folded up, but the tape dispenser on top gave her the idea that that wasn't for long.

Luc disappeared around the corner and up the stairs. There wasn't much time before he had to work. Renee hadn't thought the confrontation through and wondered if she should leave. Though, waiting all day to speak to him would torture her. This was the right decision. Get her apology out there and they could enjoy whatever time they had together.

The more she thought of him leaving, the more she started to accept it for herself.

"Sorry about that," Luc said. "I wasn't expecting you."

Renee clasped her hands in front of her, twining them together and tugging slightly as if the words were attached to her movements, and she could pull all the perfect ones out of her head. "I wanted to talk about last night."

Luc rubbed the back of his neck. "I don't know what I said to make you so upset. I'm sorry, though."

"It wasn't you. My mother . . . she said some things to me that . . . She was the one to set me off. Not you."

Luc's shoulders relaxed, and he stepped closer to her. His hands moved to her waist, and she couldn't help that slithering feeling again. It wasn't the same giddy excitement at all.

Renee realized that Isla *had* tainted this relationship. She stepped back, needing space from him. From Isla. From everyone. She had come over to talk to him, but she couldn't quite grasp the words as Isla appeared in her mind with her nasally mother-knows-best voice. *You're just like me.*

"Renee," Luc said. "Watch—"

Her back slammed against the edge of the counter. Both hands flung backward, sliding over a folder of paperwork. The world moved in slow motion as they flitted to the ground.

"I'm sorry." Renee knelt to get them.

His hands slid over hers as they reached for the same sheet of paper. "You know you can talk to me. I understand complicated parent relationships."

"I know." Renee had no trouble before, but Isla returning to town had thrown her backward in her mind and life. Following her mother's wicked ways wasn't the news she had expected out of their conversation. What would Luc think of her if she told him she only dated tourists because there was an expiration date? He would take offense to that. Anyone would. Her gaze dropped to the papers in her hands. They were from the realtor's office. Copies of paperwork with the sale price of the house reached up and gripped her throat, tightening with each second.

"Renee?"

Her attention snapped to Luc. Guilt riddled his face—forming in each of his handsome features. The small downward tug of his lips. The pull at the corners of his eyes.

"The house. It's up for sale already?"

"No." Luc stacked the other strewn papers into a neat pile. He leaned over and took the folder from behind her. His scent made her stomach turn when it usually had the opposite effect. "It's sold."

"It sold." The words coiled in her mouth.

"Yeah. I wasn't going to make a big thing about it."

"Of course not," she said, paving the bricks to form the wall around her heart. It was the only way to get through the rest of the week with him so close. The paperwork was confirmation that she had made a mistake with him. It wasn't one she would make again.

"This is a good thing, right?"

"Sure," she said.

His surprise melted into confusion. "This was the plan all along. It happened much quicker than I realized." He hesitated. "But you don't seem too happy about it."

How did he expect her to be happy with him leaving and her having to stay there with a stranger moving in? Everyone was going and she was staying. Suddenly, she had a glimpse of what her mother had yearned for. Renee would never leave West Cove, but a different perspective was all she needed.

"You don't have to come to the wedding with me," she said.

"Not if you don't want to."

He placed the folder down and shook his head. "I made a promise. I don't intend to let you go alone." His eyes narrowed, and the paperwork crinkled under his grip. Renee knew he was restraining himself, almost as much as her. "Unless that's what you want?"

"I do." *This is the only way to say goodbye. A quick, clean break. Just like all the rest.*

"Where did this change of heart come from? Is this what your mother said to you last night? Did she try and break us up?"

"It was inevitable."

Luc's body rocked as if she had shoved both hands into his chest to keep him away. His jaw dropped like she had slapped him. "Was it?"

"I haven't changed," she admitted. "I date tourists. This is no different than any other year. It always ends."

"Wow." Luc shoved a hand through his hair and stepped away from her. "I thought this conversation was going to go a lot differently."

Renee ground her teeth together, willing the emotion to stay out of her voice. "Me too."

Luc watched her as if he anticipated her to spring up and say it was all a joke. She couldn't move from under his stare.

He sighed and hung his head. "Listen, I have to go to work. Can we talk later?"

"I'm not going to change my mind." Falling for him more would only make things worse. She turned but stopped when he spoke her name.

Renee didn't turn around, even when he started talking.

"You are different. No matter what your mother says. Everyone grows up, and you aren't that scared teenager anymore. You've found your place. Don't let anyone tell you otherwise."

A shaky sob stole from her throat as she charged out of the

kitchen and into the sunroom. The boxes bumped against her leg, and her trembling hands moved to stop them.

The not-so-subtle reminder of Luc leaving filled the space.

This is right.

So, why didn't it feel that way?

Chapter 24

Renee stayed in her kitchen—the only windows that didn't face Luc's house—until his screen door cracked against the door-frame. Fixing that spring had been on his list, but she supposed it was the new owner's responsibility. After counting to twenty, she peered through the living room windows to make sure that Luc was already across the street. He stood by the net with his whistle in his mouth, blasting sharp tweets at the girls while they ran through the surf.

"I can't stay here."

Hunter popped his head up from his spot next to Brandy. Her tail surrounded his little body like an oversized scarf.

The beach was hers. It was the one place she went to think about any troubles she had in her life. While the clinic was in session, she had to find another place. It was the last day, though, and Renee would have her life back after the weekend. That thought gave her no relief, only a pooling feeling of dread. Her walks with Hunter had been easier by the day, but she could use different scenery.

Renee loaded the dogs into the back seat of her car. Hunter nearly jumped out every time she tried to close the door, giving her mini heart attacks thinking she was going to get his tiny paws caught against the frame. Once they were inside, she grabbed her bag filled with treats and water bottles and slipped into her car without one passing glance at Luc across the street. In her driveway, she was in the open, leaving herself vulnerable for another conversation with him. Luc had wanted to continue talking, but what else was there to say?

* * *

The West Cove dog park was on the edge of town. The fenced-off area was the only part of the park that was in West Cove, while the remainder of the stretch of land belonged to the town of Hampstead. Renee tried to wrangle Hunter onto the leash, but his focus was getting out of the car without restriction. Instead of fighting, she picked up the little guy and tucked him under her arm.

Brandy was much easier and accepted the leash and walked next to her.

"Will you ever be as easy as your cousin?" Renee cooed to Hunter.

His underbite gave him a strange smile, but she could swear he understood. In the time she'd spent with him, she was convinced he was smarter than he acted. Cait gave him attention for his little antics, but all it took was some tough love for the dog to listen.

There weren't many others in the park, aside from older people who probably wouldn't be baking in the sun like most of the tourists on vacation. Only one other dog was inside the park—a boxer with floppy ears and drool dripping from its jowls.

Renee curled her lip, hoping she wouldn't have to bathe the dogs after the trip.

The greenery was well manicured but didn't clear her head in the way that the sand and salty sea air did. But it would do for the time being. Inside the fence, she let the dogs loose. There was enough space for a hundred dogs inside the sprawling park.

There were rocks the dogs could climb, and Hunter went to those first—even though they were ten times his size.

Brandy trotted over to a tree and marked it before moving on to the next one.

Renee sat on the bench near the entrance and watched the dogs explore for a little while. Hunter barked incessantly at the boxer, and the larger dog bowed to Hunter, his head twisting from side to side. She could almost picture Hunter's overactive imagination making him believe that he was even close to the size of the seventy-pound dog.

As they played a game of Tag, Renee's thoughts drifted to the breakup with Luc. Was it a breakup, though? They were technically only together for a week.

In her mind, that week had moved at the pace of months rather than days. None of her other summer hookups had moved that slowly. Most of the time, she had wanted them to move quickly to get to the end of whatever vacation the guy had taken so she could move on.

Cait's ringtone blared from Renee's phone. The guy standing across the way threw a glare at her and returned to his phone. Renee stifled an eye roll, not wanting to catch any more of this guy's attention when he had been blasting music the entire time he was there.

"Hey," Renee answered.

"Nay . . ."

"You could at least say hi first."

"Hi. Nay." A slight pause. "I need your help."

Of course you do. "What's up?"

"Can you swing by the florist and pick up flowers for tonight? I need a bouquet—a small one is fine. Blair forgot the one I had made at my shower. Maid of honor fail, right?" She didn't waste a breath before jumping into her next request. "And I already called for some centerpieces for dinner."

"Can't they send them to the restaurant?"

"They could, but you're around . . ."

There were so many things Renee could have said to her sister.

What if I wasn't around?

What if I was working?

What if I was with Luc?

Cait had no idea about the breakup with Luc. Not that she expected her sister to ask about it. With them together, she couldn't tease them any longer about being around each other. Besides, her wedding was tomorrow. It was the final day for the summer of changes to settle into something resembling normal.

"Renee? Are you there?"

"Yes, I can do it."

"Good. See you at four-thirty. Bye!"

Cait hung up the phone, and Renee stared at it for a few seconds. Her stomach churned and she placed the phone on the bench. Marcus's and Luc's revelations about Cait came at her with a relatively strong sense that she had screwed something up in her life. But did it have to do with any of them, or herself? Renee had made the choices, whether it was doting on Cait or hooking up with Luc. While she could have pushed back on all of Cait's requests—including the last-minute one today—being with Luc was the happiest she'd been in a while. Isla had made her feel guilty for that.

Her mixed-up thoughts tangled together, tightening until a headache began to form. Questioning herself only made the situation more confusing. Making choices didn't usually feel that way. Once she had made up her mind about a task or project, that was it. She had prided herself on not living with regret.

Luc leaving teetered on her mind as if she might regret how she had left things with him, but she had no idea what to do next.

* * *

After about an hour, Hunter's tongue was practically dragging on the ground, and Brandy had already fallen asleep twice during her sunbathing by the tree. Renee gathered them up and brought them into the car. Hunter had insisted on her carrying him, and he was still in her arms. She popped a kiss on his head, and he looked up at her with more surprise than she had felt.

"You're not so bad when you're exhausted."

He let out a little grunt and licked her thumb.

* * *

It was early enough in the day that Luc and the girls were still across the street on the beach when she arrived home, but Renee managed to avoid any eye contact with him. The distance from the house hadn't solved the puzzle in her mind about him, but it did bring some perspective. Luc had been right about Cait and how Isla had made her feel. She should have spoken up for herself numerous times with her sister but doing what she could for her was innate in Renee's actions. In the same vein, defying Isla was instinct and that had spilled over into more of her life than she had intended.

Marcus was on the front porch, drinking from his mug and rocking in his chair. Brandy climbed the steps and swirled around twice before settling by his side.

"Where did you go?" Marcus asked.

"The dog park."

"Not the beach?" He gave a pointed look at the water.

"Not the beach."

Renee let the dogs inside and filled up their water bowls before she made her way to the front of the house. Allowing Luc to see her wasn't on her agenda, so she stood by the screen door, blocking his view of her.

"Cait asked me to pick up flowers before the dinner tonight," she said.

"Are you going to?"

"Of course I am."

Marcus rocked back on the chair, catching her eye. "You don't want to pick them up."

"I don't mind—" Renee stopped herself. She had claimed she didn't mind all month. "This is about our conversation from before."

"Sort of. Why are you avoiding Luc?"

"I'm not avoiding him."

"Of course not. Why don't you sit next to me?"

Renee sighed, keeping her stance. "Fine, we argued." The wound from him leaving was as fresh as it was earlier.

"About Cait?"

"She was included."

"Honey, you've been mothering that kid since she came out of the womb. But it was never your job to do that."

"If Mom would have raised her she would have turned out—"

"Like you? There's nothing terrible about you. Cait would have survived."

"You weren't there." Renee hadn't meant to bring up those bad years, but he wasn't seeing her point.

"I was there, Renee. Your mother and I were in constant contact when it came to you. I know it was hard, but we were both there for you."

"I'm not trying to start an argument."

"Neither am I, but you need to understand that Cait is an adult now. She can take on her responsibilities. You are also an adult and old enough to say no. You are not her mother and she doesn't need one at this point in her life other than Isla."

Renee had nothing to say to that.

"You're a good person, Renee. Almost too much for your own good. You have a big heart, but you should use it for yourself now."

Renee wanted to confide in him about how Isla preferred tourists to get her thrills instead of West Cove, but that was too much information with possible hurtful side effects. "What if I'm incapable?"

"Don't be so dramatic."

Renee shot a look at him. "I'm not."

"You're young. I didn't meet someone again for a while, and it turned out she was right in front of me the whole time."

From the beach, Luc tweeted his whistle, and Renee jolted.

"The only other time I've seen you as happy as you were this last week was when you came here for the summers. This place is where you belong. You know that. You can build a life here. It's not impossible, no matter what Isla tells you."

Renee narrowed her eyes, sharpening the lines around Luc walking the beach as the girls scrimmaged.

"I never thought that. She gets under my skin, but I don't believe everything she says."

"Good, I'd hate for one person to dictate your happiness."

Hadn't that been what Isla did? She had wedged herself between Renee and her happiness with Luc. Or had Renee sabotaged herself? Cait had lived with Isla her entire life, too, but didn't despise her.

Renee allowed all thoughts of her mother to dictate her happiness. "I think I made a mistake."

"We all do from time to time," Marcus said. "But all we can do is learn from our mistakes and move forward. That took me some time to realize, so I'm imparting my wisdom to you."

"Thanks, Dad."

Chapter 25

For the rest of the afternoon, Renee locked herself in the bedroom and focused on her work. She had taken the week off due to the wedding, but she needed a distraction from her life. The way she had treated Luc rolled over in her head with each small break she took. While she wanted to hate Isla even more for getting into her head, she needed a shift in mindset against thinking that her mother was out to destroy her life. Renee was in charge of every movement of her life, and no one could dictate that to her. Cait had always wanted Isla and Renee to get along. It was as if they were the divorced parents sharing a roof, with Cait as the child they fought for control over. But Renee could live out her life putting people in separate boxes. It was the only way she could find her happiness. Planning the wedding had been an intrusion in her life, but it gave Renee insight into the real reason for the massive party that Cait was having.

Cait's love for Jorden had caused her to come across the country for weeks so that it was perfect for him. While Renee was sure Isla's opinion was considered in the details, Cait had done this to start her marriage on a flawless note.

While Renee wasn't sold on the prospect of marriage yet, and wasn't sure she could be due to her past, there was no reason she couldn't be happy. Her fear of long-term relationships was because of Isla. If she wanted to break free from the pain in her childhood, she had to think in the opposite direction. Renee had no idea why she hadn't figured that out before. There had been many opportunities throughout her life that she had lost out on due to her trauma with her mother. The anxiety of getting close to anyone had kept her from experiences that could have led to long-term happiness. While she didn't need a partner in her life to be happy, sharing her life with another person shouldn't have been avoided at all costs.

Sitting back in her chair, she glanced out the window at the roof of Luc's house and considered her life. Before he swept into town she was fully capable of contentment. Would she look back in ten years and feel the same way? Or would she fall into the same mindset of resenting her mother? Renee had no intention of allowing Isla to take up any more of her brain space. Standing up, she took in more of the house next door. No matter if Luc wanted to stay in touch with her, she couldn't allow him to leave without apologizing. If he wanted, she would keep her invitation to the wedding in place. It was childish and reactionary to uninvite him, but she had to own up to what she had done.

The roar of Luc's truck engine sounded outside. The computer clock read three, and she hadn't even realized how long she had been working. No doubt Luc had loose ends to tie up before leaving, but she had to get to the rehearsal soon and she wasn't sure when he'd be back.

Her phone screen hadn't turned on the entire time she was working, but she debated texting him. She crafted a well-thought-out—albeit boring and toneless—message to him. It read like a novel and she eventually deleted all of it.

The words had to come from her heart, and she had to speak

to him face to face. When that would happen, she had no idea. Though she couldn't help thinking she deserved to feel uncomfortable after how she had acted toward him.

Now, it was time to turn it around and apologize to him. It was the least he deserved, even if it would end the same way.

* * *

Over the next hour, Renee religiously checked the window for Luc's return. At four, Olivia entered through the back door into the kitchen. Marcus had made her dinner, and they were spending the evening together watching a movie. Renee was used to Olivia's involvement in her and Marcus's life, once again proving that not all relationships were garbage—especially after Isla had been involved in both Cait and Marcus's lives. They were happy with a partner, and Renee just wanted to be happy and whole.

The drive to the florist was uneventful, but Renee kept her eyes peeled for Luc's truck. It wasn't at the hardware store, or the realtor's office, or the plaza offering free parking for anyone looking to stroll down the strip of stores on either side of the road. That had to be a sign of something. Maybe Luc would end up disappearing without so much as a text goodbye. She didn't deserve anything from him but would live to regret it if she couldn't at least see him face to face one more time.

By the time she reached the club, a ball of stress knotted in her stomach. It didn't help that none of the centerpieces were stable, and she had to grip on to them on the passenger seat the entire time, giving her less of a handle on the steering wheel than she wanted. She nearly hit the curb on the way into the long driveway and breathed a sigh of relief when she arrived at the parking area.

Renee balanced the bouquet and one centerpiece and rounded the building toward the patio space. She expected Cait or anyone else from the bridal party to swoop in and help her, but not one person stood outside. It was four-twenty-two when she left the car. Where was everyone? Did Cait tell her the wrong time? She peered inside, and no one was there either.

Prudence burst outside with her phone pressed to her ear. Her eyes were wild. "Where were you? I've been calling you."

"Cait said four-thirty."

"I told her four," Prudence said. "The officiant has another rehearsal at five."

Renee's arms started to ache. "Where do I put these?"

"In the dining area. Why didn't you remind her?"

Renee couldn't recall what Prudence had said at their meeting. Heat crept up her neck, but as Prudence waited for an explanation, she realized this had nothing to do with her.

"This isn't my wedding," Renee said. "I'll be right back with the other centerpieces."

Prudence let out an exasperated sigh, but Renee was far enough away that the wedding planner wouldn't be sure that Renee had heard her frustration or not.

* * *

When Renee returned to the dining area, the entire wedding party had arrived and milled around the patio space. After placing the last two centerpieces on the designated tables, Renee headed outside.

Cait spotted her. "You're late!"

All of Cait's friends turned, and she couldn't help the heat in her cheeks. Leave it to Cait to embarrass her in front of people she barely knew. "I brought the flowers, remember?"

Cait waved a dismissive hand and turned toward Jorden. Their hands interlocked as the officiant—a smiling older man with a shock of white hair on his head—led them to the farthest edge of the patio.

240

"I find it's easier to start at the end and work backward." He lined everyone up where they would end the ceremony. Prudence sought out control where she could and hushed the other bridesmaids when they were speaking over the officiant.

Cait was oblivious to her friends, as she stared up at Jorden. She listened intently to the officiant as he gave instructions on what their parts would be during the ceremony.

At some point, Isla had crept her way over to the group, sitting in the back row of white chairs, waiting for her turn. Renee had had enough of her mother and her spoiling ways for a while. Instead, she focused on her sister and Jorden. They looked like a candid picture of the most in-love couple in the world. The plan that Renee had for the wedding crumbled in her mind as the ceremony came together. They walked up the aisle in the procession they were going to follow the next day. Renee was paired up with Jorden's little brother, Edward. He was twenty and eyeing up all the bridesmaids.

"Is Blair single?" Edward whispered to her on the way up the aisle the second time. Apparently, Prudence wasn't impressed at the pace everyone walked.

"I don't think so."

"What about Dee?"

Renee shrugged as he went down the list of other bridesmaids and some of the guests. His mood soured, and his eyes started to drift toward the other women nearby. Once he was in his spot, he resumed questioning the other groomsmen for insight on who he could hook up with during his time in West Cove.

Prudence lined Cait and Isla up near the back of the chairs. They were to come down the aisle after all the bridesmaids walked, so they had some time to wait while that accrued. Renee had the urge to text Luc and tell him all about what was happening at the rehearsal but realized they weren't at that point yet. She wasn't even sure if Luc would change his mind about coming to the wedding at all. From the way he'd left the house so suddenly before, she knew he was avoiding her as much as she had avoided him yesterday. Even if he didn't show up to the wedding, she needed to tell him how she felt. There was no denying her feelings, but if there was ever a chance for them—even a glimmer of it—she wasn't going to let him go home again without telling him.

When Cait and Isla walked down the aisle, Renee's attention snapped to them. The closer Cait came, the more Renee spotted the redness in her sister's eyes and the glistening tears welling. Without Jacob there to perform his fatherly duties, there was no doubt Cait would be thinking about him.

Isla seemed oblivious as she preened and swooshed her skirt as if she were the bride.

As Isla handed Cait off to Jorden, and Cait broke down. Renee was there in seconds to hold her sister's shoulders. Sobs racked her, and Renee squeezed her tightly. "It's okay."

"I didn't want to cry."

"Don't mess up your makeup, dear," Isla said, patting Cait's back twice.

"It's fine," Renee said to her sister. Her hands curled into fists as she turned Cait slightly away from their mother. The other girls surrounded them as Cait tried to compose herself.

"I'm okay. I'm okay," she repeated.

Jorden stepped in, giving Renee a thankful smile and drew Cait from the group.

Renee couldn't help smiling back. Jorden was good for Cait. He had the protective sense to know what Cait needed at that moment, unlike Isla. His parents had passed several years ago, and Renee understood that part of their relationship was from shared losses.

"Well, I think we all did wonderfully," Prudence said as if her bride hadn't broken down on the patio next to her. "Let's head inside and see what Chef has for us."

"Where's the booze?" Edward called out. He cackled, and Jorden shot him a look.

"You're not drinking anything," Jorden said.

"Aw, come on, Denny!" Edward ran after his brother and Cait toward the entrance to the main building.

Chapter 26

Even with Prudence's insistence that they had been late for the dinner, the servers entered the dining area as the wedding group arrived with piping hot appetizers on trays. A small bar was set up near the tables by the massive bay windows, looking toward the beach and the setting sun. Each member of the wedding party and Isla headed toward the two bartenders, forming a line. It appeared like a mini-wedding reception.

Renee made her way over to Cait and Jorden. "Do you need anything?"

Cait blotted under her eyes with a tissue. Jorden stood next to her, pulling several from his pocket like a circus clown. "I have mascara all over my face, don't I?"

"You look beautiful," Jorden said.

Cait pouted. "Don't lie. I feel like a child."

"He was your father," Renee said. "It's almost your wedding day. Everyone would be more surprised if you didn't cry. And I promise, you look fine. You should go with that brand tomorrow. It holds up."

Jorden nodded at Cait, smiling. "You know I can't lie to you. You look beautiful." Jorden kissed her and Renee gazed at the floor.

"I'll get you some water."

"No way," Cait said, sniffling. "I want to enjoy myself."

"You heard what the officiant said. We can't show up intoxicated tomorrow." Jorden glanced at Renee. "He said he wouldn't marry us if he thought we weren't of a 'sound mind.'"

"I'm not getting drunk. I just want to take the edge off and enjoy myself. Is that too much to ask?" Cait flitted away, plastering a smile on as she joined the others at the bar.

"Hopefully, you won't have your hands full with her," Renee said.

Jorden sighed. "Even if I did, I wouldn't mind a bit. I can't wait to make our love official since it's not going away anytime soon." His eyes darkened as he took in his brother standing at the bar. "Excuse me." Jorden pulled his brother aside. The mixed drink in Edward's hand sloshed over the edge of his glass. Renee couldn't hear the conversation, but Edward stomped his foot when Jorden handed the glass back to the bartender.

Cait walked over to them and shook her finger at Edward before laughing and throwing her arms around him in a hug.

Renee's chest swelled. Weddings blended families. For some reason, she hadn't understood that it meant Cait would share her life with another family too. In a way, she was losing her sister to Jorden's family. After the wedding, it wasn't a permanent goodbye, but her obligations would change.

The weight pressed against Renee's heart, stealing her breath. For the first time, Renee wanted what Cait had.

Relationships were fleeting in the way that Renee treated them, but with a good one right in front of her, there was no point in thinking that it wasn't possible for her too. Had she screwed up a potential long-term relationship with Luc? Logistically, it didn't make sense. But the thought of him leaving clogged her throat with a want she'd never had before.

Nothing was stopping her from calling him and apologizing. They could meet up later that night and talk. Renee lifted the phone from her bag. On the first ring, it clicked over to voicemail.

"Everyone, please take your seats for the first course!" Prudence said from right behind her.

Renee took a step away, but a hand dropped on her shoulder. Prudence's perfectly lipsticked smile preened at her. "You too, Renee."

"One second—"

"Come on, Nay," Cait said as she bounced by her sister with Jorden in tow. "You're next to me."

The phone beeped for her to leave a message, and Renee hung up. She typed a quick text to Luc, hoping he'd understand.

We should talk.

With Renee the last one to the table, and the prime spot next to the bride-to-be, everyone had already taken their seats. The only person she could focus on was Isla—right next to her.

Renee ground her teeth together, wondering if Cait had any intention of stopping her mission of pushing her and Isla together for the remainder of their time in West Cove.

"The family is back together," Isla said, reaching for her glass of white wine. There was less than a sip left.

Lovely.

It took much of Renee's strength not to say they weren't a family anymore. Instead, she speared a piece of the crab cake from the plate in front of her. It was smeared with the most delicious white sauce, and Renee gobbled it up. With her mouth full, she could keep from talking to Isla.

"Miss, do you want some wine?" a male server asked. He had to be close to Edward's age with the darkest lashes blotting across his impossibly green eyes.

"White for me, dear," Isla cooed at him. "Don't be shy."

He cleared his throat and filled her glass.

"You're a doll." Isla lifted the glass to her lips the moment he had finished.

Renee glanced at Cait, who stared at their mother.

"Are you two separating for the night?" Renee asked to get Cait's attention.

Cait pulled a face.

Renee shrugged at her poor attempt for small talk. "It's something I've heard people do before their wedding."

"Since we've been living together, it would be silly to do that," Cait said.

Prudence came by and clucked her tongue but said nothing of her obvious disapproval. Renee knew she was an avid churchgoer, so 'living in sin' probably wasn't on her list of the perfect bride and groom.

"He hasn't seen the dress, though," Cait said. "At least that will be a surprise."

"I can't wait," Jorden said.

"I bet you can't wait to take it off." Isla cackled.

Renee curled her lip at her mother.

"Oh, loosen up, Renee," Isla said to her eldest daughter. "Tonight is about having fun, right?"

Renee wished Isla was joking. Jorden stared at his plate, most likely avoiding the fact that his mother-in-law was casually discussing his sex life with Cait.

A tinkling sound filled the air, and they all turned to Blair, who sat across the table. "Let's all raise a glass to the bride and groom? Tomorrow is going to be so much fun as we celebrate these two lovebirds?"

The room rang out with cries of "cheers!" for the couple.

Isla downed her glass and clicked her manicured nails over the side of it. Her signal to the server went unnoticed, and her fake smile faltered. "This place has terrible service."

"Mom, I'm sure they will be back in a minute," Cait said.

Isla lifted her eyes to the ceiling. "For their sake, let's hope. You should consider how much you tip Catie."

Cait frowned, and Renee flagged down the young server when he had completed taking the orders for entrees at another table. "The mother of the bride needs a refill."

"Sure thing," he said, sauntering away to the bar.

"Oh, you didn't need to do that," Isla said, shifting her mood again. Her eyes sparkled with excitement as he came back with a full chilled bottle of white wine.

Colorful expletives moved through Renee's mind, but it was neither the time nor place to explore them.

Renee checked her phone for a text from Luc, but her message went unanswered. No three dots at the bottom and no response. Had he seen it? Or was he ignoring her? There was no stretch of time in their relationship when he had taken that long to get back to her. Various scenarios moved through her mind, enough to cause her palms to sweat. What if he left, knowing where she was for the night? He could be halfway to Massachusetts by now, and she'd have no idea.

Renee had the urge to text Marcus and see if Luc was still there, but that was too obsessive. Luc wouldn't leave without saying goodbye. At least that was what she told herself.

A hand moved in front of her, propelling her back to the present. The server lifted her half-eaten salad from the table. She noticed Isla maneuvering around his hand to refill her wine glass.

"Maybe you should take it easy on that," Renee found herself saying. She didn't care about her mother much but getting trashed the night before Cait's wedding wasn't going to bode well for the next day.

"I should be able to enjoy my daughter's wedding, shouldn't I? There's a lot of pressure for a mother when her daughter gets married."

Isla's justification made little sense, but Renee didn't push it.

"Are you ever going to take the plunge?"

And end up like you? No thanks. Renee shrugged.

"You should try it at least once."

"Marriage shouldn't be something to try," Renee said, as a tightening sensation clamped on to her chest.

"Why not? That's how you can see if it will work or not."

Cait stiffened at Renee's side.

248

"That's not my intention with my life."

"Then, what is? You're not getting any younger."

Renee steeled herself again. Her mother's words slurred slightly, and her eyelids were heavy. Walking into that trap wasn't going to help either of them.

"Don't blame me when you wake up alone in ten years."

All of the feelings Renee had pent up the night before overwhelmed her until she couldn't take it anymore. "I would blame you, Mother. You're the one who made no example of relationships. You went from guy to guy, sucking the love out of marriage until you were done and then left the shell of a person behind. And I was there to witness it all. You're the person who makes marriage appear toxic, and why the hell would I ever want to get married with an example like that?" Renee shoved away from the table with trembling hands and stalked out of the dining area.

It wasn't until she was halfway across the space that she heard Isla carrying on a conversation like she had done nothing wrong.

In the hallway, the air was much cooler against her burning cheeks. Renee knew she couldn't stay out there for long. She hadn't even intended to tell Isla off, but the words had flowed out of her. The thought of Luc leaving without saying goodbye or her apologizing would ultimately be her own fault for letting Isla get under her skin. The pressure inside of her had made her snap, and now she was ruining Cait and Jorden's rehearsal.

Renee went into the bathroom and blotted her face with a damp towel. She didn't want to smear her makeup or show her mother that she cared so much about what she thought that she was crying in the bathroom. That wasn't the case. But the longer she stayed away, the harder it would be to convince any of them that she wasn't bothered.

Taking a deep breath, she left the bathroom and headed back inside. Enough conversations were going on throughout the three tables that Renee's outburst was already forgotten or entirely ignored. The air around her table was thick, even as she sat down and faced her sister.

Cait tried to convey a conversation with her eyes, but Renee didn't understand what her sister wanted. Instead, she said a silent apology to her sister and cut into the salmon on her plate.

"I never knew that was how you felt," Isla said softly. For once, it didn't seem as if her mother was desperate for attention.

"What else did you expect?" Renee hissed.

Isla opened her mouth and closed it. "I-I don't know, Renee. I didn't think it had anything to do with me."

"Well, it does." *And I screwed up a perfectly good relationship because of it.*

Renee could no longer blame Isla any more for her own mistakes. Isla had never intentionally pushed her ideals on Renee. She was a grown woman who didn't need to make excuses for herself or her actions. As much as she wanted to blame Isla for her life choices, they were hers and hers alone, no matter if her mother had put the ideas in her mind or not.

Cait and Jorden chatted with Blair next to them, but Renee could tell Cait was listening to their conversation as well.

"Like I said the other night, I do apologize if I put those thoughts in your head. Mother and daughter relationships are complicated, but I never expected you to believe that partnering up with someone long term was a bad thing. I expect I'll have more to discuss with my therapist when I return home."

It was as much of an apology as she was going to get. Reverting the conversation to herself was always Isla's thing. It wasn't a final resolution for everyone, but Isla's awareness of her lack of parenting to her children was the best she could do.

* * *

They managed to make it through the rest of the rehearsal dinner without any family drama. Cait surprised her bridal party with gifts—and not just the smaller, personalized gifts she'd found in town. No one was more surprised than Renee that Cait had kept a secret like that from her. The monogrammed canvas bags were stuffed with an oversized fluffy robe with their names embroidered on the backs, complete with matching slippers—for all the pictures they were to post. Each of the girls also got stemless wine glasses with their names and the wedding date.

Cait gave Renee a picture frame with seashells glued around the edges. A photograph of them as kids stared at her, and Renee's vision blurred before she tugged Cait into the tightest embrace.

Renee wiped a tear from her eyes. "Thank you."

"Your desk could use more décor," Cait squeezed back.

Jorden gave the groomsmen personalized cooler bags filled with individual six-packs based on the taste of the guys. Edward was sorely disappointed with soda, but the night ended on a higher note than that saggy middle.

On the ride home, Renee reflected on what her mother had said. For once, Isla appeared sincerely apologetic, and all it took was confronting her. It was a simple concept but it had eluded Renee for years. Being more upfront with Cait and Luc would have spared her a lot of frustration over this last month. While Cait was oblivious to anything other than her wedding, Luc was her next stop. She had to be sure that he wouldn't leave without her apology.

* * *

Renee slowed as she approached Luc's house. The lights were off, even though it was only around nine. There were no flickering lights from the television, but his truck was in the driveway. When she parked, she grabbed her phone again, and he hadn't returned her text. She could go over and demand to talk to him, risking him turning her down. Or she could give him one more day and hope that he would show up at the wedding.

Another night without talking to him wasn't going to help her sleep. Instead, she decided to go over there. She had her speech prepared and was ready to tell him everything, leaving her fate up to him.

Renee steeled herself and knocked on the door. One minute turned to three. Renee knocked again. Nothing. She rechecked her phone and debated on texting him. She turned to the beach and noticed the volleyball net was gone. This was really happening. A tightness settled in her chest.

Renee walked toward the road and spotted a figure further down the beach. It was faintly Luc-shaped, and as he neared, she noticed the dip in his chin against his chest before he turned to the ocean. It reminded her of last night when she needed space. As much as she wanted to talk to him, he had given her the time when she needed it. Renee would talk to him tomorrow. Tonight, he deserved a final night on the beach before he left West Cove.

Chapter 27

Nightmares of the wedding plagued Renee through the entire night. Waking from each of them gave her a start, but she fell back into a mixed-up land walking down the aisle in her bra and underwear and rain pouring buckets over the wedding with a crying Cait in a soaked wedding dress.

The last vision before she woke was standing in the center of the dance floor during the first dance without Luc. Everyone stared at her, and she almost would have rather been naked.

Renee's eyes flung open, and she knew she wasn't going back to sleep. Granted, it was already six-thirty in the morning. The bridesmaids were to get to the country club around eight to start preparations.

Hunter slept soundly by her feet. While neither of them was the hugging type, Renee yearned for a little comfort. With a click of her tongue, Hunter's head popped up and he trotted over to her. After plopping his butt on her hand, she reached with the other to scratch his chin. He let out a low sound in his throat.

"You're not so bad, are you?"

He responded with a lick against her mouth, and she rolled over on the verge of gagging. Hunter's tail wagged and he hopped around the bed, yapping.

"I changed my mind."

He responded with another yelp before flying off the bed and skittering toward the stairs.

After starting the coffee, Renee peered out the dining room window with the view of Luc's place. His truck was there, and she had the urge to visit again. If it was six-thirty at night, maybe. But if he was still upset with her, she wasn't going to make the conversation easier if she woke him from a dead sleep.

Renee would go over there at a decent time, right before the wedding. She would apologize, whether or not he was coming to the wedding. After the way Renee had confronted him, she would understand if he didn't.

While she showered, Renee thought of the dream that had woken her earlier. Cait had wanted the wedding party to join the first dance after the first minute of the song, and Renee's option for dance partner would have to revert to Marcus if Luc didn't show up. Marcus would never miss a chance to dance, but Renee could still feel the weight and warmth of Luc's hand in hers. She wanted him. And she had screwed it up so badly that her chest hollowed with a missing Luc-sized piece.

Other than blow-dry her hair, Renee didn't bother with her regular routine. She did slather a good amount of lotion onto her body, though. Beach life led to dry skin, and today was a marathon instead of a sprint. The pictures of her would last beyond today and she wanted to make sure everything was perfect for Cait.

The idea of someone else doing her makeup gave her a little thrill, as she would appear more put-together than she had in a while. It was the least excitement she could feel at the idea that Luc might not show up to be with her.

Think positive thoughts.

The sentiment was there, but the sinking in her gut gave her a dose of reality that she hadn't asked for.

* * *

Marcus had stayed the night at Olivia's. Renee glimpsed how different her life would be after the wedding. The last month had seen significant changes for her family, and she hoped to continue them. While it was a small step moving forward with her own life, Luc was still a possibility in her mind. No matter who bought the house next door, she wanted to stay in touch with him. She even dared to think that he would visit West Cove after the sale was finalized. His connection to the town was as strong as hers and even he couldn't shake that.

It was almost seven-forty-five by the time Renee fed the dogs, and herself breakfast. She took Hunter for a short walk—similar to the night when Luc had first arrived. Reflecting on the changes overwhelmed her. Summers were magical in that sense and experiencing another short time with Luc had changed her as much as he had the summer they had met. Wherever they left off after today would dictate the rest of her life.

Once she locked Hunter inside with Brandy, she grabbed her dress, tote, and locked up the house. Renee glanced at Olivia's place, debating on if she should tell Marcus that she was leaving. Instead of interrupting two people that morning, she decided to text him when she arrived at the country club.

After hanging her dress in the car, a weight lifted from her. It was heavier than the dress itself, but now was the time to confront Luc. His truck was still in the driveway, so there was no avoiding her. Movement from the kitchen window caught her eye. It was bright enough outside that she only caught a glimpse of Luc's outline standing by the kitchen sink. She moved to the side, not wanting him to spot her before she was ready.

If it were a few days ago, Renee would have been comfortable enough to stroll through the back door to give him a good-morning kiss. As quickly as their relationship had flourished, it had also faltered. Enough that she wasn't sure even a polite knock on his front door and an apology could fix it.

Cait's ringtone blasted from her purse, stopping Renee

mid-step. Luc's outline moved out of view, and she wasn't sure if he had seen her at all. She turned the ringer off and hesitated on picking up.

The phone call ended, then the ringing started again.

It was the last day that Cait needed her. Renee picked up. "Happy wedding day—"

Cait's sobs filled her ear, and Renee sprinted to her car.

"Cait, what's wrong?"

"M-m-m—" Cait couldn't even get the word out.

"Are you hurt? Is Jorden there?"

As if he had heard her, Jorden's voice sounded in the background. "I'm sure she's fine," he said. "We can try calling again."

"Cait," Renee demanded. "Talk to me. What's wrong?"

"Mom," she moaned. "I can't. She's not—"

"Isn't she in the bungalow?"

A shuffling sound filled her ear, and then Jorden's loud and clear voice came on the line. "We've been calling Isla all morning. She was supposed to meet Cait an hour ago. Cait stood outside the door for a few minutes. She didn't hear the phone ringing, but—" His voice cut off, and Cait's sobs lessened. It sounded as if he had gone into another room. "Last night, Edward and I had to bring her back to the bungalow. She was wasted, Renee. Can you go down there? I can't have Cait see her like that."

"Cait has no idea?"

"Without Jacob around, she's counting on Isla. Renee, Cait's been through a lot lately."

"Tell me."

"She's been seeing a doctor for severe panic attacks."

"What?" Why hadn't Cait said anything? Renee thought of all the weight that Cait had lost. The reason she came to West Cove—because it was a place with good memories for her. Why the wedding was difficult to plan. Renee was an idiot for not realizing it sooner. She hadn't been there for Cait in the ways that she needed.

"I can't leave her when she's like this. I have her medication, but she needs time to calm down. If Isla doesn't get it together, Cait's going to lose it even more than she already has."

"I understand," Renee said through gritted teeth. "I'll handle it."

* * *

Renee had never sped through West Cove faster than she had that morning. All thoughts of her conversation with Luc were pushed aside as searing heat pierced through her. Even at her daughter's wedding, Isla had to make it about her. Her mother had drunk a lot during the rehearsal dinner and eaten very little. Renee had been in her head at the time and didn't say anything. But it wasn't as if Renee's opinion ever mattered to Isla. Renee didn't expect that Isla would remain unconscious during Cait's wedding, but she never failed to surprise her eldest daughter.

At the club, Renee parked in the visitor lot behind the resort and as close as she could get to the bungalows. There were only ten of them, and they were set far enough away from each other that Renee's conversation with her mother would remain uninterrupted.

Outside bungalow number three, Renee stood for a moment, composing herself. She let out a small snort. Less than a half-hour ago, she was outside Luc's place with the same intention in mind. Again, Isla had interrupted that.

Renee strode up to the door and slammed her hand against the wood. The small window to the left of the door gave only a view of a small entrance with a closet. After a few seconds, she knocked again, harder that time.

A voice floated over to the door before Isla tried to open it from her end. It opened a crack, straining the chain which, somehow, she hadn't seen.

Isla let out a groan, and Renee stepped back before the door opened. "What is it?" Isla held up a hand to shield her eyes from the sunlight.

Renee barged into the bungalow. "Do you know what today is?"

Isla moved aside after Renee bumped into her. Her reactions were slow, and she backed away from the door, licking her dry, cracked lips. "Renee, what is going on? I was sleeping." Isla still wore the dress from the night before, and the heels she had worn were toppled over by the door.

"It's Cait's wedding day," Renee said. "You were going to meet her early this morning."

"I know that," Isla said, but the widening of her eyes betrayed her. "It's not until—"

"Yeah, *Mom*," Renee said, emphasizing the name Isla always insisted she use. Standing there like a train wreck made her look the part less than ever before. "What is wrong with you?"

Isla scoffed and wandered into the living space. She perched on the edge of the bed, smoothing her hair over her shoulder. "Nothing is wrong with me. It's you who needs an attitude adjustment. Now, leave me to get ready."

"Cait deserves more than you ever gave me. She doesn't have a father she can go to when she's sick of you."

Isla tutted, and Renee's hands clenched into fists. The more her anger grew, the more she took in the state of her mother. She was a sad and lonely woman who used people and alcohol to get through her life. Renee wasn't sure why she'd ever cared for Isla's opinion when she was the worst person she knew. Her hands unfurled and she allowed a sigh to seep from between her teeth. The binds between them severed with an audible *snap* in her mind. No, that was Isla's hair tie breaking as she tried to wrestle her matted locks into a bun.

Her mother's mask of indifference shaded her expression. "Be a dear and call Cait for me. Let her know I'll be by shortly."

Renee walked to the door, spotting Isla's phone on the side table. "Call her yourself."

* * *

Renee walked the beachside toward the resort. After the argument with her mother, the air seemed fresher in her lungs. The sand was softer against her feet. It hugged her sandals, spilling over her toes, and filled her with a calmness she hadn't ever experienced in Isla's presence before. Breaking bonds with her mother was easier than she had expected, yet it had taken so many years. Renee tried not to think of the time she had wasted, allowing her past trauma to overcome her life. That was over now. Isla would never have the same power over her again, but it was up to her to fix everything with Luc.

Since she hadn't had time to speak with him that morning, she pulled out her phone. She hadn't heard anything from him in over twenty-four hours. It was a long shot, but it might be her last opportunity. It wasn't how she wanted to talk to him, but she hadn't been given a choice. It was as if fate was trying to keep them apart, but she still insisted on attempting to make it right.

I want a chance to talk to you before you leave. I understand if you don't want to come to the wedding. Don't leave town yet. I'll stop by the house after the reception. Please understand that today is about Cait. I will (hopefully) see you soon x

It was the shortest—and least pleading—version of the thoughts moving in her head, but it would have to do. Today was Cait's day, and unlike Isla, Renee wasn't going to spend all of it worried about herself. Whatever mistakes she had made with Luc were hers alone. She only hoped that he would give her the second chance that she needed to attempt to make it all right.

* * *

When Renee reached the bridal suite, laughter and shrieks filled the air. She hesitated by the door and listened. Cait's voice wasn't among the others, but the other girls were as supportive of Cait as Renee. Did Cait have that smile that barely reached her eyes, or had Jorden calmed her down enough to enjoy her wedding day? Renee debated on finding Jorden, but she was already late.

Pushing inside, the other girls barely turned around at her presence. Mostly because half of them were in chairs at various stages of getting their hair and makeup done. Renee scanned the open area for her sister.

Cait was by the windows, staring at the ocean. Her hair was still in curlers and her face was without makeup. Renee crossed the room, ignoring Dee and Fiona holding out flutes of champagne and telling Renee she needed to "catch up" with them.

"Hey," Renee said when she reached Cait's side.

Cait blinked and turned to her sister. "Is she coming?"

Renee hated how Cait was so stuck on Isla even after she had disappointed both of them repeatedly. But, as she said to Isla, Cait had no other living parent. Having Marcus had saved Renee from turning out worse than she had. He was the calming force—in the same way West Cove was for her.

As much as Renee had done for Cait, no one could replace a mother, not even a sister who had tried.

"She's coming," Renee said.

"Good."

Renee's snaked her arm over Cait's shoulder. "How are you doing?"

"I'm—"

"Fine? Don't bother."

"I am fine," Cait said. "Jorden and I can deal with this."

"You don't have to keep it between you two. I'm here for you. Do you know that? In more ways than just as a wedding planner."

"In more ways than a knight in shining armor?"

Renee cocked her head to the side.

"You keep coming to my rescue when it comes to Mom. I know she's not the best, but—"

"She's all you have."

Cait sighed. "Yeah."

"I understand."

Cait leaned closer to the window, and Renee followed her gaze. Isla trudged up the sand toward the hotel. Without knowing anyone was watching, her slumped shoulders, and hard footfalls were apparent, even from that distance.

"What did you say to her?"

"What she needed to hear." Renee wasn't going to trash their mother. Nothing would taint this day with Cait. Not even if Isla deserved it.

Cait wrapped her arms around Renee and held her tightly. "I love you, Nay."

"Love you, too."

* * *

Cait walking down the aisle was everything Renee imagined, and more. Even with a preening Isla hooked on her arm, a swell of pride moved through Renee as she watched her sister float down the narrow path to a new future.

Renee glanced at Jorden, who couldn't take his eyes off his bride. Tears welled in his eyes, bringing more emotion to Renee than she had anticipated. It took staring at the arch and the gorgeous roses cascading down to the ground to stave off her own urge to cry as Isla handed Cait off to Jorden. When the officiant asked everyone to sit, Renee turned slightly, facing Cait and Jorden for the start of the ceremony, which would begin their life together.

One person in the crowd stood for a few seconds longer than the rest, catching Renee's attention.

Luc was in a full suit with his normally unruly hair slicked back against his head. Without any of it hanging over his eyes, his gaze was clear and purposeful. He looked only at her as

261

he sat. The rush of her heartbeat in her ears overpowered the officiant's words.

Renee's hands tingled as they gripped the bouquet. A quirk of his lips made her knees wobble, and she fought to stay upright as her view of the entire day changed before her eyes.

Chapter 28

Renee couldn't take her eyes off Luc for a good two minutes. Her pulsing heartbeat drowned out the officiant until his words muffled in her ears. Luc's expression was stoic, and when the momentary shock wore off, Renee wasn't sure what to think of his presence. Had he come because he was obligated? Or did he want to be there with her? The happiness from seeing him burrowed in her gut until the tightening in her throat became too much to bear.

A rush of the salty air filled her lungs, calming her mind. Whatever the reason for Luc's arrival—as refreshing as it was— had to wait until after the ceremony. Her duties to Cait were almost done, and there was no use thinking about why Luc had come until she could ask him herself.

Renee turned to her sister, watching her more intently than she had all summer. The secret of her anxiety disorder had caught Renee off-guard, but she was confident in Jorden's ability to care deeply enough for Cait that she would be okay—even in Isla's presence.

Cait and Jorden's hands were clasped between them as the officiant read the passages that they had chosen to seal their love with. Jorden's smile never wavered, and Renee caught a few

263

glimpses of her sister's smile several times when she glanced at her family and friends around her.

The ceremony itself was only about twenty minutes, but as Renee's thoughts shifted to Luc, the minutes seemed to carry much more weight than usual.

After the rings and first kiss as wife and husband, the movement of the procession startled Renee enough that she almost tripped over her dress. The thin material clung to her in the afternoon heat, and when she caught Luc's gaze that blaze intensified within her.

Renee passed his aisle, gnawing on her lip because she couldn't talk to him just yet. Pictures and obligations to the bride before the cocktail hour took precedence. After the pictures, Renee would be free to do whatever she wanted.

Marcus and Olivia walked over to Luc. Her father shook Luc's hand, and Luc offered a pat on Marcus's shoulder too. Renee tried to read lips but found it impossible.

Blair stopped in front of her and Renee moved to the side to avoid a collision. "Sorry!"

"I can't wait to get these things off?" Blair said. "My feet are killing me?"

At least she wasn't upset with Renee. Earlier, the bridesmaids left their phones with Prudence, who would return them after all the professional photographs were taken. While it was a good idea to keep the girls focused, Renee desperately wanted to check it to see if there was any hint of why Luc had come to the wedding. His expression had given her no understanding of his decision. Renee wanted to feel prepared for the inevitable conversation with him.

Sullivan and his team were professional and quick to take the photographs for Cait, so they could enjoy what was left of the cocktail hour.

Renee smiled for the camera, but after each one, she glanced at the crowd milling outside the ceremony area. There were high-top tables set up, and servers circled the guests with trays filled with food. She had lost track of Luc and her father but continued to look for them after each shutter flash.

"Just the bride and groom now," Sullivan said, leading Cait and Jorden toward the edge of the property and to the water.

Renee couldn't move quickly enough as her heels punctured the ground with each step. Eventually, she pranced on her toes, not wanting her shoes to deter her from getting the explanation from Luc that she needed.

Marcus, Olivia, and Luc stood by one of the tables. Luc's back was to her, but Marcus's expression must have caught his eye. He turned, giving her a full view of him.

Renee wasn't sure what she expected. Indifference? Annoyance?

He had settled for a blank face, rendering her useless to figure out what his reasoning was for coming to the wedding. Now that she was on the firm, concrete patio, she walked with steadier feet toward them.

"It was a lovely ceremony," Olivia said.

Marcus pressed his lips together. "You look great, Renee."

"Thanks," Renee said, waiting for Luc to say something.

The four of them stared at each other before Luc broke the silence. "Can we take a walk?"

Renee steeled a breath. "Sure. How about the beach?" It was her comfort spot and being there would give her the confidence to tell him her true feelings.

"Yeah, that sounds good."

The walk down the patio and steps toward the beach was mostly silent, other than the sounds of the crashing waves intensifying by the second.

Renee compiled her thoughts, wanting to tell him everything that had been on her mind since their fight the other day. Isla's name danced on the edge of her tongue, but she would no longer blame her mother for her actions. That part of her life was over, and now she'd spend the rest of it on her own terms.

They were on the edge of the beach. If it were up to her, she'd stay there for the rest of the day. It calmed her enough to put everything she wanted to say at the forefront of her mind.

"Renee—" Luc started.

"No, Luc. Please, I want to get this out."

He pressed his lips together and nodded.

"My mother, she put these thoughts into my head about what relationships look like. They were very black and white. She was always someone different when she was with a new person. I thought, stupidly, that that was happening to me. I thought I would lose myself in you. But, it turned out that you were the one to bring out a side of me that I had kept hidden away for so long. It took some time to realize it. I know you're leaving soon, but I wanted to see if we could make the best of the time we have together. I'm even willing to keep going after you leave for Massachusetts. Fate has brought us together twice and ignoring it would be turning my back on something special. But I do understand that this isn't all about me. I want to know what you think."

Luc licked his lips, and they curled into a smile. "I can talk now?"

Renee fought back the urge to chuck him in the arm. "I had a lot to say."

"I know." The corners of his lips tugged downward.

The walls around her heart were down, and she fought to keep them that way. She wasn't going to hide from the hurt anymore. That wasn't living, and after today, all she wanted to do was live.

"I appreciate you wanting to make this work."

Renee waited for the inevitable "but".

But, I have a life in Massachusetts.

But, I can't see this working.

But, this was only for the summer.

"I want the same thing."

Renee blinked hard. "You do?"

"I'm not going anywhere, Renee."

That gave her more pause than him wanting to be with her. "I don't understand."

"I didn't either until I saw your text, and then I talked to Marcus."

"What does my dad have to do with it?"

"Renee, I bought Audrey's house."

"*You* bought the house?"

"Yeah," he said. "I thought you knew that."

If she knew that, the last two days would have gone differently.

"That day, you looked at the paperwork," he continued. "I thought you were upset that it was me."

"What? No. I wouldn't be upset. I'm not."

He chuckled. "I figured that out eventually. Your text told me not to leave. I knew you were here, so I talked to Marcus. He was surprised that I was staying as well, and then I started to wonder."

"Luc, I'm sorry." Renee was such a fool, allowing Isla to cloud her judgment about Luc. She'd held the paperwork in her hands. If she hadn't allowed Isla into her mind, she could have taken the time to realize it was Luc who had bought the house and not some stranger.

Luc took her hands in his. The same zips of electricity coursed up her arms as she had experienced the last time they were together. "Stop being sorry, Renee. You don't need to apologize for anything."

Renee nodded. "I know. But the last two days—"

"They're over. But we're not. That is, if you still want—"

Her mouth covered his, stifling his words. As his hands moved over her waist, she tugged him closer. She was tired of talking about her life and wanted to start living it. Her hands dug into his arms, holding him against her. The sands below them shifted, but she was more grounded than she'd ever been before.

A ringing bell sounded in her head. But as Luc slowed his kiss, she realized she wasn't the only person who heard it.

Closer to the building, Prudence held a bell above her head like a town crier. The guests shuffled together, toward the reception.

Luc licked his lips. "Are you needed up there?"

Renee smudged her lipstick off the corner of his mouth. "Probably."

"Shall we?" Luc offered his arm, and they walked up the beach together. The shore always held significance for her, but Renee had never felt more connected to her favorite place than she did at that moment.

"How did you make all of this work?" Renee asked. "Your job?"

"I have a job at the high school," Luc said.

"When did this happen?"

His chin dropped to his chest. "I wasn't forthcoming with my entire reason for coming to West Cove." He scrubbed a hand over his mouth. "West Cove always held a special place in my heart. For the last few years, I've asked Aunt Audrey about the house."

"You did?"

"She wasn't exactly easy to pry the information from, especially since her memory has become spottier. But she promised me that if I could restore the house and prove to her that I was worthy of it, then I could stay."

"That's why you renovated it this summer?"

"Yeah. There's still a lot of work to be done, but I secured a teaching job earlier this year. I don't know if I'm going to be coaching the team, but I'd like to make the beach volleyball clinic available again if they'll have me."

Luc wasn't leaving. There was no reason for them to break up. Yet, a niggling sensation curled around her heart and squeezed. "Why didn't you say anything to me?"

"I'm superstitious. It all hinged on Audrey's decision to give me the deed to the house. I didn't want to say something to you, and then have Audrey not sign off. I hope you're not upset with me about that. The more we reconnected, the worse I felt, Renee. That's the truth."

Renee squeezed his hand and tucked her body against his side. "I'm not upset. At all."

"Good."

Renee didn't miss the mix of excited glances at them as she and Luc entered the building. The guests were already inside the hall while the bridal party waited outside for their official announcements.

Luc pulled Renee to him again, planting a slow kiss on her mouth. She melted against him as her skin lit up at his touch.

"See you in there," he said after breaking apart from her.

"There's a dance," she blurted. "For the wedding party. I—"

He silenced her words with another kiss. "I'll be there," he murmured against her lips. "Wherever you need me, I'm there."

Renee watched him enter the room before Prudence closed the door. "Line up, everyone."

Cait appeared at Renee's side. "What happened between yesterday and today with you and Luc?"

"He's staying," Renee said, unable to move from her spot.

"He's what?" Cait shrieked. The rest of the girls gathered around them. "Luc is staying in town," she explained to them as if they were discussing an episode of one of her favorite TV dramas.

The other girls squealed with excitement for Renee. She wondered how much Cait had talked about her and Luc behind her back. Though nothing could bring her down from the high of Luc staying.

Prudence tutted and ushered the girls to their spots. "You have all night for these conversations. Everyone is waiting for you."

Cait wrapped her arms around Renee, and Renee put all of her love into the embrace.

"This is the best day," Cait said.

"It really is." They held each other as the DJ announced for everyone to stand for the entrance of the wedding party. Renee held on to Cait a little longer, wanting to burn that memory into her mind.

A sharp tap on her shoulder made Renee turn. Prudence's eyes were wide. "You're next."

Renee kissed Cait's cheek and locked arms with Edward before entering the room. She scanned the space, spotting several family members from Jacob's side at one table, while her family was at the next. Marcus and Olivia cheered the loudest, with Luc's whistling cutting over the group.

Renee's body heated up as she took her spot on the dance floor.

It took everything inside of her to look away from Luc as her sister entered the room. Cait and Jorden pumped their arms in the air in time with the upbeat music before they settled against each other in the center of the dance floor. The room quieted, and the first notes of their song floated through the speakers.

They started to move together as if they shared the same mind. Renee glanced over her shoulder at Luc, and he gave her a thumbs-up. She yearned to be closer to him again, and her opportunity came quicker than she expected. The others moved toward the floor, and Luc slid away from his seat.

Renee backed onto the dance floor as Luc approached. His hands reached for hers and smoothed over her skin. Luc grasped her firmly in his arms, holding her tightly against him as they started to move together. Slow at first, then building up to the tempo of the song. They were not professional dancers by any means, but they moved with each other.

Luc's cheek dipped to hers, as they swayed to the music.

A shiver rolled down her spine at his touch.

It was the first time in Renee's life that her future seemed promising and not an obstacle in her way. It opened up in front of her, vast and expansive as the ocean through the windows behind Luc. There were endless possibilities for her, and for once, she wasn't going to shy away from taking them.

Luc kissed her cheek and pushed her away before flourishing her in a twirl. Their intertwined fingers locked together as he pulled her close to him again. Their movements slowed as their eyes never left one another. Possibilities of a different and exciting life stared back at her. Through Luc's eyes, she saw the happiness she had always kept away from herself.

This summer was about to change once more, and more than anything, she was ready for it as she lifted on her toes to embrace Luc and the life she wanted to share with him.

Acknowledgments

As always, I want to thank the HQ Digital team for making my stories come to life. Thanks to Belinda for helping me through this book even when it didn't want to crack. Your unwavering patience is greatly appreciated and your feedback (as always) has really brought this story to life.

TSAG – you are the support system that holds me up when things don't necessarily go the way I expected. I will forever appreciate all of you.

Thanks to Susan & Jenel, for connecting with a fan to give all the outlining advice. Susan, I'm "borrowing" your methods moving forward, and I couldn't have written this book in the way I wanted without your kind and thought-provoking guidance.

To Julie and Amber, thanks for pushing and motivating me to get this book on the page. You're the best sprinting partners!

Thanks to Katie for heading to Panera with me as often as possible for our writing sessions and helping me get the work done.

Thanks again to my readers, Mom and Leigh, for being there even when I give you no notice to read my book. Love you both!!

And last but certainly not least, my readers. Thank you for supporting me through my writing career, and I appreciate you much more thank you could ever know!

Summer is here!! I hope you enjoyed falling in love with all the characters in West Cove. This book took a while to come into my mind, but when it did, these characters consumed my life. I loved writing the complicated relationships between all the people in my story, especially the women.

I'm humbled and honored that you've chosen to add *Barefoot on the Beach* to your shelf, and I hope you got all the beachy feels from this story.

If you enjoyed this book, I would be forever grateful if you left a review. Reviews are how readers find books, so even one or two sentences helps immensely in getting Renee and Luc's story into more hands.

I love being in touch with my readers, so feel free to contact me on Facebook, Twitter, Instagram, or on YouTube to chat about the story or books in general.

Thanks for reading,
Katlyn

Dear Reader,

We hope you enjoyed reading this book. If you did, we'd be so appreciative if you left a review. It really helps us and the author to bring more books like this to you.

Here at HQ Digital we are dedicated to publishing fiction that will keep you turning the pages into the early hours. Don't want to miss a thing? To find out more about our books, promotions, discover exclusive content and enter competitions you can keep in touch in the following ways:

JOIN OUR COMMUNITY:

Sign up to our new email newsletter: hyperurl.co/hqnewsletter

Read our new blog www.hqstories.co.uk

🐦 : https://twitter.com/HQDigitalUK

📘 : www.facebook.com/HQStories

BUDDING WRITER?

We're also looking for authors to join the HQ Digital family!
Find out more here:

https://www.hqstories.co.uk/want-to-write-for-us/

Thanks for reading, from the HQ Digital team

Keep reading for an excerpt from
Wrapped up for Christmas . . .

Chapter 1

The Christmas song blaring from the pocket of the man in front of Angie was the last straw. He turned off the ringer of his phone, but that was it for her. She hadn't even reached the end of the jet bridge before heat surged behind her eyes for the dozenth time that afternoon.

Don't you dare cry, Angie Martinelli.

At least not until she'd buried herself under the covers in the room she hadn't slept in since high school.

A day ago, she had lain in her queen-sized bed with eight hundred thread count sheets. When she wasn't in her apartment, she was in Brett's California king, treating it like a twin. She recalled the firmness of his body, snuggling up against him—

'No,' she hissed, startling the family of four next to her. The parents tucked their children closer to them, away from the crazy woman talking to herself. 'Sorry.'

The mother grabbed onto her daughter's backpack and steered her into the airport.

Angie tried to take a calming breath, wanting to push Brett and his cheating self to the farthest reaches of her mind. She gripped her rolling carry-on bag and adjusted her handbag on her shoulder.

With her belongings accounted for, she swiped away a stray tear threatening to fall and dipped her chin against her chest as she made her way through the waiting area toward baggage claim. Angie was determined to keep everyone out of her business – even strangers. She was adamant that they weren't going to see the tortured expression she wore on her face. As an only child, she prided herself on being a strong and independent woman.

Or at least, she used to.

Once she reached the food court, the scent of greasy cuisine filled her nose. Her stomach ached for something to eat; she had waited too long on the flight to get one of the prepared meals and they were sold out. Nothing on the plane went her way. She sat behind someone who reclined their chair the entire time and the three complimentary bags of chips did nothing to ease her emotions as her mind and stomach churned across the country.

Angie stopped in front of a pub and hesitated, thinking of her bank account. Dollar signs filled her vision for the charges she'd had to pay for the three extra suitcases she'd brought with her. Only one more deposit would come through her account for her severance pay and then nothing. She shook her head, her long dark hair swooping across her face. It clung to her damp cheeks as she tucked the stray strands behind her ears before heading to baggage claim. She could wait to eat until she arrived at home. No doubt her mom would have prepared a feast for her already.

As she followed the signs toward the first level of the airport, she managed to hold back the dam of tears that threatened to break. She was doing well until she saw a handwritten sign on lined paper which read 'Aunty' taped to the huge belly of her best friend standing next to the unmoving carousel.

Tears burst from her eyes as Angie sagged into Reese's arms and sobbed against her shoulder. The ugly, snotty cry that only a best friend or mother could take without feeling utterly disgusted.

Reese patted Angie's back. 'Let it all out, girl.'

'How was the flight?' her husband, Jeremy, asked.

Angie choked out a laugh and wiped her nose with the sleeve of her shirt. 'Hi, Jer.'

The tall and still handsome high school football champion of their day stood a few feet away, clearly freaked out by the tears coursing down her face. Ten years after graduating, he had aged well. His mother always said youthful genes were a blessing in their family despite the lighter strands now peppered throughout his jet-black hair.

Men had it so easy.

A flash of Brett's blond locks and million-watt smile threatened to crumple Angie's composure.

Reese flipped her caramel hair over her shoulder. It seemed smoother than ever. Reese had been over the moon when she found out what pregnancy hormones did to her body. Her warm brown eyes peered down at Angie, filled with concern and warmth.

Angie couldn't imagine starting a family, never mind getting married, since her life was already over. The dramatics were unnecessary, but it was hard to think of anyone but Brett at the moment. He had been the vision of her future. Now what?

'Why don't you grab Angie's bags?' Reese said to Jeremy.

He backed away as if Angie was a bomb ready to go off.

Angie stood straighter and wiped her face with her sleeve again. 'Do I look okay?'

Reese raised an eyebrow. 'I mean, I could lie and say you look great.'

Angie snorted a laugh, and more tears streamed down her face.

Reese folded her arms over her chest. 'There are only two ways that dating your boss could go. Unfortunately, you got the short end of that deal.'

'I never thought it would end like this.'

Reese patted Angie's back before pulling her as close as she could, avoiding the basketball-sized lump under her shirt. 'Love is a funny thing. Sometimes it blinds you.'

Angie wrinkled her nose at her friend. 'That still doesn't make me feel any better.'

Reese gently scratched the side of her belly. 'It's not supposed to. You're hurting, and nothing I say is going to help until you start to heal. Right now, you can't do anything about it. Brent—'

'*Brett*,' Angie corrected, even though the sour taste of his name made her already sensitive stomach quiver.

Reese waved her hands dismissively. '*Brett* lied to you. Now you need to learn from it and move on. You've been on the go since you graduated from college. Take some time for yourself. Slow down and appreciate life.'

'I can't,' Angie said.

'Why not?'

'Keeping busy is going to help me forget about him.'

'Why not enjoy the time off and a chance to have a break? It's Christmas, and you haven't been home in forever.'

Angie shouldered her overpacked handbag she'd dropped at Reese's feet. 'Is any part of this conversation going to be helpful?'

Reese's smile fell. 'Were there any signs?'

Angie considered that question. It was all she had thought about when he informed her the day before Thanksgiving that they weren't going to work out because of his fiancée. Fiancée!

The return to work was incredibly awkward. Angie didn't flatter herself to think that every employee knew about her breakup, but all she could think about was where Brett was in the building and how she could avoid him. There was no way that she could watch Brett and his fiancée – soon, wife – strut around the hotel in front of her. Determined for them both not to get the better of her, she decided to quit and demanded proper severance pay to tide her over the Christmas period.

The signs, though? Angie spotted them immediately after coming out of her love cloud to stare them in the face.

Brett was away at least two weeks a month on business. She had made excuses for him, putting it down to work since he had a hotel to run. It had worked out well for her as she was busy planning events. Her work had started to pick up as Thanksgiving approached; everyone wanted a holiday party in the hotel during December. Every night she had passed out fast asleep well before ten to get up and do it all over again the next day. But that had been their routine.

'He wasn't around much lately,' Angie admitted.

'I guess absence didn't make the heart grow fonder.'

Angie shot her a look.

'Sorry,' Reese said. 'I can't control it sometimes.'

When Reese's family moved to Brookside, Connecticut when they were in the second grade, Angie liked her plucky attitude immediately. Her best friend's sarcasm didn't earn her many friends in high school or beyond. But Reese's bluntness kept Angie down to earth, giving her a reality check as her mind tended to float up to the clouds. Even though it hurt to realize how idiotic she had been with Brett, she needed the truth now. It was the only way she could move on.

They walked over to Jeremy as he searched through every bag that passed him on the baggage carousel, much to the annoyance of the other travelers.

'What color are your bags, Angie?' Jeremy asked over his shoulder.

Angie wiped the residue streaks of tears from her face. 'Green.' When she had left for college, her dad insisted she had a set of suitcases for coming home. Even though they were a hideous shade, it was his way of helping her out when she traveled.

Jeremy rocked on his heels. 'How festive.'

Reese lifted a small bag of trail mix from her back pocket. She ripped it open and started to snack. 'I bet your mom is thrilled you're coming home for Christmas. What did she say when you told her?'

Angie chewed on her lip. For the past five years, Angie had flown her mom out to visit her in San Diego for Christmas. It wasn't the white Christmas they were used to at home, but for Angie, it was better than returning to a place which reminded her of her dad's absence. Her mother didn't complain too much when she sat on the terrace of Angie's apartment, soaking in the sun. If all had gone well with Brett this year, everything would have been the same. It would have been the first time that Brett had been able to meet her mom.

'Considering she hates flying, she was thrilled,' Angie said, picking up one of her bags as it came by. Jeremy took another. 'It finally gave her a chance to decorate the house. The Thompsons next door helped her with the tree and lights.'

'The Thompsons?' Reese asked with a snort. 'I bet that was a struggle.'

Angie laughed and lunged for another of her bags.

'I've got it!' Jeremy appeared beside her and grabbed the handle before she could.

Angie stepped back and glanced down at Reese, licking her fingers for the last morsels of salt. 'How are you feeling? Are you ready for the baby?'

Reese answered without looking up. 'As ready as we'll ever be.' Reese snaked a hand around Angie's waist. 'I'm glad you'll be here to meet her first.'

'Wouldn't miss it for the world.'

Reese raised an eyebrow.

Angie sighed. 'It was going to be a surprise, but I did book a flight home after New Year's.' Another plan in her life she had to cancel.

Reese snorted. 'You better have. Or else I would have kicked Brett's butt for keeping you across the country.'

A break from California would get Angie's head on straight again. Her life couldn't get much worse, and she was determined to break her unlucky streak as soon as possible.

* * *

'They've outdone themselves this year.' Reese craned her neck to peer around the driver's seat. The Thompsons next door spared no expense to make their house light up like a Christmas tree from December 1st through mid-January every single year.

Angie had forgotten how brightly their house shone and the memory caught her by surprise. Each polished ornament from her childhood stood in the same place as if they were stored in a snow globe. Though there were a few new ones, including the six – no seven – elves appearing to prance along the sidewalk. She didn't need to roll down her window to hear the joyous 'ho ho ho!' from the mechanical Santa surrounded by his famous reindeer.

Angie's mom had always tried to keep her dad away from accepting Mr Thompson's annual request for assistance with their display for fear of him breaking his neck falling from the roof. Her mom had aligned their Christmas tree shopping that same weekend for many years to avoid the argument. As a child, Angie had sometimes woken weeks after Christmas, hearing the sound from the Santa on the neighbor's roof.

As they drove by, Angie smiled, fondly thinking about her dad grumbling to himself for the entire month and a half about the outrageous display. The image of his face burned into her eyes, imprinting on her memory as Jeremy pulled into the driveway of her childhood home.

Colored lights climbed the highest peaks of the house and sloped toward the ground. A swooping sensation filled her, stealing her breath. Coming home was what she needed. She knew that now more than ever.

A familiar station wagon sat in her old spot on the driveway. The rusted edges of the wheel wells had extended to the back bumper. She was surprised it still ran. Angie's mom must have invited her nonni over for dinner, knowing Angie was coming home. She braced herself for tight embraces and sloppy cheek kisses, but couldn't help smiling. Her home had been a place to run away from for years. Now she wanted nothing more than the familiar.

Reese yawned and turned in her seat as much as she could. 'We would love to visit, but I'm exhausted. This little angel sucks up all my energy. Let's meet up tomorrow?'

Angie leaned over and kissed her friend on the cheek. 'Definitely.' She opened the door and hopped out of the car. 'Thanks for picking me up.'

Jeremy grabbed two of her bags before they walked together to the porch with Angie rolling the last, and her carry on. She wasn't sure where she was going to put everything.

'How is she doing?' Angie asked as they approached the house, out of Reese's earshot.

'She's having trouble sleeping,' Jeremy said, massaging the back of his neck. 'I've been on the sofa.'

Angie spotted movement from behind the living room curtains. 'Let me know if you need help with anything.' *Not like I have much to do anymore. I'm jobless, homeless, hopeless . . .* She shook the negative thoughts from her mind.

'Sure thing,' he said. 'It's nice to have you back. Reese will never say it, but she misses you. Even more now with the baby on the way.'

'Hormones?' Angie tried to make light of the conversation. She hadn't been the best best-friend since moving to California.

'She's become more emotional. It's an adjustment for everyone.'

Angie sighed. So much had gone on the last few days, she wasn't sure if she could handle more emotion from herself or her friends. 'Thanks again for the ride. I'll come by the house soon.'

'No problem.'

Jeremy leaned forward, and they awkwardly hugged. Even though Jeremy and Reese had been together for years, he and Angie had never quite mastered the closeness either of them had with Reese. She was their glue.

The front door opened just as she reached for the knob. Donato grabbed his chest as if she'd knocked the wind out of him. His wheezing breath billowed above them. 'Jesus, Mary, and Joseph, you scared me. I thought you were a damned ghost.'

Angie smirked. 'I'm not a ghost, Nonno.' She took the cigarette and lighter from his hand and put them in the pocket of his thick knitted sweater. 'Those things are going to kill you, you know?'

'That's what your nonna says, but my ticker is as strong as it was when I was fifteen!'

Angie steered him inside and closed the door behind her, taking in the blazing heat of her home. It was worse in the summer as her mom insisted on cooking the same amount of food all year round. At least since Dad died. He had always been the grill-master, and after he had passed away, her mother saw no reason to change her cooking habits away from the kitchen. She hugged Nonno, sturdy as ever.

A loud cackle caught her attention.

Angie's nonna, Emilia, held her hands in front of her, gesturing for Angie to come closer. As if she hadn't been the one creeping behind the curtain. 'Angela! Angela!' The thick Brooklyn accent filled Angie with a warmth she hadn't expected. The round woman pressed herself against Angie's middle and squeezed. Even now, in the later end of her seventies, she still made Angie breathless with her hugs.

Angie leaned her cheek against the top of Emilia's head. Her gray-streaked hair was shorter than she remembered.

'I think you've shrunk.'

Emilia pressed her hands against Angie's waist. 'You too.'

'It was so nice of you two to come and visit me,' Angie said. 'I missed you.'

Emilia stiffened and took a step back, keeping her hands on Angie's waist. A version of the terrible stink-eye that could send any man in a ten-foot radius skittering away had befallen Angie.

'What's with the face?' Angie looked at Donato who suddenly found his hands fascinating.

'Maria!' Emilia barked, making both Angie and Donato jump.

'You've done it now.' Donato rubbed a hand over his stubbled cheek.

'What did I do?' Angie asked.

Emilia darted from the room, and Angie followed her toward the kitchen. She barely had a moment to take in the boxes of Christmas decorations on the floor before approaching the raised voices of her mother and her nonna going at it.

Angie peered into the kitchen, not wanting to get in the middle of whatever was happening. 'Ma?'

Emilia placed her hands firmly on her hips, and her bottom lip jutted out. 'Tell her.'

Angie's heart warmed when she saw her mom, pear-shaped as ever, holding a wooden spoon tipped with gravy. Her mouth watered thinking of a home-cooked meal for once instead of take-out or airplane food.

'Tell me what?' Angie thought of all the possibilities of horrible situations. Was one of them sick? Dying? Did it have something to do with her coming home?

Maria rolled her eyes. 'Mom, can you give me a minute to say hello to my daughter?' She darted across the room and kissed Angie on the cheek. Her skin was softer than Angie remembered. 'Welcome home, Angela.'

No one could stop Emilia when she was about to scold someone. 'You had plenty of time to tell her, now you're going to disappoint your only daughter.'

Angie huffed. 'Can someone fill me in?'

Emilia crossed her arms and avoided eye contact by staring at the ceiling.

Maria took Angie's hands in hers. They were warm. 'I told Nonna it wouldn't be a big deal to you.'

Angie's gaze darted between her mom and Emilia. 'What wouldn't be a big deal?'

'Nonno and Nonna had to leave their apartment.'

'Rodents!' Donato said from the doorway.

'Disgusting,' Emilia spat.

'So, they're staying with us for a little while.'

Angie waited yet no one else spoke. 'Is that all?'

'Well,' Maria said, dragging the word out longer than necessary. 'They're staying in your room. It's bigger and more comfortable for them.'

'I told Maria we could stay in the guest room,' Emilia offered. Maria glared at her mother.

Angie mustered a smile to appease her family. 'I'll stay in the guest room while I'm home.' She had no intention of staying longer than necessary and moving her nonni out of the room for a week or so didn't make any sense.

'See!' Maria shrieked and pointed the spoon at Emilia. 'I told you it was fine.'

Emilia grunted and sat at the table set for four.

Maria led Angie to the chair she had sat on since she was a kid, gesturing her to sit. 'Tell us all about your trip. I'm almost finished with dinner. I made your favorite.'

Angie sat at the table, allowing the warmth of the house to envelop her into a tight hug. She was used to the wide-open space of her and Brett's apartments. The house where she grew up felt smaller than it had the last time. But the laughter and happiness shining in her family's eyes lulled her into a sense of security she hadn't realized she had missed.

* * *

Angie could barely keep her eyes open during dinner, even though her brain was three hours behind. She guessed the exhaustion from moving her life across the country and breaking up with the man she had expected to marry had finally caught up with her. At least she would soar over the potential jet lag.

After saying goodnight to everyone, Angie headed upstairs to

291

the guest room. She wearily carried her heavy feet down the long hallway toward the last door, lugging her suitcase behind her.

Angie had slept in smaller confines in college, so she didn't mind the change in her plan. The moment she pushed open the door, it rebounded back, smacking against her arm. Pain zipped through her elbow and she frantically rubbed the spot to make the radiating ache stop.

Angie pushed the door open again, slower this time, and flicked the light switch. Against the back of the door, a folded-up treadmill blocked her way. She squeezed into the room, turning her suitcase to pull in behind her.

In the far corner was a table, covered with scrapbooking supplies, and on the floor were about twenty photo albums. Next to that were even more Christmas decoration boxes, which her mom usually stored in the attic. Angie guessed that she hadn't dared to pack them away since her dad had died. The rickety pull-down ladder to the storage space always terrified her mother.

A headache formed behind Angie's eyes and she rubbed the side of her temple, willing for it to go away. Adding physical pain to her mental anguish wasn't going to help her get any sleep. She abandoned her other suitcases in the hallway, turned the light off, and flopped onto the bed. Moonlight poured into the room, throwing shadows across the walls.

It wasn't long before a single tear slipped down her cheek. Even in her own home, she couldn't help but feel cast off. Days ago, she was a successful event planner for one of the most prestigious hotel chains in the country with a sexy, wealthy boyfriend and a fantastic apartment. Now she was back at home, in the town she had always wanted to escape from.

Angie thought of the giant rock on Brett's fiancée's finger, and her skin prickled. Hot tears coursed down her face and she tightened her grip on the blanket around her as the memories of her relationship with Brett flooded her mind. He was the perfect boyfriend. When they were out together, he never seemed interested in other women. Though, they did keep their relationship a secret since he was her boss. Was that the appeal for him?

Angie wasn't the type to throw herself pity parties, but her chest had felt empty from the moment she boarded the plane in California.

Gathering all the memories of Brett, she mashed them into an ugly ball and shoved them into the darkest reaches of her mind. Her breathing slowed as her eyes became heavy.

Angie was a list-maker, which was a big part of her job. If there was ever a time to make one, this was it. Her eyes squeezed shut as she worked out the next step of her plan. She was on the other side of the country, so she doubted she would see Brett again. Not that she ever wanted to. Before she left, she had demanded a glowing recommendation letter to help in her new job search. It was part of her request in the severance package.

Her job had been a coveted position at the company, and she knew the vultures would be there after the holidays picking up the pieces of her previous life. This was a tough time of year to search for another job. But, with the New Year on the horizon, there wasn't a better time to start over.

First, she would update her resume and scour job openings in New York City and surrounding areas.

Angie never intended to stay on the East Coast, but it would have to do while she could get back on her feet. After bouncing back from this, she would leave again on a new adventure.

This was all temporary, and with a plan in mind, she snuggled under the covers with visions of job offers dancing in her head.

If you enjoyed *Barefoot on the Beach*, then why not try another delightfully uplifting romance from HQ Digital?